Additional Praise for Paul O'Brien and the Blood Red Turns Dollar Green Trilogy

"Loved them, the inside kno⸺ ⸺ wrestling business is amazing." ⸺T/WWE superstar

"I'm in awe of the research and I w⸺ ⸺ales. Gripping stories, great characters and villain⸺ My cup of tea with two sugars."
—William Regal, N⸺ ⸺ manager

"Amazingly well written story. I loved the characters, especially Ade who is like several bad ass wrestling women all rolled into one. This book is straight fire!" —Becky Lynch, WWE superstar

"Gripping . . . hard to put down . . . just so much to enjoy here."
—*Pro Wrestling Torch*

"Unique, thrilling reads." —1Wrestling.com

"Like nothing else we've ever read." —*Calling Spots*

"Every wrestling fan needs this novel." —*Monday Night Mayhem*

"Full of twists and turns." —ProWrestling.net

"This is a major piece of crime fiction." —*Brit Alley*

"I was burning my fingers getting through this. I was ecstatic that the story kept on deliver until the last line." —*Slam*

"A marriage of wrestling and literature that has never been seen before." —OrderofBooks.com

"Captivating. An instant classic." —*Collar and Elbow*

"Top notch, stylish . . . the first professional novel about professional wrestling." —*Fighting Spirit*

"Fifty pages in and we were hooked." —*Ministry of Slam*

"O'Brien nails it overtime. . . . This is how you create a wrestling universe." —*Wrestling Observer*

"Epic and intimate. Intense and involving." —*Pulp Pusher*

"Trust me, you'll want to read this book. At least I can say I knew Paul before it was cool."
—Todd Barnes, Sundance Award–winning writer and producer

"Blood Red Turns Dollar Green is one hell of a novel, with shades of Mario Puzo, Elmore Leonard, and Michael Connelly. The action is relentless, the characters are shady, and the justice is swift and final. Paul O'Brien is the real deal and a rising star in the crime arena."
—Eoin Colfer, *New York Times* bestselling author
of *Artemis Fowl*

BLOOD RED TURNS DOLLAR GREEN

BLOOD RED TURNS DOLLAR GREEN

A Novel

PAUL O'BRIEN

Skyhorse Publishing

Skyhorse Publishing books may be purchased in bulk at special discounts for sales promotion, corporate gifts, fund-raising, or educational purposes. Special editions can also be created to specifications. For details, contact the Special Sales Department, Skyhorse Publishing, 307 West 36th Street, 11th Floor, New York, NY 10018 or info@skyhorsepublishing.com.

Skyhorse® and Skyhorse Publishing® are registered trademarks of Skyhorse Publishing, Inc.®, a Delaware corporation.

Visit our website at www.skyhorsepublishing.com.

10 9 8 7 6 5 4 3 2 1

Library of Congress Cataloging-in-Publication Data is available on file.

Cover design by Owen Corrigan

ISBN: 978-1-5107-0933-1
Ebook ISBN: 978-1-5107-0936-2

Printed in the United States of America

For Úna, because if I said I was building a zoo, you'd try and find me an elephant.

CHAPTER ONE

September 30, 1972.
New York.

Lenny Long was minutes from history but miles from home. He lay silently, his mind scrambled, and tried to focus on the broken cooler in front of him. Both he and it had just been on the same short, sudden journey. As his eyes closed, he remembered what his young wife felt like beside him. He pictured her sleeping. Lenny wanted to sleep too. He could finally relax, forget about everything.

He smiled as he thought about how he had made it. He had proved he could be trusted with the most important job in this whole dirty, dangerous business. Now he could get some sleep. Nothing more to do. Home soon.

Except one thing.

What the fuck?

Lenny's eyes snapped open. His cheek was pressed against the dark, wet street. He had no idea how he got there. He sucked in a large breath and lifted his head.

What the fuck?

Left wasn't familiar. Right wasn't familiar. He slowly turned around to see a brand-new VW Kombi van overturned and mashed into the railroad bridge halfway down the street. His brand-new VW Kombi van.

What the fuck?

He struggled to his feet and limped toward the van, dragging his uncooperative right leg with him. He still had no idea what had happened, or why, but the awful weight of dread in his stomach told him it wasn't good.

They can't still be in there.

He tried to move faster but the excruciating pain shooting from his leg held him back. He slid his hand down to where the pain was originating and could feel a hard, foreign protrusion coming from his hip socket.

Lenny's panic grew as he approached the van. The passenger door was jammed shut and the smashed glass popped under his feet as he slid around to the back window. He gingerly stooped and saw the giant form of Babu unconscious in the back. His other passenger, Gilbert King, sprawled limply across the ceiling of the overturned van. Both men were unconscious.

The radio, like a shocked victim, continued to babble out soft music in the background. Lenny could see the hole in the windshield where he and the cooler had torpedoed through.

There was a faint smell of burning as a tiny stream of dark smoke piped out from under the steering column.

Painfully but hurriedly, Lenny entered the back of the van and slid his way up to Babu's massive face. Even a totally disoriented Lenny knew he was going to need some serious help moving a seven-foot-five, four-hundred-and-seventy-two-pound man.

On the other side of the unlit street, Lenny could make out a graffitied phone booth. He was in the kind of neighborhood where there was just as much chance of being killed over there as there was of dying in an explosion if he stayed in the van.

The smoke grew darker and thicker.

Being blown up or being murdered in a phone booth were only *possible* ways he could die that night. One thing Lenny was *sure* would get him killed was to sit there and do nothing. There was too much distrust, too much money invested in the two people lying unresponsive in his van.

Confidence had been put in Lenny to deliver. He at least had to try.

He pinched the giant nose in front of him and rose up onto his haunches to get in position to administer the kiss of life. All the pressures of the situation began to beat on him. *What happened? How was he going to explain this one to the boss?* There were a lot of people expecting these passengers to get to their destination. Their not getting there would start a quiet war if Lenny didn't do something.

What the fuck?

And then clarity, sudden and serene. Absolute peace. Lenny knew exactly what to do. His natural survival instincts took the wheel. Like a mother that just knows how to nurse her child, he just knew the perfect response.

He raised his hand to the heavens and brought it right down on Babu's big unconscious face.

Nothing.

And again. Same deal. He paused and waited. Nothing. Lenny then grabbed a handful of the giant's hair and yanked it. Twice.

Nothing.

Lenny's panic and the sensation of *notfuckingknowingwhattodo* quickly returned and peaked when he saw that the smoke under the steering wheel was now accompanied by some angry electrical sparking.

"C'mon, you big fucking lug," Lenny pleaded as he hopelessly shook Babu.

There must be fucking something . . . He wormed back out of the van and looked around for some inspiration. Anything. His hip was in agony. He grabbed the van and attempted to lift. His modest arms tightened and his back strained. He had no chance of lifting a giant, but maybe lifting a van that housed a giant and a grown man in it would be easier.

He exploded with power and roared with endeavor, but only managed to tweak a hamstring—and pop his hip back into place. The pain was strangely calming. The sound was a little sickening. Lenny raised and lowered his leg a couple of times to make sure everything was okay. It was. But he was still fucked in general.

He yelled in frustration and hit the van with a volley of slaps. The back of his shirt was attracted to him like a shower curtain in a cheap hotel. Lenny felt the back of his head; it was busted wide open and blood was running down his back.

"Time for something different," the smooth voice from the radio said as Lenny walked toward the pay phone. He had no more options, no more choice.

I have to call someone.

"Hey?" moaned a voice from the wreckage of the van.

Lenny stopped, not sure if he was hearing things.

"Hey?"

Lenny turned back to the van.

"Hello?" Lenny said.

Lenny could hear movement up front in the van. He scurried back.

"Hello?" Lenny said again.

"Don't call the cops. You hear me?" demanded Gilbert's weak voice from inside.

Lenny quickly grabbed the door handle and tried to force it open.

"You hear me, Lenny?"

Lenny put his hand through the broken side window and unlocked the door from the inside.

"What happened?" Lenny asked as he opened the battered door. The smoke now was so thick and black it made it hard to see. Lenny

grabbed Gilbert by the collar, the pain of which immediately emptied Gilbert's lungs.

"What the fuck are you doing?" Gilbert gasped.

"Sorry," Lenny said.

Gilbert, too, was becoming more aware of the danger in staying.

"No, no, get me out of here," he said.

"I'm trying, man." Lenny approached Gilbert's torso from several
different angles but couldn't find two handfuls of him that weren't
torn or broken.

"No, I mean get me out of here altogether."

Lenny stopped. He looked around for prying eyes and leaned in to
Gilbert's partially missing ear. "You mean . . . kill you?"

"No, you fucking fairy. Get me a cab or something. I can't be here
with him when there's other people around."

Lenny looked Gilbert up and down. He was no doctor but things
didn't look good from where he stood. "I should get an ambulance . . ."

Gilbert grabbed Lenny by the inseam of his trouser leg, which
pinched a little, but Lenny thought it was inappropriate to wince
given the circumstances. "You call anyone and you'll be done. Me
and the giant can't be seen together under any circumstances."

Lenny nodded as he again planned his hand placement. Gilbert
raised his arms like a child looking for comfort. "Drag me. Quickly,
you asshole."

Lenny carefully but swiftly scooped his hands under Gilbert's
armpits and began to drag him from the wreckage.

Gilbert moaned involuntarily. Blood was dripping from his mouth
and he was slipping in and out of consciousness. Lenny managed to
get his whole body free. He slowly dragged Gilbert inch by inch to
the other side of the road.

"Hurry," Gilbert said as his eyes rolled in his head.

Lenny grabbed him tighter and lugged Gilbert across to the curb
with less delicate drags.

"Fuck me," Gilbert breathlessly mumbled in pain.

Lenny gave one last pull to get Gilbert's dead weight fully out of the road. They both fell, weary, with Gilbert between Lenny's legs, like two entangled lovers watching the tide come in.

Lenny choked out a laugh of pure relief. No explosion. Not yet. And Gilbert looked to be still alive. The only thing lost was one of Gilbert's boots that must have caught a divot in the street on the journey over.

The van began to move. Babu was coming to and Lenny had no idea how he was going to react to whatever had just happened.

Lenny rested Gilbert's head on the ground and called from a good, safe distance.

"Babu?" he said as he cautiously approached the van.

Lenny picked up Gilbert's stranded boot. The weight of it in his hand caught his attention. *That's very heavy.*

Lenny weighed the boot in his other hand.

What the fuck?

He turned back to Gilbert and saw that his right leg stopped cleanly just at the end of his shinbone.

Holy shit.

Lenny instinctively flung the boot away from him. His legs deserted him and he cracked his head off the ground. There was no way they were going to make it to their destination on time.

Lenny's prone body was drowned in light as the flames from the van sparked to life and grew beside him.

This was bad. Really fucking bad.

The boss walked the corridor, listening to the white noise above him turn to booing. He worked the only job in the world where booing was not only a good thing but was encouraged at every turn.

After fifteen years running his own business, Danno Garland could identify a "good night" for the audience just by listening, and he knew that this was one hell of a good night. For the audience.

"Where are they, boss?" a worried-sounding voice asked as he strode past.

Danno ignored the question, but he really wanted to stab the inquisitor in the temple. Instead he continued at pace to the upper deck.

The full stadium presented herself with the grand reveal of an unfinished circle. Even with all that was going on, the spectacle and energy of 65,417 people took his breath away. It was a beautiful sight—in fact and in business. A reason to be proud and a little bit emotional.

Danno Garland had finally made it to Shea Stadium.

Her sweating beauty wrapped around his creation in a giant protective huddle. The collective masses thundered down their applause and disgust in equal measures.

All these years Danno had waited for the right time to go big. And it didn't get much bigger than this. With another look at his watch, he reluctantly conceded that this was the setting for him to lose it all.

Merv Schiller was right. He did fuck it up.

"Do you want to make another call on the finish, boss?" Ginny Ortiz respectfully asked from behind.

Danno shook his head without turning around.

"But the—"

"I know," Danno interrupted. "I know." He tried to answer Ginny a little more gently than he would anyone else pressing him—because of what happened. Because of what Ginny had to go through to get here.

"Just gimme a sec, Ginny."

Ginny waited patiently for a nod in one direction or the other.

What could have possibly gone wrong out there? It was only a thirty-minute drive from the hotel to here.

"The cops want to know if there's going to be trouble, boss," Ginny said.

Danno was instantly angry that word was leaking out to the front. Angry, but not a single bit surprised. It was one of the cornerstones of this event. Loose lips filled the stadium. Most of the time Danno used those loose lips to his advantage. Now, he just didn't know how to control them. He didn't even know where to start, and Ginny really didn't want to push it, but he knew that if something wasn't done soon there was going to be a major issue with the crowd. "Sir?"

Danno wasn't being mysterious on purpose; he didn't know what to do either.

It was time for strategy, a plan B, even. Who else did he have that could send the sticky, rabid crowd home happy? His advertised main event was a war that had been years in the making—and everyone in those seats knew it. They came to see blood.

Fuck.

If they didn't show up soon he'd be ruined. He'd never sell another ticket again. The state of New York wouldn't have to try to shut him down anymore, because he'd effectively do it himself.

He removed his sweat-stained tweed cap and rested it on his bent knee.

I should have kept things simple.

"Sir?" asked a voice again.

"Fuck off, Ginny," Danno snapped back in his rounded New York accent.

"Sir, we just got a message from Lenny."

Danno turned to see a soft, conservative-looking man he vaguely remembered hiring. The messenger stood rigidly and respectfully with a note in his hand.

"Message? From where?" Danno asked, confused.

The man bowed his head and handed over the note. Danno turned away and topped himself up with a steadying breath before opening it. He placed his cap back in its familiar spot. "I haven't got my fucking glasses. How bad is it?"

The messenger opened the note and read it slowly. "Lenny is refusing to come to the stadium, sir. He said he'll only talk to you," the man said without lifting his eyes.

"He's refusing to come . . . what?" Danno squinted closely at his watch.

"Everyone wants to know what to expect now, sir."

Danno trawled through the thousands of bad situations he had been in over the years. The endless real-world experiences. The hundreds of possible outcomes. The thousands in the crowd.

It was completely out of Danno's hands. He was as paralyzed as everyone who wanted answers. But to one man out there, something like this would look like Danno fucked him over by design. And that made Danno more edgy than anything else.

"Tell them that I have no fucking idea what to expect."

A train roared past on the bridge over his head. Lenny stood in the derelict phone booth as his pencil-like body shook like a pup in the rain.

After only a few years in this business, he sure was getting sick of phone booths.

He used his rolled-up nylon jacket to stop the bleeding from his head as he compressed the pay phone between his shoulder and ear. His hair and face were blackened by the smoke of the van. The cops and emergency crew milled around the mangled Kombi van as Lenny watched in a daze through a tiny patch of unsprayed glass. The fire was out. The van was unrecognizable as the one he had bought in Queens a short time before. He thought about how he'd had to forge his wife's signature to buy it in the first place.

But the van was the last of his worries. For now. His racing mind turned to the bosses. None of them wanted this kind of attention, this type of spotlight on their business.

This was the worst kind of bad.

Past the zigzag of abandoned police cars, Lenny could see Babu sitting silently against a wall as an officer interviewed him. Trying to push Babu for answers was probably not the wisest thing to do.

Lenny was at a loss as to whether he should leave the phone call and smooth over the interrogation, or wait on the line to be fired, abused, or much worse.

"Where are you, you little fuck?" Danno suddenly yelled from the other end of the line.

"Hello?"

"Where?" Danno shouted.

Lenny struggled to keep himself together. "Hello? That you, boss?"

Danno could tell by Lenny's voice that he wasn't firing on all cylinders, so he steadied himself and picked a different approach. "Where's the champ, Lenny?"

"I can see him . . . the giant . . . he's right here . . ."

"Good." Danno laughed in a release of tension. "Now where the fuck is here? I can get someone to you right now."

Lenny took one last look around. "I had Gilbert too. I think I had Gilbert."

"Did you say you had Gilbert? As in Gilbert King?" Danno was puzzled as to how his man, Babu, ended up with their man, Gilbert. They weren't meant to be anywhere near each other.

Lenny answered, "Yeah. He was with us. He wasn't going to show . . . It's . . . I just want to . . . we got him in the van."

"Lenny?" Danno tried his most calming voice. "Lenny, this bit is very important. Did anyone see those two together? Think about it before you answer."

Lenny desperately tried to slap the pieces of his journey, the crash, and now his phone call together. "I don't know. The van . . . they were . . . I . . ."

Danno could feel his stomach sinking and his blood pressure rising. "What happened? Where are you?"

"I can't remember, sir. The van crashed. It looks like we hit a couple of cars and rolled into the bridge. And now I can't find Gilbert King."

Danno's heart thumped unevenly in his chest. "He's missing?"

Lenny could feel this whole situation getting way too big for his position in the company. "I was talking to him, trying to pull him out. I can't remember. I think I have a concussion. Things—"

Danno cut him off with a more even tone. A tone like people who try to remain calm in a fucking traumatic situation might use. "Is he in the van?"

"I don't think so. I thought I . . ."

"Lenny, is your fucking van invisible?"

"No, sir."

"Is it so far away or so damaged in the crash that you can't look into its windows?"

"No, sir."

"So. Is. Gilbert. Fucking. King. In. The. Van?"

"No, sir."

"Perfect." Danno thumped the receiver against the chipped walls in the bowels of Shea Stadium.

Lenny turned away from all the flashing, noisy distractions in front of him. He was sure there was a simple and logical step to piece together what he was missing. "I'm sorry. I was knocked stupid myself, and I can't even really remember what happened. I would do anything to make this right, boss. You know that."

Lenny waited for a response. He was fully aware that saying that he'd do anything for Danno Garland was a dangerous offer at this stage in the game.

"Are you still on the phone?" Danno asked calmly. Too calmly.

Lenny paused, unsure of what to do. "Yes, sir."

"Fucking find him. Do you hear me? You've got ten minutes to get them both here, otherwise do you know what will happen? The—"

The phone abruptly disconnected. Lenny's mouth fell open with shock. He desperately checked the receiver and phone cable running to the box for an obvious breakage. "No, no, no, no." He dug through his pockets, looking for more coins. He stuck his head out the door and asked no one in particular, "Anyone got any change? Anyone?"

Lenny turned away from the circus on the street and shook his jacket, listening for the sound of coins rattling. "Fucking fuck." He dropped the dead receiver and warily trotted toward the overturned van to see if he had imagined dragging Gilbert from the passenger door. A female police officer noticed Lenny's dubious path straight to the crime scene. They locked eyes as Lenny moved closer to the cordoned-off vehicle.

"Sir?" she more demanded than asked. "Sir?"

"Have you got a quarter?" he asked her.

"Sorry, sir?" she replied.

"Nothing." Lenny suddenly changed direction—like he was never walking to the van in the first place—and walked toward the giant who was being forcefully questioned.

Lenny knew that wasn't going to last long or turn out well.

Babu was not paying much attention to the pushy officer in front of him. The giant was dressed in a rainbow-colored traditional African agbada with a matching cap. His right arm was in bad shape, but you could never tell by looking at his demeanor.

"Officer?" Lenny interrupted.

The police officer put up a single wait-a-minute finger in Lenny's face.

Lenny Long wasn't cut out for this. That familiar feeling of wanting to go home crept up on him again.

How could you lose someone, Lenny? A whole fucking person.

"Are you certifiably mute, sir? Do you have any papers to prove that as fact?" asked the name-tagged Officer Tyler standing in front of Babu. "'Cause it looks to me like you're just being uncooperative."

"Officer? He can't talk," Lenny tried again.

Babu stared silently into the distance over the officer's shoulder.

"He can't talk," Lenny insisted.

"You already told me that, sir. We need him to confirm it."

It had been a long night and Lenny was starting to doubt his ability to judge irony, sarcasm, or stupidity. "You want a mute person to tell you he's mute?" Lenny asked.

The cop knew his request was absolutely stupid when he heard it out loud, but there was no way he was admitting it. "That is correct."

Lenny sighed in acceptance. What else could he do? This whole thing was way beyond his power. "I have ten minutes to get this man to Shea Stadium. I will literally do anything to make you let us go. Please."

"Are you trying to bribe me?" the officer asked, agitated.

"No," Lenny said, backing off completely. "As a matter of fact if *you* could give *me* a quarter, I'd appreciate it."

"Excuse me?" the cop said.

Babu signaled to an invisible watch on his wrist. Lenny looked at him, almost defeated. "I know."

"Well?" asked the officer, chewing on nothing in particular. "You two going to come clean about what happened here? Drugs? Maybe you two were . . . distracted by each other."

Lenny could feel himself reaching for any reasonable argument to get them off the hook. "No one was hurt here and we'll cover the damage."

Babu stood. This seemed to put the police officer on high alert. "You better sit again, chief, or I'm going to have to bag me a rhino," he said as he patted his sidearm.

Lenny stood in front of Babu to try to gently defuse the situation. If he was to get the giant to Shea, this had to go smoothly.

"You know who this is?" Lenny asked. "Huh? You know who this is, right? The champ?"

The young cop looked Babu in the face. "Of course I do."

Lenny's eyes lit up. "You do?"

"Yeah."

"And, you probably know that the biggest match of all time is happening in Shea tonight," Lenny said as he moved closer.

The cop folded his arms. "I know who he is. I also know what he does for a living. And we're staying here till I find out what happened, because I don't have the luxury of faking my way through my job, like he does."

Babu's ham-like left fist launched from its hanging position—past Lenny's head—and hit the cop squarely in the face. The impact dropped the cop instantly. Such was the speed and power of the hit that Lenny wasn't even sure what happened until he turned and saw the uniformed body spasming on the ground.

"Oh, fuck," Lenny said.

There was one thing that Babu would never let be said aloud: he was no fake. And neither was the business he was in.

Danno slammed down the phone backstage at Shea Stadium and tried hard to contain his rage.

"He just hung up on me," Danno shouted in disbelief before turning around to see that everyone in the company had lined up expectantly behind him.

"Get someone to see if they can find out where they are," Danno snapped.

A few bodies at the back of the room jumped up at Danno's request. Wrestlers, ring crew, and referees all stood silently, like they were waiting to hear the dire prognosis of a loved one.

The weight of the situation hit Danno. "Alright, there's no way to sugarcoat this: our main event isn't going to happen."

The waiting collective dropped their heads in unison. A few deeper voices in the middle somberly cursed their luck. This was the big one—the one they had been working toward for the last few years. The one that was to produce the big payoff for them all.

"We still getting paid, boss?" a brave but anonymous voice asked from the back. Danno ignored the question.

"It's time to make a call on the finish. We're going for a big shmoz, clusterfuck finish with everyone in the ring. Everyone who isn't booted up—get so," Danno ordered the waiting crowd. "We're going to load the ring with everyone we've got and I want them to beat the shit out of each other."

Ricky Plick was leaning his stocky frame against the wall just behind the rest of the troops. "Why aren't you going to let the natural thing happen out there, boss?"

Even though Danno had given a direction, nobody on the roster moved before hearing his answer.

"No. We're going to go out there to finish. It might not be the finish they paid for, but we will give them everything we have," Danno said.

Danno hurriedly grabbed a paper tablecloth from a nearby table and thrust it at the chest of a hairless wrestler in the front of the pile. He pulled the top off a Sharpie and began to write out different match scenarios on the tablecloth. "I need a list of everyone who is ready to work. Ricky? Go and find yourself some gear."

Ricky tried again. "If they riot then we might at least get paid after all the shit we've been through."

"I fucking know that, Ricky," Danno snapped. "We can still work our way out of this. Get booted up."

"With all due respect, Danno . . ." No one in that room had dared to call Danno anything other than "sir" or "boss" before. "This whole place paid to see Babu versus Gilbert King, and I don't see either of them here."

"Do you not think I fucking know that?" Danno said.

The pressure in the room was immense. Out on the pitch, the heat from the floodlights added that extra weight of closeness. Word had traveled from the backstage area to the ring that Danno was being questioned in public by closet soldier Ricky Plick. The older wrestlers had been in sticky situations further south before. They had to deal with overzealous fans who brought knives, bottles, or cups of piss to throw at them. In all the collective years in the dressing room, no one had seen anything approximating what was surely about to happen. What was developing in the stands was far and above annoyance or passion.

This match was years in the making. Personal shots had been taken. "Wrestling" was put aside. All the stuff that was usually kept behind the curtain had been dragged out in front of everyone to see and read on national TV and in newspaper columns. This was to be the match that all the hardcore fans could point to for years to come as proof that wrestling was real. Everyone had bought their tickets for tonight because they knew this match was a shoot fight—a real grudge. They all knew this match was personal. If they only knew just how much.

"You sure you still want to work this angle, boss?" Ricky asked as he approached Danno.

The crowd of spectators around the boss and his right-hand man had doubled in the seconds that had passed since Ricky questioned the owner. It was not the wrestling norm to have so many people watching this kind of argument. Interactions like this usually happened behind very closed doors. Wrestling's number one rule was "protect the business." That meant that no one outside of the inner circle got to see or hear any discussions about matches, decisions made, or anything at all about how the business worked.

"I don't want to talk about it here, Ricky," Danno replied.

Most of the wrestlers were drama queens at heart. They loved to gossip about each other and tear each other down. They usually luxuriated in confrontation and commotion. But this was different. What they were watching was a challenge to the boss. In public.

"There's nothing to talk about, Danno," Ricky replied. "We can't give the crowd what they paid for, so now we have no choice but to make sure they riot."

The long-standing theory for a doomsday scenario had been to incite the crowd, let them riot, and you could slip out the back with the box-office money while the people in the crowd were busy kill-ing each other. If you let a group of civilized fans out early, they usu-ally stop at the box office for their money back on the way out. Make them riot and no one can be blamed for leaving in a hurry. Including the box-office staff. With the box-office takings.

Danno wanted to address this in a stand-up manner. Ricky was more about the business.

"I have no other choice now, Ricky. We stay and finish the card," Danno said.

Ricky butted his head against Danno's. "You've done nothing but fuck this territory since you got your greedy hands on it."

Some members of the roster growled their displeasure at Ricky's disrespect. But they did it from the safety of the crowd.

Danno pushed his closest confidant away. "Don't ever get in my face again, Ricky."

A few half-dressed wrestlers silently stood between both men.

Ricky paused and looked around the room. "You people realize what's happening here? No payday. After all that's happened. Years of fighting. Some people getting fucked up, never to wrestle again. The biggest pile of money we've ever seen and he's going to give it back."

"I'm not fucking this crowd over." Danno continued to write out his revised card on the tablecloth.

"But you're willing to fuck us over. The truth is, you couldn't draw money with a green fucking crayon. Asshole."

Ricky spun on his heel and sucker punched Danno hard in the side of the head. The old promoter stumbled helplessly into the tables, which collapsed under his considerable weight.

Tiny Thunder, an Asian midget wrestler, grabbed Ricky around the waist as some of the roster hurried to Danno's aid.

"Are you fucking crazy, man?" Tiny shouted. Ricky shrugged him off easily and moved for the exit. His strides exploded into a sprint when he saw some of the other wrestlers running toward him with bad intentions.

"Did everyone forget we're here to make money?" Ricky shouted as he bolted through the exit door.

The room melted into chaos.

Danno immediately rose up and tried to steady himself. There was a nasty gash above his left eye and a lump was already starting to form. He pushed his revised plan into Tiny Thunder's arms. "We go out there and finish the card. We take what is coming our way. Then we are going to rebuild. No matter what happens out there, we can come back from this."

Danno staggered out of the room and used the stadium walls to steady his shuffling movements toward the restroom. He opened the door and hid in one of the dirty, smelly stalls. He knew there was no way this was going to remain a secret. Everyone was soon to hear about the moment that Danno Garland lost the wrestling company that had been in his family since 1924. His failure to deliver would make him weak among the other wrestling bosses in the other territories. And Danno stood atop of bunch of promoters who would routinely cut the weak from their pack.

From outside a panicked voice shouted, "Boss, Proctor King is looking for you."

Proctor King was exactly the one who would spearhead Danno's elimination. It was Proctor's son who had gone missing from the front of Lenny's van.

"You didn't tell him I was here, did you?" Danno shouted back.

"I meant on the phone, sir."

Danno exploded, "Well, say that, then. There's a big fucking difference."

The messenger paused. "What should I tell him?"

There was no way that Gilbert King not showing up to the biggest match in history didn't look suspicious. And based on what happened to get the match in place at all, Danno knew he looked the guiltiest. And if the previous four years had taught Danno anything, it was that the one person you didn't want to fuck with was Proctor King.

January 9, 1969 — Four Years Earlier.
New Jersey.

His father never ran Moose Hall. When he took the company to Jersey, he would run Union City, Patterson, Newark, Jersey City, Passaic, or Highland Park. His father never ran Moose Hall, so Danno had to run Moose Hall.

The thirteen people in attendance were glad that he did.

"It's okay, boss. You go ahead," Ricky Plick said as he warmed up in the corner. He was wearing his wrestling gear, which consisted of long black tights and red glossy boots with his initials on both sides. He had dyed black hair with a matching mustache. He wasn't old looking, but his middle-aged body moved like it was too old to be doing this for a living.

"Thirteen people?" Danno said. "I could nearly give them all a ride home when we're done here."

Ricky changed to squats—slow and traumatic ones. "They seem to be into it."

"Fucking depressing. The guy at the door said there were about twenty more, but they thought it was bingo night."

Ricky suddenly stopped and felt around the base of his spine.

Danno continued to watch the match in the ring. It was a midget wrestler match. The four children standing up at the front seemed to be enjoying it. The wrestlers in the ring were working their hardest to pull some excitement from the minuscule audience.

"I'm going to have to do something, Ricky. What's going wrong here?"

Ricky held himself straight against the wall. "It goes in cycles, boss. It was like that for your old man too."

Ricky had been a loyal wrestler and advisor for Danno's father before Danno came on as boss.

"This bad?" Danno asked.

Ricky didn't respond. Danno knew the answer anyway. His old man always managed to turn chickenshit into chicken salad. He always had a plan working in the background. Even when no one else knew the plan, Terry Garland knew the plan.

Danno turned back to Ricky and saw the pain etched on his face. "You okay?" Danno asked.

Ricky immediately continued his squats. "Yeah. Never felt so good."

Out in the ring, the handsome white-toothed midget stamped his foot on the mat and clapped his hands to try to get the audience to follow. They didn't. He took a drop kick to the face instead.

Danno pulled the curtain shut. "I can't watch anymore. The sooner I get to Portland, the better."

"You think it's going to go your way over there?"

Danno smiled for the first time. "The deal is already done. They've seen the giant and they all see money in him too."

"I'm delighted for you, boss. You taking Mrs. Garland?"

Danno nodded. "Yeah. Another ticket I have to buy."

Ricky took out a couple of tubes of lipstick from his bag.

"Speaking of extra tickets. You know anything about the guy who's coming to drive the car?" Danno asked as he sat beside Ricky. "I think it's important that we give the rest of the bosses . . . at least the impression that we're still big time enough to have the world heavyweight title down here."

"Yeah, a driver would be good for that image. We had a couple of the new guys that were willing to do it for nothing," Ricky replied, crushing the lipstick into his hands. "The guy we picked is outside waiting for you."

Danno closed his eyes to visualize the packed houses and the rabid crowds in his future. "This giant will be the biggest draw in our history. I know it. He's a once-in-a-lifetime type of wrestler. No offense."

Ricky laughed. "None taken. He should be champ. A blind man could see that."

Danno knew the task ahead of him in Portland. "It wasn't a blind man I had to convince. It was a cartel full of snakes and con men. But even they could see the money in our guy."

Ricky opened a bottle of baby oil with his teeth and squeezed some into his lipstick-covered hand.

"What are you doing?" Danno asked.

Ricky rubbed the mixture of lipstick and baby oil all over his body. "It adds tone and sheen. Looks good for the people out there."

Danno picked up his travel bag. It was nights like this one that made him regret taking up the wrestling business at all—but he knew he only had to wait one more day to get exactly what he had wanted for the last fifteen years. The world heavyweight title.

"Good luck," Ricky said sincerely. "Have a good flight."

Danno smiled and nodded in the doorway.

Outside Moose Hall, Danno could see a car waiting. He passed his bag from one hand to the other and walked carefully down the poorly lit steps. He could see the face of his new driver—a blond-haired twenty-something with a beginner's mustache.

Why isn't this guy getting out to open my door? Danno wondered as he approached.

The rookie driver looked nervous. Too nervous. His brow was speckled with flop sweat and he didn't raise his eyes to meet his advancing boss. Danno slowed down and discreetly looked around. Something was off. He patted his pockets, mimed that he forgot something, and turned back around toward the building.

As Danno walked back he could hear the car door opening behind him.

"Mr. Garland?" the driver called.

Danno didn't turn around.

"Boss?"

Danno briskly took to the steps, but misjudged the raised, broken last step in the darkness. He stumbled and fell to both knees as his bag slid along the cold concrete in front of him. The fall tore his knees and ripped his suit trousers—but the sound of the skittish driver approaching from behind was of far more concern. Danno tried to get to his feet.

"Are you okay, boss?" asked the voice directly behind him.

Danno slowly looked back over his shoulder. The blond-haired driver stood behind him, completely naked, cupping his crotch.

"They told me that everyone does their first pick-up naked," the driver said.

Danno could feel himself moving from fear to rage. "What?"

"They said that if I wanted to be your driver, that I had to . . ."

"Who said?" Danno shouted.

From his knees, Danno looked back toward the building and could see the faint silhouette of his wrestlers ducking out of sight.

The driver said, "I'm sorry. I thought . . . I just wanted . . ."

Danno lifted himself gingerly from the ground. The naked driver offered his hand. Danno slapped it away.

"Don't fucking touch me with that," Danno said.

"I'm sorry, I have my clothes in the car."

"Yeah? Well go get them and find yourself a bus outta here."

"Sir?"

Danno glared at his wannabe driver. "You're fired."

The rookie stood motionless and silent.

"You hear me? Get out of here," Danno said.

"But . . . the car is mine."

Back inside Moose Hall, Danno walked the hallway with his knees bleeding, his trousers ripped, and his teeth gritted. He was late, pissed, and out of patience.

"Does anyone have a fucking car? Anyone?"

"What's this guy's name again?" Danno asked his wife as he watched Lenny approach them.

"Lenny Long," she answered.

Danno really didn't give a fuck. The hardened blood from his knees was now sticking to his fresh pair of trousers. He was waiting to board a flight with his wife and some guy Ricky had recommended as loyal, reliable, and someone who would work free of charge.

"Lenny Long? Sounds like a blue movie star," Danno mumbled to himself.

"How would you know?" she asked.

"What?" he said as he stood and walked away from the conversation.

He didn't want his wife to hear what he was about to say to Lenny. "You're near the front. Wait until last before you board. My wife and I will be in first class, so don't bother looking for us. You understand?"

Lenny nodded. Danno handed him his ticket.

Danno continued. "You get on the flight, you put your head down, and when we hit Portland you wait for us by the luggage."

Lenny nodded again. With a little smile this time.

"What are you smiling at?" Danno asked.

Lenny dropped the smile.

"This is serious business and you're here to represent New York. You understand?"

Lenny understood.

"Someday you might get to ride first class too," Danno said as he walked away.

Danno rushed to his window seat near the middle of the plane and dropped himself into it. They weren't in first class. Nowhere near it.

"What's wrong with you?" Annie asked her husband.

"Nothing. Tired." Danno peeked between the seats, watching for Lenny to board.

Danno watched as his new driver politely moved out of people's way, said hello to his fellow passengers, and generally oozed happiness at simply being on the flight.

Lenny took his aisle seat near the front. Danno crouched down when he thought Lenny might look back and see them.

"Why are you hiding?" Annie asked.

"What? I'm not." Danno studied his wife's face as she looked away. He watched her covertly slip a pill into her mouth and draw a deep breath. She needed to steady herself. Someone other than her husband might have thought it was because she was afraid of flying. But Danno was her husband—and he knew her better than that.

He sat and waited for the plane to fly and for her to sleep, but he never took his eyes off Lenny. Danno wanted their relationship, no matter how brief, to rest on the "fact" that Danno was first class. That was how he lived; that was his position in life. If he couldn't convince his driver of that, then there was no way he was going to convince the pack of snakes and cutthroats he was on his way to do business with.

The owner who wanted the world champion flew first class. Even when he didn't.

January 10, 1969—The Next Day.
Oregon.

The National Wrestling Council was a cartel of nine men who owned the largest wrestling territories in the Americas, set up to prevent other wrestling outfits from starting up and eating into their pie. The NWC would give each "boss" their own territory that only they would trade and promote their matches in. For many years, the bosses successfully patrolled and promoted without too much of a challenge.

People knew better than to try.

Merv Schiller had sat as president of the NWC since its inception in the mid-forties. Over the years, he had positioned himself so as to own the table that all the other bosses only dined at. His reasons for drawing breath were to make money and to keep control of the outfit he had helped start.

"So, Romeo Roberts has finished his program with us in the Carolinas and I don't have anything else for him," Tanner Blackwell informed the meeting. "He bumps good but has a problem keeping his dick in his pants."

"I remember him coming out of New York. Good hand. I'll have him," Joe Lapine immediately offered. "I see money written all over this guy down in Memphis."

"So who do I get in return?" Tanner asked.

Joe thought for a second. "Well, we just did a scaffold match with Mad Mark Mars, so he's done with us. He fucked up his ankle pretty bad, but he said he'll still work."

Tanner scoffed at the suggestion. "Is he the guy who has the insane astronaut gimmick?"

"The crowds loved it. We positioned him as a spaceman whose helmet cracked during training on Mars and it made him psycho."

"Training on Mars?" Tanner laughed and ran his comb through his slick black hair. "Fuck me. And that made money?"

Merv intervened. "He's a good worker. Change his gimmick if you don't see money in it."

"Okay," Tanner agreed. Both men shook hands on a deal done.

To the owners it was just like swapping baseball cards. Both would return to their respective territories to tell their respective wrestlers that they were moving next week—with no way of knowing for how long, or what their pay would be. That would all depend on how "over" the wrestler was with the paying public in their new territory.

All eyes were now on the main item of the agenda. Danno's stomach was upset just thinking about it.

Merv rechecked his notes as he rolled his fat cigar around his brown fingers. "We move on to the world heavyweight champion. Danno Garland wants the belt to come to New York where he has that giant waiting."

Danno watched as the other bosses smiled and nodded encouragingly in his direction.

Merv picked up a piece of paper and slid his huge, black-framed glasses onto his face to read. "The National Wrestling Council has decided via traditional unanimous vote that here will be no change in the . . ."

The small, smoky back room acted like the outcome was a shock. Danno did all he could to hide his devastation.

"Excuse me. Excuse me," Merv said, trying to retain order in the room. "There's no need," Merv continued above the mostly feigned disquiet. "Sal Pellington is a good champ for us and a good draw along the West Coast. So, no change."

Merv, it just so happened, owned the West Coast territory.

"What about the rest of us, Merv?" asked aggressive Curt Magee from Texas. "How are we supposed to eat?"

"With your fucking mouth," Merv snapped back.

Curt looked around the room for anyone as shocked as he. "Did you say '*with* your fucking mouth' or '*watch* your fucking mouth'?"

"Both." Merv wound up and knocked out his most worn-out lines: "None of you are tied to this council. You all had a free vote and the outcome is the outcome."

Danno knew he had been screwed over again. He had brought Missus Garland and put her up in the Governor Hotel, such was his confidence this time. She even wore those under-britches that very seldom saw anything but the bottom drawer.

Eight months previous, Danno had scraped together some money and flown the whole NWC to see his giant kid beat Ricky Plick in a hell of a main event in the New Jersey Armory. He knew it was a small crowd, but a great match and a true attraction wrestler gave Danno the nod over the other potential champions in line.

The giant was also a heel—a bad guy—and everybody knew the big money was to be made from the local heroes trying valiantly to take the belt from the giant bully in their hometowns. Danno had finally found a draw that could turn his ship around, maybe even set him up for retirement. This was the type of talent that his father had always talked about, but never found. All he needed was the backing of the other owners to make the giant the champion.

It was all sealed by a crystal clink in Danno's backstage office. Everyone was going to get rich off this huge find. The members of the NWC were happy and unanimous that the belt be dropped to the giant after their next official meeting in Portland.

This meeting.

"We don't feel it's the right time to move on from Pellington," Merv explained. "He's pulling in some numbers that have us confident that we'd be leaving money on the table if we jobbed him out now."

It had been over fifteen years since Danno had replaced his father on the NWC, and in all that time he never once had the belt in his territory. Even the other promoters around the table would grudgingly admit that it made no sense for a territory like New York to go so long without the belt. It was where most every wrestler wanted to be in Danno's father's day.

"Okay, let's move on to any other business," Merv said as he pulled his glasses off and shuffled some papers.

Danno cleared his throat and the meeting left a respectful silence for his potential input. He stood up.

"We had a deal, Merv." Danno looked around the room to see which of the other eight owners had knifed him in the back. "But more than that, I have someone who we know people are going to pay to see. I have someone who you all watched work a few months ago—someone who could make us all a lot of money. Now, I've kept him off TV, kept his appearances low profile, because I was waiting for the nod today. I was going to explode this kid onto the scene and get the world talking."

"He was green as goose shit and we need to move on to other business, Danno," Merv interrupted.

"But I have a question," Danno fired back.

"Make it quick," Merv said.

Fuck it. Danno had nothing to gain anymore by being polite anyway. "Yeah, just one point. Would you still be reneging on our deal if the giant jumped to your company like you quietly offered him to do several times last week?"

The occupants of the room turned squarely to Merv to hear his response. Danno had simply asked what everyone else was thinking.

"In my life I've never been so insulted and . . . and . . . what's the word?"

Danno instinctively finished his sentence. "Crooked?"

Merv picked up his ashtray and unsuccessfully threw it at Danno's head. "You be fucking careful what you lay at my door, you Mick fuck. Where's your evidence that I tried to sign your guy? You didn't get the belt today 'cause you'd only fuck it up if you did. Simple as that."

Danno could have been standing in front of his old man. The same old man who kept him away from the business at every turn. The same man who trusted Danno with nothing and left him even less when he died.

You didn't get the business, Danno, 'cause you'd only fuck it up if you did.

Merv was so sure. His words were so definite that Danno was instantly persuaded that Merv and his father had already decided that he was a fuckup many years ago in some backroom deal.

Who else in the room thought of him that way? The hanging heads told him nothing.

"You're the worst-earning member of this council, Danno. I'd keep my fucking mouth shut if I were you," Merv warned.

Danno slowly sat down.

Merv reigned over the silence in the room. He wiped the spittle from his mouth and watched everyone else's reaction, waiting to take on any more of this uprising bullshit. "In case anyone forgot the procedure in here, there was a vote taken on this decision, just like every time we have someone who thinks they have the next champ. So please, do me a favor and stop with the bleeding heart routine in here. I'm getting all fucking emotional."

Merv was right. And in that vote he had just enough of the other bosses on his side with backhand deals and co-promoting perks that he never had to worry about losing a ballot.

"Anyone else like to say something?" Merv asked.

As small and as old as Merv was, the whole wrestling world knew that he had come to this business from another, dangerous one. If that old cunt didn't want you around anymore, you'd stop being around.

"Well?" Merv glared at Danno. "Are we moving this meeting on?"

Danno hesitantly nodded. There would be no celebration, no victory speech, and no blowjob from Missus Garland that night.

Merv, in turn, also sat down. "I was going to inform the meeting that Sal was going to tour your territories again this summer as champion. Boost your gates."

The other owners smiled and nodded at the scrap of generosity, and everyone turned attentively to his next item. Everyone except Proctor King, who winked at Danno.

Business was about to pick up.

Proctor King was a former circus strongman-turned-wrestler-turned-owner. He constantly squinted, as though staring at the sun, even at night. His hair was clinically dead from years of Florida living, but he still managed to remain more blond than a man of his years should be. He had a face made of lacquered leather and a right forearm that entertained an anchor tattoo without irony.

He was without a neck on first inspection. He owned a pair of freckly shoulders that connected to his head, just under the ears. This gave him a squareness that you don't usually associate with a human. Proctor was a brick that sat atop some legs.

He was also the youngest-ever owner of a territory when he got Florida in the fifties. This didn't sit well within the NWC.

The Florida State Athletic Commission had already sent in two of their officials to investigate professional wrestling after the *Sun-Sentinel* ran a story about a blacklisted wrestler who was willing to tell all. A week later, and after a hefty collection, the agents found that wrestling was "true and honest in every way in every venue in

Florida." A week after that, they found most of the tell-all wrestler's body in his home. Most of it.

But the commission had spoken and put an end to the "fake" rumors for another couple of months and the NWC wasn't going to have a kid ruin those reprintable words. There was no way someone Proctor King's age could keep a quiet locker room, and that would be bad news for the bosses. Wrestling existed because enough people believed that what they were doing was "real."

One night at a charity ball, the word was given in the restroom that Proctor had to go. Merv gave the nod and the other bosses nodded along. The only thing that saved Proctor's life was a terrified Gilbert King, who heard the whole thing by chance from his bathroom stall.

Gilbert immediately informed his father. The early tip-off gave Proctor the chance to get ahead of the herd. There were only two things that would stop the order—to walk away from the business, or to start earning serious money.

One night inside the Hollywood Legion Stadium, Proctor jumped the rail and blindsided that territory's owner, Niko Frann. Niko was taken out on a stretcher and filed suit against Proctor. The arena erupted at the sight of an owner from another territory jumping the rail, and many people ended up in the hospital. One was Proctor himself.

He was stabbed in the stomach by a fan as he got mauled in the back of the arena.

Proctor's territory became hotter than ever after that. Fans traveled from all over to see what the Crazy King would do next. He booked himself as his top star. The word was out—no more messing with the owner from Florida. That kid was legit.

Niko, however, never forgot. He waited.

Proctor turned half of the money made on those gates over to Merv.

"Money makes everyone forgive everything," Merv told Proctor. "Everyone in this is here to do business. It's the first thing that we should ask ourselves every time we make a decision. Does this move make me money?"

Proctor listened. And Merv's words would come back to haunt him.

CHAPTER TWO

Danno lost the vote, but he had one more piece of new business to attend to that day before he left Portland for New York.

Lenny stood at the back door of the hired Continental and waited for his boss to leave the Governor Hotel. Lenny noticed that the boss was quiet and surly now, the complete opposite of how he had been before his big meeting.

Lenny wondered what had happened.

Danno just wanted to check out and take himself and Missus Garland back to New York. Not that they didn't need a break. And Portland was nice to look at. The white peak of Mount Hood looked pink when the sun was setting—which was nice enough.

Lenny opened the door and Danno got in the car.

You didn't get that mountain view where Danno came from. He was kind of happy about that; nothing good ever came from anyone who lived around a mountain. Most of them were retards, in fact. People do awful things to each other in the absence of a TV.

Gimme the junkies of New York any day.

Lenny slid into his seat and started the ignition.

"How are you now, boss?" Lenny asked.

Danno looked up. "What's your name again, kid?"

"Lenny, sir. Lenny Long."

Danno quickly disconnected from any further conversation and ran the day's events over in his head. As different as everything was in Portland, the business stayed the same. Well, except that look he got from Proctor King. It was hard to shake. Hard to read. But it was different. And the hushed invitation that followed, that was different too.

"Where are we headed, boss?" Lenny asked.

Proctor and Danno had never traded a single word outside the meetings before. That was about to change.

Lenny tried to catch Danno's distracted eye in the rearview mirror. "Boss?"

Danno immediately tuned back in and answered like he had been listening the whole time. "Bancroft Street. There's a new restaurant opening there. Look for the signs."

"Yes, sir." Lenny reversed slowly.

"Wait," Danno said. Lenny stopped the car.

Danno watched Missus Garland walk through the lobby without turning to wave him good-bye. She was beautiful, elegant, soft-spoken. Too good for the business her husband was in.

"Okay. Drive on."

Lenny headed out of the hotel driveway.

What could Danno call his monster rookie? Something exotic. Something wild. The wrestling world had Stompers and Crushers. Mongolians and Samoans. Beasts and Barbarians.

"It's pretty nice around here, huh, boss?" Lenny said. "I don't get out of New York much. I really appreciate the opportunity to be here with you today. If you need me again, anything at all, just let me know."

Danno nodded. Maybe he should have brought a gun with him and, when Merv stood up, blown his Jew fucking head off. Danno sometimes wished he was that sort of man. Life would be easier.

"Are you the ring guy who brings the sandwiches for the Boys?" Danno asked.

Lenny was half surprised and half embarrassed that the boss knew. "Well, my wife makes them, and I . . ."

"Sell them," Danno said, finishing Lenny's sentence.

"Well, yes, sir. I do."

"What's your angle?"

"Sorry, boss?"

"Explain the business of the sandwiches to me."

Lenny settled more comfortably into his seat and tilted the mirror in place. "Well, I take some of the wrestlers up to their next town after my shift is done on the ring crew."

"Why? Are we not working you hard enough?"

"Well, sir, I'm new here and I'm not . . ."—Lenny cleared his throat—". . . making much." Lenny looked to Danno for some sympathy. He didn't get any, so he continued. "One night, as a favor for Oscar Dewsbury, I took him to the town he was wrestling at. So my wife said I should charge them two cents a mile. It gives me some extra money and it gives them the time to do whatever it is they want to do between towns."

Lenny smiled. "You know what wrestlers want to do between towns. And it ain't driving."

Danno smiled too.

"So I did that," Lenny continued. "And now I have a waiting list, kinda, it's so popular. Then my wife made me some meatball sandwiches, but I was too embarrassed the first time to try and sell them. So my wife gave me the next batch, punched some holes in the bag for the Boys to smell. She's a great sandwich maker."

"How much do you get?"

"Two dollars a sandwich, and a dollar a soda."

"She's a smart lady."

"We've got a kid and another on the way. We're saving for our own place, is what I'm trying to say."

Lenny sensed that Danno wasn't as measured as he might be back home in New York. Maybe he could talk his way through some of the legendary secrecy of the wrestling business. "They don't say much of anything around me, though. The Boys. They kinda talk in their own language."

Danno looked Lenny in the eye just long enough for Lenny to know it was too early to try to jump that fence. "The wrestling business reveals itself slowly. There's always something happening under the table that you can't see."

Danno smiled as he heard his own words leaving his mouth. He wondered if something was happening under the table that he couldn't see himself. Proctor King was as ropey as Merv, if not more so. The kind of guy that can wait ten years to slit your throat. The sort that would be comfortably agreeable until he forked you in the eyeball.

One thing Danno did know for sure was that he was getting sick of being stepped on and passed over.

For an opening night, the Old Spaghetti Factory sure was quiet. Danno read the menu for the second time at a table under a big stained glass window. He skimmed the room and quickly counted the potential money at each table by multiplying the average meal price per head. It was a habit he was sure all promoters couldn't switch off. He watched through the window as Lenny pulled the Continental into a parking spot and walked to a pay phone.

Right on time, Proctor walked through the front door and pointed Danno out to the waitress.

"Fucking place, huh?" he said as he approached Danno's table.

"Have a seat, Proctor."

"You in a hurry?" Proctor asked.

"I've got some things, but nothing too, you know . . ."

Proctor was still standing. A waitress passed by and smiled at him.

"You back again, sir?" she asked Proctor.

Proctor just stared at the hospitable waitress until she walked away.

"Are you going to sit?" Danno asked.

Proctor took a long look around the restaurant. "No."

"No?"

Proctor was even more sure the second time. "No." He turned and signaled for Danno to follow. "I think we'll go outside."

"Where are we going?" Danno asked.

"There's something I want to show you."

Outside, Danno tapped on the phone booth glass. Lenny hurriedly said into the phone, "I gotta go. Bye, honey. Love you," and hung up.

"I'm going somewhere with this guy," Danno informed Lenny as he pointed Proctor out with a nod. "So, you know."

Lenny didn't know. "Isn't that Proctor King?"

"Yeah."

"He's on the front of my magazine this month." Lenny pulled a wrestling magazine from his back pocket and unrolled it to show Danno.

Danno wasn't impressed. "You're not a fucking mark, are you kid?"

"A what, sir?"

"A mark. A fan. Nothing, forget it." Danno shook his head and walked toward where Proctor was waiting.

Both men marched to the end of the nearly empty parking lot. Behind some thick bush at the edge of the lot there was a river. Proctor led the charge, ducking under the hanging branches in their way before he slid down the small bank toward the river. Danno stopped.

"Where are you going?" Danno asked from the top of the bank.

"Somewhere quiet." Proctor continued until his feet were covered by the water. He could sense Danno was wary. "You want to make money or not?" Proctor asked.

Danno looked around and saw Lenny waving at him. He didn't feel any sense of comfort that only a newbie driver knew his whereabouts.

"You could always turn around and go home to the way everything is set up now, if you like," Proctor said.

Danno took a second to think before he slid slowly and awkwardly on his ass down the bank. Proctor reached into his pocket and took out a cigarette. He broke the filter off and threw it into the brown water. "Nice view, huh?"

Danno tried to assess the situation and the geography without making it obvious he was doing so. He also watched the water's edge so as not to get his feet wet. "What did you want to see me about?" Danno asked.

"I want to do some business that will make us both rich," Proctor replied as he inhaled. "Big money."

"Haven't you got an office or a phone for this kind of stuff?" Danno asked.

"Not this kinda stuff."

Proctor waited for Danno's response and enjoyed the power of watching him digest the broken information.

"Well?" Danno asked. "What are we talking about here?"

Proctor took one last look up the bank before gravitating toward Danno's ear. "I want to get you the belt."

Danno leaned back to recapture his personal space. "You were there today, Proctor. You saw the room vote with Merv. Maybe you voted with him too. I don't fucking know who is with who in that room."

Proctor smiled and nodded at Danno's naïveté. "Fuck Merv and those monkeys who follow him. I can get you the belt by the end of the month. That'll give you time to put a program in place for that giant golden goose you found—you lucky bastard."

A rush of hot and cold ran up and down Danno's back. He knew that Proctor was serious and could get it done. This both delighted and terrified him. After all these years, he could finally have the belt. But there was the other issue that was providing the coldness. "What are you planning on doing with Merv?" Danno asked, not sure if he really wanted to hear the answer.

Proctor dodged the question. "Listen, I want that belt—we all do, but everyone knows you've got the guy for now. The other owners had already signed off on it, except fucking Merv snapped his fingers and frightened them back into line. When he's removed from the situation, you get the belt. And my reward for doing it is that you drop the belt to me next. I pay you two hundred thousand dollars up front and another two when your giant does the job to my son in a few years' time."

"A few years?"

"Yeah."

"Why a few years?"

Proctor offered a cigarette. Danno declined with a shake of his head.

Proctor answered, "I'm going to be honest with you. If I had all my pieces in place now I would just do this and get the belt for myself, but . . . my son just went inside." There was noticeable pride in Proctor's voice.

"Oh."

"It's his first time and I want to give him something to look forward to when he gets back out. You're going to have all the time in the world to make your guy a fucking unbeatable monster. You send him the length and width of the whole fucking country, beating everyone in every territory. You get filthy fucking rich. And when my boy gets back to town, he'll do major business defeating the giant that no one else could beat. He'll be a hero. Have a legacy."

It sounded nice. Too nice, to Danno.

"It's a win-win." Proctor flicked his exhausted cigarette butt into the river. "We got a deal?"

Danno felt he needed more time. It made total sense as Proctor laid it out, but he knew this was as close as his mortal self was ever going to get to shaking hands with the devil.

"Danno?" The pitch of Proctor's voice raised—he was seemingly surprised that he had to chase an answer.

Danno opened his mouth and paused. Even if it meant getting himself in even further with Proctor, money and fancy under-britches were powerful motivation.

"On one condition," Danno said, the water now running over his feet.

"What's that?"

"I call the angle when the time comes."

Proctor smiled and offered a handshake.

Proctor and Danno shook hands.

"What's your giant's gimmick?" Proctor asked as he climbed back up the bank.

Danno tried, unsuccessfully, to follow Proctor. "I think I'm going to make him an African Savage."

"He's white, Danno."

"He's going to be from South Africa." Danno stopped at the bottom of the bank and watched Proctor wave good-bye. "You're going to leave me down here?"

"Do I look like someone that rescues fat Irishmen?" Proctor said.

Lenny jumped out of the car when he saw Proctor come over the bank. He dusted off his nerves and walked toward him. "Mr. King, can I get your signature, sir?" Lenny pulled out the magazine from his back pocket.

"Go and help your fat boss, you fuckin' mark," Proctor said as he marched straight past and to the phone booth. Lenny didn't expect anything less from Crazy King. He thought he might have been disappointed if he had turned out to be a nice guy.

"Lenny, Lenny!" shouted Danno from the riverbank. Lenny couldn't immediately place the voice or where it was coming from.

"Lenny!"

Lenny stuffed his magazine back into his pocket and ran toward Danno's voice.

Proctor dialed the last digit on the pay phone and made sure no one was listening. "We got him."

CHAPTER THREE

January 24, 1969 — Two Weeks Later.
San Francisco.

Mickey Jack Crisp was a former heavyweight contender. He was quick and solid, and everyone had backed him to fly up the ranks after he left the amateurs. Thing was, he was a bit of a dirtbag. He liked dropping acid and fucking all kinds of women more than he liked training. The title never came Mickey Jack's way, but hardship did. His life was full of late-night fighting and early-morning dodging. He was getting older and growing more tired of that kind of life.

He needed to get a job.

A guy who knew a guy whispered something about something back in Florida where Mickey lived. The whisper sounded like something Mickey could do, *and* there was travel involved.

Mickey had found himself a job. The pay was good, and killing an old man didn't sound too difficult.

Mickey took a flight out to San Francisco. He stood in a phone booth at the top of a huge unfurled hill and scanned the bay view. The bridge, the island, all the boats meandering left and right. The air was the kind that helped with a good night's sleep. Micky already felt like a new man.

Pity he wouldn't be here long.

He pulled Merv's picture from the inside pocket of his coat and studied it. Mickey knew what his orders were, but wasn't sure about this situation.

"Yeah, I'm just outside the place, but there's something going on over there." Mickey said into the phone.

He waited for the response.

Mickey grew impatient. "No, there are cars and people everywhere. You told me it was supposed to be just the old man and his wife at home."

Mickey didn't seem to be painting a good enough picture. "Tell your guy that I'm out. I came here to do what I was supposed to, but there's twenty people milling around his house, and he ain't one of them."

The voice on the phone made Mickey take a breath and look again.

"Yes, it looks like a doll's house. Franklin Street. I'm in the right place." Mickey heard some movement in the direction of the house. "Wait. Wait." Mickey put the phone down for a closer look.

"Are you fucking serious?" he mumbled to himself as he pieced together what was unfolding in front of him.

January 21, 1969 — Three Days Earlier.
Memphis.

Merv owned shares in a few prize horses. The trick was picking them before they came to peak, or stealing them when everyone else said they were finished. He took this approach to betting on his human investments too. In the wrestling business, Merv could pick the talent early and then get rid of them before their bodies broke down. He prided himself on his eye for squeezing the last drops of money from any investment. Even if this one was a broken-down singer.

There was very little difference in how he treated all his investments. He was always hands-on and always opinionated. Sometimes it worked and other times it got him removed from the process.

Like this time.

This investment was based on a track record gone to shit. The price to buy in was cheap because everyone outside a small pool of investors thought this asset was finished, no good. Merv didn't think so. He put down his good money and placed a bet. A bet that The King could do it again.

If he was right, he was about to be part of a very rich consortium. Unfortunately for Merv, that same fucking consortium was more interested in getting autographs and taking pictures than they were in making money.

Fucking marks.

That was how he found himself outside the American Sound Studio one bitterly cold night. It was only on nights like this that Merv knew exactly how old he had gotten. He hated the fact that he needed gloves in public. He thought they made him look like a fucking woman. He also had this thing lately that made his nose drip for no reason. If he bent down to tie his shoe, he would leak all over himself. Picking up the newspaper was the same. Even when he was taking a seat, he had to pretend that something on the roof caught his attention so he could compensate and tilt his head back to stop the snot running out. But nothing shut Merv down like that cold.

Where's my fucking car?

Only the job of protecting his money could get Merv away from *Rowan and Martin's Laugh-In* on a bitter night. But the way things were going inside the studio, he didn't see much of that coming his way, either. If this were his show alone, Merv would have The King grinding his cock in girls' faces again.

That's what worked the first time, and that's where the money is. Not this sensitive song shit.

Merv took an aggressive pull on his cigar and chaired an angry session in his head. He looked around the area where he stood. The whole place was falling apart. Closed shop fronts, chain-link fences where houses used to be. He could hear arguments in the distance.

They brought him to a dive, too. What is this place? You want to be a star, you've got to act like a star.

It was the same in the wrestling business. Presentation was everything. This was bullshit. Merv knew he didn't know all that much about music, but he was sure that people wanted to dance.

It's not my fucking fault that the momma's got another mouth to feed. What are we singing about it for? No one is going to buy this shit.

Merv shook his head in bewilderment and flicked the cigar butt as his driver turned the corner at the end of the street. He clasped his hands under his armpits and danced on the spot until his head was cracked open by a tire iron from behind.

Merv fell forward, but he was dead before he could even raise his hands to break his fall. In that one swift move, wrestling's tightest grip was released.

January 24, 1969 — Back to the Present.
San Francisco.

Mickey left the phone booth and watched the hearse pull into Merv's driveway. A legion of pasty old white people dressed in black walked into the house. A coffin emerged from the back door of the hearse.

Some of the women cried, but mostly it was a silent affair. A woman, looked to be the widow, was helped from another car with a black veil over her face. She was placed behind the coffin as it was marched in through her front door.

Mickey watched the proceedings in shock. He slid back into the phone booth and raised the phone to his mouth.

It took a couple of seconds before he could say, "Someone else got there before me."

January 26, 1969 — Two Days Later.
San Francisco.

There were midgets, beauty queens, tattooed faces, gold sunglasses, new white suits, hugely obese twins, a bald old woman, toothless mountain men, islanders, a one-legged man, and a widow. San Francisco welcomed difference admirably. But even it raised an eyebrow at this funeral.

The outer fence was lined with people who wanted to know what the spectacle was. Some younger voices chanted their favorite wrestler's name. When the time came, they all tried, with varying degrees of success, to bless themselves.

"John Merv O'Reilly, may you rest in peace."

Niko Frann leaned toward one of his wrestlers and whispered, "Was this guy faking the Jew thing too? Fucking asshole."

No heels or villains were present. The funeral was held in a public cemetery and the bad guys could never be seen in civil company with the good guys.

Danno and Lenny stood at the back of the crowd. Danno took a small bottle of mustard from his pocket and positioned a little dab on his ring finger. Lenny watched with interest. The crowd turned and walked away from the grave. Danno tapped the inner corners of both eyes, which produced a string of words not suitable for the Lord's ears.

One after the other, the rest of the promoters came and shook Danno's hand. Each was forcibly crying and testifying to what a wonderful human Merv was.

"He had two huge balls," Jacque Kaouet, the owner from Quebec, admirably tried to say. The others nodded in agreement.

It might have been Merv's funeral, but all of a sudden Danno Garland was the prettiest girl at the dance. And every one of them knew that he was next in line for the belt. Every one of them wondered if Danno was involved in causing the day's events.

Danno wondered that, too.

Merv's backyard was awash with black and somber tones. People spoke in hushed sentences and trays flew around like silver frisbees.

Merv's wife, Ade, sat on her back steps smoking and thinking. It was the kind of thinking no one wanted to interrupt.

Lenny was thinking, too—thinking that she was a fine woman. Much too elegant for what he heard about Merv.

Only the owners and the family had been allowed to go to Merv's house. Wrestlers were sent off to wherever it is they go. In truth, most of them had second and third jobs to be at. Wrestling was a great living if you were at the top of the card, but a soul-crushing paycheck if you weren't. By the looks of Merv's house, he had been earning far more than all the others put together.

Danno walked down the steps past Ade and made his way over to Lenny. "Where did you put the car?"

"I got it right beside the house," Lenny said.

"Good. I want to get out of here soon. Have you seen Proctor anywhere?" Danno noticed all the drinks lined up on the low wall beside Lenny.

"Everyone is coming over every two minutes with drinks and sandwiches for you, boss," Lenny said.

"They're all so generous when the drinks are already free," Danno answered.

He searched the crowd and the other bosses were all saluting him with their drinks. Danno raised his in return. "Ever get the feeling you're being fattened up to be eaten, Lenny?"

"Can't say that I have, sir."

Danno spotted Proctor staring in his direction. "And here's the cook himself," Danno said as Proctor got closer. "Go and wait over there, will you?"

Lenny walked away and Proctor shook Danno's hand. "Terrible tragedy, Danno. Who would have wanted it?"

Proctor toasted nothing in particular and demolished his drink. Danno quickly shushed him.

"What?" Proctor asked.

"You fucking know what. Be quiet," Danno said.

"What?"

"I didn't want this," Danno said under his breath without moving his lips.

"Want what?"

Danno turned his back to the gathering. "I've been in this business for fifteen years and I've never let it change my ethics or morals, Proctor. I didn't sign up for this."

"Me either. I mean, I'm not fucking crying that it happened, but . . ." Proctor sucked the remaining drops from the ice cubes at the bottom of his glass. "You think I did this?"

Danno walked a few steps away from the nearest set of ears. Proctor followed.

"You expect me to believe that this just happened?" Danno asked.

"What, that a rich old man got robbed in a bad neighborhood?"

"You telling me that's what happened?"

"Fucking right I am. My plan didn't involve any cracked heads. I'm telling you. Seriously. Fuck you, then. You won't be wanting the belt, I suppose?"

Danno began to soften in his suspicion. "I didn't say that."

"I thought so." Proctor nodded over Danno's shoulder and let him know with one simple old carnival word that someone outside the business was approaching—"Kayfabe."

Danno immediately changed the subject. "You can't say that Nixon doesn't have that something that Johnson didn't. He's clean and on the . . ."

Ade Schiller locked onto Proctor, ignoring Danno. "You staying?"

Proctor warned Ade with his eyes. "No, why would I do that?"

Ade waited for Proctor to say something else. He didn't. She shook her head with disgust. "Fuck you."

"Is everything alright here?" Danno asked to break the tension. Ade walked away.

"Must be the shock or something," Proctor said as he watched her leave.

"Yeah, shock," Danno half-heartedly agreed.

CHAPTER FOUR

January 27, 1969 — The Next Day.
San Francisco.

They couldn't let an opportunity go to waste. They were all in the same place at the same time anyway; they might as well do it now and add some stability to the business before anything got too loose, or potential challenges arose now that Merv was gone.

"To Danno," Proctor announced, standing at the end of the rented room with a glass in his hand.

All the other owners stood and joined the toast.

Proctor continued, "I'm not Irish like you, so my toasting abilities aren't as . . . flowery. But, may your giant visit my territory often and bring with him a wave of fucking money."

Everyone cheered in unison and lowered their drinks.

Danno sipped. This was the first minute of his life where he knew the clock had started; he would never be able to let his guard down again. Especially around these people.

"To doing business the right way," Curt Magee from Texas said simply.

Danno stood as all his colleagues walked over to him and slapped his back. There were offers of help and advice if he needed it. Some wanted him to come to their territories and stay for the weekend. Others brought wrapped gifts.

He didn't feel like it yet, but Danno was the boss now. All the other men in the room would depend on him to make his champion an attraction and then bring that attraction to their patch so they could sell tickets.

Danno had wanted the position, and he got it.

Proctor smiled at him from the other end of the table.

It was time to get to work.

CHAPTER FIVE

February 1, 1969 — Less Than a Week Later.
San Francisco.

"Cut the crying, Ade. Let's get down to business," Ricky said across the table.

Ade took the handkerchief away from her face and dropped the facade. "Fine."

They sat opposite each other in Ade's drab, miserable, dark-wood kitchen. Ricky picked up a sheet of paper and carefully read from it: "As Merv's closest kin, you are entitled to his San Francisco territory. You become a member of the NWC with voting privileges. If you do not want the territory, the NWC will handle the sale to a suitable buyer. As you may know, your husband was chairman of the NWC, but you, of course, cannot fill that position."

Ade shook her head. "Will I be able to survive on the money from this territory?"

Ricky looked around at Ade's palatial surroundings. "Without the champion, your gates are going to be bringing in less money. A lot less." Ricky went back to his sheet. He didn't get any pleasure from laying this out there, but he continued nonetheless. "On January 27 of this year, the NWC voted in favor of Danno Garland. He gets the world heavyweight title from San Francisco to bring to New York."

Ade stood up to get her cigarettes. "So he finally got it?" she said with a smile as she flicked her lighter. "I always liked Danno."

Ricky got the keen sense that Ade wasn't as out of the loop as she portrayed herself to be.

"Why isn't he here doing this himself?" she asked.

Ricky sat stone-faced at her table.

"I see. He won't talk to me about the business 'cause I'm not in the secret club yet."

Ricky looked at the rest of the sheet. He could see that all this formality was bouncing off Ade's head and going out the window.

"Listen," he said as he stood. "There's a couple things you have to know if you're going to be in this business. One, you're always, always going to have to protect it. Be careful of who you trust with the mechanics of what we do. And two, this whole setup we have begins and ends at making money. No friendships overrule that, no relationships, no circumstances. If one territory isn't pulling with the others, we all go down. And no one is going to let that happen, no matter the cost."

"Did Proctor King have anything to do with it?" Ade asked.

Ricky knew what she meant but didn't want to acknowledge it. "With what?"

"My husband."

"I thought he was mugged in Memphis."

"Mr. Plick, my husband was a fuckface. I am not like my husband. I have no love for this business. Unfortunately for me, my husband had no love of banks, telling the truth, or informing me where he squirreled away all of our money."

"So, we're clear?" Ricky held out his hand for Ade to shake.

She obliged. "I need to get people's attention quickly, don't I?"

"Transition in a territory is always hard. It's advisable to give the audience everything you have tonight."

Ade put a locket around her neck and kissed it as she grabbed her purse. "I will."

Sal Pellington used to have matinee-idol good looks. Shiny hair, a square jaw, a big chest, and a small waist. He used to be like Superman. Used to.

"Ladies and gentlemen, after forty-four seconds, we have a new NWC world heavyweight champion: The African Savage, Babu," shouted the appropriately mustachioed announcer through the house mic.

"It's the other way around, you fucking idiot. Babu, the African Savage," Danno shouted from the back.

Babu shoved the announcer through the ropes and dropped another elbow on the defenseless ex-champ. He might have won, but he wasn't finished yet. Not with the camera from KTXL in the arena.

The Cow Palace was rowdy about the decision, but they were livid about Babu's lack of class in victory. Their former champion was a stand-up guy who shook hands with the kids and posed for pictures after his match.

Babu dragged Sal to the corner and sat him up against the bottom turnbuckle. He turned his huge frame around, looked to the crowd, and backed his ass into Sal's face. Some irate spectators in the crowd started to flow over the barricades and toward the ring. The local cops weren't about to try too hard to protect the big stranger from New York from the punters they had to see every week. Besides, most of cops thought that was a piece of shit move, too.

"Okay, let's get him out of there," Danno ordered from the curtain. "Heels only."

Danno's men lined up and filed out into the arena like a gang of huge personal bodyguards. The boss only let the bad guys out to punch and manhandle the locals; that was no type of work for his good-guy characters to be seen doing.

Ricky Plick was the first down the aisle. He was dressed in hooded street gear, which made it easier for him to sucker punch members of the audience as he passed. Lenny sat in the crowd. Most of the other ring guys were doubling as referees, but he hadn't even graduated to that stage yet. So there he was, cheering and screaming like everyone else. Waiting for his chance to get in that cherished eighteen-by-eighteen-foot ring.

Ade Schiller stood with Danno at the curtain in the back of the arena. It was her time. She knew she didn't have any power to keep the heavyweight title with her husband gone—but she could try to keep her territory strong.

"Thanks, Danno," she said as she walked through the curtain. He nodded and smiled in return. He had always liked Ade, too.

All the wrestlers in the back jockeyed for position to see what she was going to do on her first night as boss. Danno knew the angle and he didn't want his promotion to have anything to do with what was about to happen. Promoters would do anything to keep their business strong. But women were different.

Ade jumped on Sal in the ring to protect him from any further attacks from Babu. She stood and slapped the giant right across his face. The crowd stopped instantly and focused on the ring. Ade grabbed the mic. "Get out of here, you giant piece of shit." The crowd roared their approval. "'Cause if you don't, I'm going to show these good people what a woman whooping a giant looks like in real life."

Fourth row center, Lenny was enthralled.

Babu picked up his belt and held it up one last time for the crowd to boo. He backed through the ropes and blew kisses to Ade as he left, surrounded by other wrestlers protecting his back.

That was what Ade was thanking Danno for. The new champ backed away and made her look strong. They didn't have to do that and she knew it. It was a mark of respect to get her on her way as new boss.

In the ring, Ade helped a battered Sal Pellington to his feet and held his arm skyward as the crowd ate it up.

"This is what a true champion looks like," she shouted into the mic. "Merv would be so proud."

The crowd calmed down and respectfully clapped at Ade's raw emotion. She and Sal triumphantly walked the four sides of the ring, pointing up to the sky.

Sal then dropped Ade with a punch. "You think I need your help to be a champion, woman?"

The crowd turned instantly riotous again.

"Holy fuck," Lenny shrieked with excitement.

Sal quickly grabbed the house mic that his limp new boss had dropped on her way to the dirty, bloodstained canvas. "If I had a crowbar, I'd crush your head in too, woman."

Sal spat on his new promoter and ran from the ring as the entire front block jumped the rails and gave chase. Ade lay on her stomach in the ring, covered in spittle and smiling to herself. It was the first angle that she had ever come up with, and it had worked perfectly. Merv wouldn't mind her using his memory to make money. And fuck him if he did. Sal Pellington, who was out of steam as a baby-face, had just been turned into the biggest heel in San Francisco.

That was the cake—now it was time to drop the cherry.

Ade took a piece of a broken razor blade from the locket Merv had given her when she found him sleeping with a whore a couple of years ago. Even though she had seen the Boys do it thousands of times over the years, she was still terrified. She positioned its sharp side and cut a small score at her hairline. Merv's voice rolled around in her head like he was talking it through with the rookies and greenhorns.

"Plenty of aspirin to thin the blood before you go out, run a deep cut along your forehead and hold your breath till you feel the fucking money rolling down your face."

Ade could feel an unfamiliar warmth running past her eye and down her cheek until it dropped off and colored the ring in crimson droplets.

"Red is green," Merv whispered from memory.

A wall of wrestlers let Sal in through the backstage curtain and fought off the oncomers. Business was done.

Ade stood up and fell around the ring to sell her attack. Her white blouse was soaked in red and members of the audience ran in horror to her aid. She found it hard to maintain her disorientation because, inside, she was overjoyed.

Lenny, still buzzing with pure excitement, jumped the railing and offered to help Ade out of the ring. She instead was escorted to the back by her wrestlers, who created a protective cocoon around her. Lenny slid under the bottom rope and stood watching the sea of people making their way to the exit. He loved being in the ring. He walked backward until he could feel the corner turnbuckles at his back.

For that one second, this was his ring and all the people had paid to see him.

Backstage, Sal waited at the curtain for Ade to stumble through. They embraced and shook hands. The house would be full again for the next few months to eventually see Sal get his. Even without a belt, smart owners knew how to draw money.

"Thanks, Sal, for looking out for me," Ade said as she tried to stop herself from bleeding on the floor.

Danno wasn't comfortable. He'd never seen a woman do that before. Or maybe he was uncomfortable at a first-time owner hitting the jackpot on her first time out. He hoped the big angle he had planned back home in New York would be as successful.

Sal and Babu shook hands too. New York had come to San Francisco and won the belt. It was their turn to run with it. Sal knew that being classy now meant he might later get a run as challenger in New York.

"Thanks, Champ," Sal said before lifting Babu's arm into the air. "For Merv."

Ade led the applause as she was getting looked over and patched up. She didn't feel anything for Merv, but she knew that there were those in the San Francisco territory who were still loyal to him.

Outside, Lenny slid the last of the ring into the truck and took out a smoke. He didn't really like the taste of tobacco, but he wanted to fit in with all the other crew. As he rested and took an awkward puff on his cigarette, he looked at a picture of his wife and son. It was well worn from late-night inspections. He was so happy to have met Bree. She was one of the great joys of his life, but he knew she was starting to hate his fucking guts.

Maybe a bracelet or something would bring her around?

Danno, Ricky, and Babu walked calmly to an empty room backstage. Their giddiness was pumping through one another. Ricky closed the door and all three hugged and jumped around in a circle. Danno merrily reached into his inside pocket and pulled out a hastily rolled brown envelope. "Look," he said, as he ripped it open.

Several rolls of hundred-dollar bills hit the floor.

All three men looked at the money and simultaneously cheered.

"We made more money here in one night as champion than we did in the last four months combined," Danno said. He head-locked Ricky Plick into his chest. "This is the man who got us here," Danno said as he kissed Ricky on the forehead. "You worked the crowds for fifteen years to get us here, Ricky. For my father before me, and me now. I won't forget that."

"Thanks, boss." Ricky shook Danno's hand and they hugged warmly.

"I wish the Sugarstick was here to see me now," Babu said, as he sat down and laid his belt on the floor.

"He'll hear. Everyone hears everything in this business," Danno said.

The significance of being champ was beginning to settle in on Babu's large shoulders. Many, many great wrestlers never got their hands on the title. Including his original trainer and mentor, the Sugarstick, Shane Montrose.

"You did a great job out there, and you're going to be a great champion," Ricky said, patting Babu on the back.

Ricky knew his own time had passed on getting the belt. Danno had told him about Proctor getting the strap next, and Ricky's body didn't feel much like holding out for another go-round.

"Now, where are we going to celebrate?" Ricky asked.

"I'll send the car back for you when they're all gone," Danno said to Babu as he opened the door.

Babu was clearly emotional. "We did it, boss."

Ricky left the room and waited in the hallway. Danno closed the door. "You're going to be everywhere now. You're going to be rich and you're going to be hated. You're going to have to do things that might turn your stomach. But most of all, you're going to do business. 'Cause that's all this is about."

Babu nodded.

"You did great tonight," Danno said as he left the room.

Ricky stopped Danno in the hallway. "Your father would have been proud of you, you know?"

"Wait till you see what I have planned next," Danno said with smile.

"Well, whichever way this angle with Proctor goes, you have in that room a giant fucking bank that's going to be around for a very long time."

Ricky was wrong.

"Hey, Mom. Did you see Bree tonight? She's not answering," Lenny asked. He was standing in a pay phone under a large freestanding sign that read: BIG TIME WRESTLING.

"Lenard. Oh, Lenard," Lenny's mother sobbed. "Where have you been? She's in the hospital."

Danno walked by and tapped the glass of the phone booth. "Get the truck out of here."

Ricky followed the boss. They both slipped into the waiting car. The fans were milling around the large parking lot, making noise and re-creating the scene they had just witnessed. They were still angry at their guy losing the title.

"What's wrong, Mom?" Lenny asked.

"She's had your daughter."

"She's had the baby?" Lenny asked, trying to hear over the shouting hordes.

"Two days ago. But . . . we didn't know where to get you. Oh, Lenard."

Danno's car horn sounded.

"I . . . what's wrong with her? Is she going to be okay?"

The car horn sounded again, more impatiently this time. Lenny tried to signal to the car, but he didn't know if Ricky or Danno could see him.

"I'm in San Francisco. Is she alright? Mom?"

"The little thing is trying so hard. You need to come home, son."

Ricky, with his hood up, exited the car and knocked on the glass. "Do you know how much that reinforced ring costs? We need to move the gear before we get killed."

Lenny nodded and gave Ricky the thumbs up, but Ricky didn't move. "Now. The boss is waiting."

Lenny's mother continued on the phone. "She's . . . they don't know, son. We're watching little Luke for you, but you should really come home."

Ricky thumped on the glass. "Move it." Some of the fans grew more curious about the commotion at the phone booth.

"I'm going to call you back, Mom." Lenny hung up and tried to gather himself. A curbstone smacked off the glass at the foot of the booth. Lenny looked up and saw a group of fans gathering as they approached.

"New York! They're over here!"

Ricky jumped into the car with Danno in it and Lenny ran to the truck. A loud bang sounded a few feet away as Lenny put his foot down. Ricky swerved between charging bodies and sped toward the bus stop and past the late-night liquor store. Lenny drove the truck on Ricky's tail.

"Was that a gun?" Danno asked, lying down on the backseat.

"I think so," Ricky said.

"What the fuck was Lenny doing back there?" Danno asked.

"I have no idea. He wasn't listening to me, that's for sure."

"Wave him down when you get a chance."

Ricky wasn't sure that was a good idea, but faithfully followed his boss's request. He pulled in beside Sunnyvale public housing and Lenny's truck pulled in behind them. Danno angrily disembarked and marched toward Lenny.

"Is there something wrong with you?" Danno shouted.

Lenny dropped out of the cab and stood with his head bowed in front of Danno.

"I said, is there something wrong with you?" Danno asked again.

Lenny thought about how to even begin to answer. He wasn't even sure that he could. "Trouble at home, sir."

"Bring her home some fucking perfume or something. The next time you put us all in danger like that, we're going to leave you there. You hear me?"

Lenny could feel his chin begin to twitch. "My new kid isn't doing well." He tried to hide his tears of worry. "She's . . . I don't know. Doesn't sound good."

"What?" Danno asked.

"My little girl is . . ." Lenny couldn't finish his sentence.

Danno fell silent.

"I don't know what to do," Lenny continued.

"She's going to be fine. You hear me?" Danno said.

Lenny nodded. Danno turned back to Ricky to see if he had anything to offer in this alien situation. Ricky just shrugged.

Danno checked his watch. "Now, we're going to go to the airport and get you on a plane."

"What?"

"We're going home," Danno said. "We'll take the car and Ricky can take the truck."

Ricky approached and whispered, "What about Babu?" into Danno's ear.

Danno pulled out a stack of cash and split it in half. He handed one half to Ricky.

"We need to talk when we get settled back in New York, boss," Ricky said.

Danno put out his hand and Ricky shook it. "I'll see you back there."

Danno opened the driver's door of the car. "You want to drive? Take your mind off it?"

Lenny entered and took the wheel. "Thank you."

Ricky pulled himself up into the truck and pointed it back toward the Cow Palace to collect the new heavyweight champion of the world. He'd find himself somewhere dark to wait until all the fans were gone first.

"Let's go home and meet your little girl," Danno said as he lowered himself into the passenger seat.

Lenny Long wasn't born into, or made for, the wrestling business. He was born in Long Island in the forties and grew up without fanfare or incident in a cul-de-sac neighborhood.

All his life he had wanted to be in the wrestling business. He had abnormally small hands for a man—small enough that his father used to call him Diane—so he never tried out for anything athletic.

Magazines, clippings, and programs—he collected a mountain of wrestling memorabilia before he eventually moved from his parents' home and tried to make it in the city. His everlasting dream was to stand in a ring and be booed by thousands.

Two weeks later, when he moved back home, Lenny met Bree Hominick outside his father's shop. She was small and cute and she was a session singer for Velvet Records. She was the best thing that Lenny had ever seen anywhere.

She was also Catholic, so Lenny did his best to get her pregnant as soon as possible. A pregnant Catholic girl signed a contract for life, and a woman this good looking was bound to get better offers than Lenny when she eventually moved to the city.

One child and one ring later, Lenny was safe in the knowledge that the devil rode the subway with Bree every time she went into Manhattan without him.

Amen.

She wanted to move her small family back to California when the singing jobs dried up. She was a West Coast girl and missed her folks, but Lenny wanted to remain in the heartland of wrestling country—New York.

At least it used to be, when he was growing up.

He didn't want to be a wrestler—and he certainly didn't have the body or athleticism for it—but Lenny wanted the chance to work a crowd. Just once. He wanted to be good enough to make them believe that what was happening to him was actually real, just like it was for him when he saw the Sugarstick get slammed on the concrete in Madison Square Garden when Lenny was a kid. The gasp of horror when Sugarstick hit the floor was a sound that Lenny would never forget. For days, Lenny had begged his parents to take him to the hospital to see if his favorite wrestler was okay.

That was when it all began for him.

He started out working for free as a program seller in Sunnyside Gardens. He would do two nights on the weekends and they would let him in, free of charge, for the wrestling shows. Lenny had been selling there for a couple of years before one night some of the ring crew had been jailed in New Jersey. Ricky Plick offered Lenny some extra cash to work the get-in and the tear-down. When he was done, he was told to follow them to White Plains and then to Trenton.

The work just kept on coming, and Lenny kept showing up.

Danno made things busy for him on the road and things began to slip at home. It wasn't right to be calling the house at three in the morning when the kids were asleep. When Lenny did call, Bree wanted to know things that he couldn't tell her.

Lenny just wanted to do right by his family and the earning potential was pretty big if you got fully in. He would also be one step closer to working that crowd.

CHAPTER SIX

February 2, 1969 — The Next Day.
New York.

The pink teddy bear was half hidden by Lenny's side as he walked down the busy hospital hallway. He was ready to either present it or drop it. Truth was, he didn't know which he was going to have to do.

He had no idea what was going on with his own family; it was time to ask a stranger.

The nurse at the desk tilted her head slightly to the right as she explained where Bree was. It seemed that both mother and child had been in trouble. Lenny didn't have the heart to ask about the outcome. He walked through the halls, taking the directions given, until he came to the ward's seating area. Lenny's mother and father both rose immediately and held out their arms. Lenny dropped the bear and felt his body begin to abandon him. His father had never hugged him in his whole life.

"Where's Bree?" Lenny asked.

Lenny opened the door and saw his beautiful wife lying still and awake. She didn't even turn her head to see who it was that entered. She immediately began to sob. "She didn't make it, Lenny. She tried. She did her best."

Lenny's world blurred. He quietly cried above his wife's head as he held her.

"I'm sorry," he said.

His wife's sobbing opened up and her whole body shook as she wailed. "Where were you?"

"I'm sorry."

"She waited to see you as long as she could."

Lenny could feel the actual pain of his wife's words choke him and rip at his chest. Night after night he convinced himself that his working in the wrestling business was all for them. All for his family. He worked harder so they could have a better life. If he worked more, he would get to go home sooner.

Maybe that was all bullshit.

Lenny and his wife held each other as the noise from other people's lives soaked in through the thin walls. Outside of his little family, no one knew or cared that his daughter had died. They walked the hallways with their own problems and candy from the vending machines. Little boys slid on the shiny hallway floor and little girls skipped along it.

Other families—happy families—walked the same ward smiling and carrying balloons and new, small, soft clothes and blankets.

"Where were you, Lenny?" Bree asked.

Lenny couldn't answer.

February 4, 1969 — Two Days Later.
New York.

Lenny carried the little white box in the crook of his arms. The weight of nothing to carry. All he could do was assure her with a whisper that they'd never forget her. Never. "I should have been there. I'm sorry. Please forgive me, little girl. Daddy loves you. Daddy loves you."

All the family, dressed in black, waited over the hole in the ground. Lenny could see that his wife could barely stand up any longer.

He knew it was tough for Bree when he was on the road. She and their young son had to live in his old bedroom in his parents' two-bedroom house. The same room where he'd hung pictures of the Sugarstick on his wall. The same room where he had abused himself in the eyes of the good Lord. This was the same room where he had tried, in vain, to get Bree naked before they got married. It was the same room where he'd put on his wedding suit. The same room where an unassembled crib lay in the corner.

The same room where he waited for his wife to cry herself to sleep after their daughter's funeral.

No one knew more than Lenny how hard it was to live in bedroom number two of the Long house. You slept six hours a night if you were exhausted; his father patrolled on insomnia and coffee. He was up at four forty-five and opened the store at six, then home at nine to grouchily disapprove of whatever his son was doing. Except today. Today, everyone was invited back to eat sandwiches, fumble over what to say, and leave very quietly.

Lenny had to make a change. His family needed their own space. Especially now. But what the fuck kind of chance did they have? He didn't even know where he was going to scrape together the money to pay for the funeral.

This was a different kind of pain. The kind that people sometimes don't come all the way back from. And certainly not in the spare bedroom of your in-laws' house. If Lenny didn't start earning soon, he knew his wife was going to leave for California.

Danno knocked at the porch door and stood waiting for an answer. Mr. Long popped his head out from the kitchen to see who was in his doorway.

"I got it, Pop," Lenny said as he walked to the door.

"How are you doing?" Danno asked.

Lenny was surprised to see Danno at his house. It felt kind of like seeing your teacher on a Saturday. "We're okay. Come in."

Lenny stepped aside, but Danno stayed outside. He slid his hand into his coat pocket and took out an envelope. "Sorry for your troubles."

Danno pushed the envelope into Lenny's hand. It was thick and heavy. Lenny was taken aback at Danno's unexpected generosity. "Thanks, but I'm going to pay you back."

"I'm sorry I wasn't there today. I can't handle anything happening to children. But it's done now, I suppose. We need to head to Boston tonight. I need a driver full time now. Maybe Mrs. Long could handle matters from here on out?"

Both men still had their hands on either side of the envelope. Lenny swallowed down and cleared away any pain that lay on the surface.

"Yeah. Of course, yeah."

Danno released his grasp and Lenny secured the money.

"Thank you, boss."

"You're welcome. Let's go to work."

CHAPTER SEVEN

April 10, 1969 — Nine Weeks Later.
New York.

Cadillac Coupe DeVille. Sounded great. Drove even better. Tough to corner sometimes, compared to other cars, but she was a pleasure on the open road. Especially with the top down. Stunning red on the outside and snow white on the inside. This was where Lenny wanted his family to be. Maybe if he kept working hard enough, he might get there. In the meantime, his job was to deliver this beauty to the Garlands at two thirty in the afternoon.

Lenny was never late. He pulled into the complex and looked for the Garlands' condo. A waiting Mrs. Garland signaled Lenny to pull into the driveway where she was standing. Lenny was surprised at how modest their home was. He wasn't sure what he had expected, but it certainly wasn't the simple duplex in front of him.

"You have a wonderful taste in cars, Mrs. Garland," Lenny said as he pulled into the drive.

"He's just finishing his sandwich and then he's coming down. Is everything running okay?"

"Perfect."

"He's going to be beside himself. His father used to have a Caddy, too," she said.

Inside the house, Danno chewed the last bites of his sandwich angrily. The newspaper in front of him read: BOY (12) CHOKES MOTHER WITH WRESTLING MANEUVER.

Danno knew he could ill afford this kind of attention right now. The money was starting to mount, but it was only a drop in the ocean compared to what was potentially on the table.

"Fuck." Danno balled up the newspaper and flung it in the trash.

Mrs. Garland heard Danno coming closer to their front door. "Wait, Dan." She ran to the door and covered her husband's eyes.

"What are you doing, woman?"

She leaned in close to his ear. "Shut up, you old fart."

Danno tried to claw her hands from his face.

"Happy anniversary." Mrs. Garland removed her hands to reveal the huge red convertible in their drive.

"Holy fuck."

"Dan."

"Sorry. Jesus Christ, that's beautiful." Danno slowly crept down his drive as if he was afraid he might scare the car into reverse. "Is this for me?"

Mrs. Garland proudly nodded.

"We can't afford this, woman," Danno said.

Lenny cleared his throat to let his boss know that he was there.

"Do you think a man of my husband's stature should have a car like this, Lenny?" Mrs. Garland asked.

"Absolutely. I couldn't agree more, Mrs. Garland," Lenny replied.

"Oh, well, if Lenny, my new accountant, says so," Danno said.

Danno delicately opened the driver's door.

Lenny said to Mrs. Garland. "My only concern, ma'am, is that he will like this car so much, he'll want to drive himself everywhere."

"If the price of gas rises above forty cents, I'm firing you and getting a bicycle anyway."

"Danno."

"Sorry, darling."

Danno molded the shape of his ass into the seat and adjusted the mirror just right. "It's not even our anniversary till Saturday."

"No—our anniversary is today, our party is on Saturday."

"Get in here," Danno said to his wife.

Mrs. Garland joined her husband in the passenger seat. "We should call Ricky and get him over here. I want to show off."

Lenny felt a little self-conscious just standing there in the middle of the Garlands' tender moment.

Danno slipped the car into reverse and backed it out of his driveway.

"What about Lenny?" Mrs. Garland asked.

"Fuck him."

"Danno."

"I'm only kidding. Get in here, boy. Very carefully, too. I don't want you soiling my new machine."

Lenny ran from the driveway to the car. "Pleasure, sir."

Danno clasped his wife's hand. "I know why you did this, but I love you for it."

"You're every bit the man your father was, Dan. And more. Don't forget that."

Danno put his shiny red gift into drive and pulled out, just like his father had in his 1950 red Cadillac Special Series Sedan nearly twenty years before him.

"It's good to have the belt," Danno said as he punched his foot to the floor.

Danno felt like a kid with a new bike in the drive. Maybe he could take his Caddy out again later. After the business was done. He craned his neck out his office window to see his anniversary gift shining in the Connecticut sun. His desk was smothered in huge gifts of all shapes and sizes from the other bosses, and the room was filled with cards and balloons.

He was on the phone with the last boss on his list. All the rest had replied to his invite weeks ago. Just one more piece of business and he could relax for the night.

"Fifty years married, Danno," Proctor shouted excitedly over speakerphone. "You're fifty fucking years gnawing on the same pussy. You the man, Danno. You the fucking man. You bet your fat ass I'll be there. I'll leave Mrs. Proctor here in Florida and bring some of the Boys instead."

Lenny mashed the button for Danno's speakerphone to mute, but Proctor hung up before he could. Besides presents and cards and balloons, Danno's room was also filled with wrestlers and a horrified Mrs. Garland holding a cake. "Who was that, Dan?"

Danno stood up and walked directly out of the silent room.

"Can you get a knife, Lenny?" Mrs. Garland asked.

They could all hear Danno roar with frustration at the end of the long corridor.

April 15, 1969 — Five Days Later.
New York.

Danno had part of his crew lined up in the empty bar downstairs. The Folsom Nightmare, a handsome black wrestler; Ginny Ortiz, a bleach-blond aging powerhouse; and Oscar Dewsbury, a massively obese bald man, lined up against the wall.

Danno walked back and forth in front of them like an old army sergeant going over the drills. "Now, I want me and Mrs. Garland to have a good anniversary party with no issues. We all remember why I had to ban the Christmas party last year."

Folsom bowed his head. "Sorry, boss."

Lenny entered the room with more giant gifts from the other owners.

Danno tossed Lenny the keys to his car. "Can you throw those in the trunk?"

Lenny nodded at Danno, but stayed in the room. He was hoping he might be included in the business of the evening.

"Now, Lenny," Danno said.

Lenny reluctantly left the room.

"Now, all the other bosses are going to be here, but there's always one to avoid. I'm not going to mention any names. We fucking know who that is."

"Proctor King?" asked Oscar.

Danno gripped his temples. Ginny elbowed Oscar for being stupid.

Danno continued. "We stay away from him and he stays away from us. Him and his crew are coming and they haven't a clean hand between them. Pass it around. No drama tonight." The gathered few nodded. "Okay," Danno said. "Ricky's going to run the room while I let my hair down. Anything that looks funny or sounds off, you let Ricky know."

The troop nodded again.

"I don't want no one playing Bullitt out there."

"So don't be afraid to loosen your ties is what I'm saying. I'd say that fat Mick will have plenty of alcohol," Proctor explained from the passenger seat of his van. "So drink as much as you can and be the life of this party. You hear me?"

Proctor was traveling to the party with Pee Chu Ming, a sneaky Japanese wrestler from North Carolina; Beguiling Barry Banner (he was named ironically); and the driver, the Professor of Pimposity Wayne (they couldn't think of a surname that suited).

"So treat this like a celebration, men," Proctor ordered while opening a bottle of Mac Dugan. "You'll be welcomed by your fellows with open arms. And if you're not, then fuck them."

At the end of the function room, all the other bosses were neatly and quietly facing their wives at specially laid out tables. A small pool of mid-card and enhancement wrestlers were cornered in at the fire exit. Danno sat at the head of the room and was the only boss who allowed his wrestlers to be at his table. Maybe it was old age, but lately he had been insisting on having his crew around him.

"All the other bosses politely replied via letter. Proctor, the ass-hole, had to pick up the phone and call me 'fat ass' in front of my fucking locker room," Danno said to Ricky Plick across the table. "I'm starting squats with you on Monday, Ricky."

"You might just have misheard him, boss," Ricky replied.

Danno stood up. "Maybe I should go and ask him."

Ricky covertly nodded to Ginny and the Folsom Nightmare on either side of Danno. Both sat their boss back down gently and respectfully. Danno threw back a shot of whiskey. "I mean, that was cruel. Wasn't it?" Danno asked.

His whole table nodded. Danno hid his frown in a whiskey glass.

In the restroom, two prototypical bleach-blond wrestlers were gleefully recounting the drama. "Did you hear that Proctor disre-spected Danno on his anni-fucking-versary?"

The other one replied giddily, "Yeah, I heard; this should be good."

Nothing made wrestlers happier than potential conflict and drama. Another lower-card wrestler was on the phone in the lobby. "Danno Garland is going to do something tonight. I'm telling you," he said as he looked around to make sure he wasn't being listened to.

Back in the function room, Proctor was tearing up the dance floor and stumbling into passersby. He grabbed the women dancing behind him and roughly spun them, held them, and slapped them on the ass. He was having a great time.

"You feeling okay, Proctor?" Ricky asked from the edge of the dance floor.

"Can't hear you."

"Why don't we get some air?" Ricky shouted.

"Why don't you fuck yourself?"

Proctor's traveling wrestlers stood up from their seats. They weren't sure what was going on, but they knew that something was starting. The remaining gossipy wrestlers at the other tables could hardly contain their joy. Ricky gestured for everyone to calm down.

"Now, why don't you go and get me another drink, sweetheart?" Proctor shouted to Ricky.

Ricky chewed on his boss's words of "no trouble." He turned and walked back to Danno's table. The other bosses looked on in shame. They didn't mind anyone becoming a drunken mess, but it just wasn't done in front of the wrestlers, and it certainly wasn't done in front of the wives or ordinary people at a family party. One by one, they made sure to catch Danno's eye and act out their disgust at Proctor's behavior.

Ricky retook his seat.

Danno threw back another shot. "What did he say?"

"He's just having a good time, boss."

"I should have left him at home. Nothing nowhere says I have to invite all the bosses. This is what I get for doing business with Proctor in the first place."

Oscar Dewsbury and the Folsom Nightmare stood up and excused themselves from the table.

"Did you hear that?" Folsom whispered as they walked a pace away from the table.

"You bet your black ass I did. They're doing business?" Oscar answered.

"Holy fuck, that's super kayfabe. That's top-secret shit." Folsom said as they split to share the latest gossip around the room.

Mrs. Garland walked elegantly between tables. She was playing the hostess, even in a closed hotel function room. She thanked people for coming and took their compliments with grace and humility. She was enjoying being the champion's boss's wife.

"Cheryl . . . Cheryl," Proctor called to her from across the floor. Annie Garland looked over her shoulder to see exactly who this man was addressing.

Ricky turned Danno away from the dance floor and signaled to Ginny to talk to Danno and keep him busy.

"Cheryl, you like to—" Proctor cut off and sang along with the chorus that was playing through the room, "This fucking song is about me!"

The whole room watched as Proctor wrapped his arms around Danno's wife and dragged her onto the floor. "Sing it, Cheryl."

Proctor ground his hips against Annie. She tried her best to smile and unlock Proctor's grip, but he wasn't about to let go. "You hold on, baby, and see if can you feel my Apollo 9."

She walloped him across the face. Lenny walked up to Proctor from behind and wrestled him off Mrs. Garland. Proctor drove his forehead into Lenny's face, which crushed Lenny's nose and loosened his teeth. Lenny fell to the ground. Proctor stomped on Lenny's torso and kicked him in the liver when he instinctively rolled into the fetal position.

Ricky Plick jumped from a chair and drove Proctor forward into an area of tables where the wrestlers were. Drinks and food detonated into the air. There was a confused second of silence before an instant mass brawl exploded.

Danno rose and turned to see the madness unfolding at the end of the room. All his family were running and tripping toward the doors. Women were screaming, windows were being smashed. Grown men were getting tossed over tables and imprinted into the stud walls.

"What the fuck happened?" Danno asked.

Ginny ran faster than his legs had ever carried him and gleefully launched himself into the spaghetti of human flesh. Proctor slid himself out from the bottom and threw a chair at the vacated DJ's booth. The decks hit the ground; the music stopped. The sudden jolt of quiet stunned the wrestlers into stopping their melee.

The other bosses marched in a group, with their wives, out of the room. There was no way they were getting caught up in this. Ricky grabbed Proctor from behind. Proctor put out his hands in a show of surrender.

"Get the fuck out of here," Ricky said as he marched him to the door.

"Are you going to let him treat me like this, Danno?" Proctor asked.

Ricky stopped and waited for his boss's nod. Danno looked around at the demolished room. His wife was crying and Lenny was bleeding and moaning loudly on the floor.

"Danno?" Proctor said. "Think about what we shook on."

Danno straightened himself up and cleared his throat. "Get rid of the cunt."

Proctor shrugged off his handler and began to walk himself to the door. His small posse followed behind, all staring at Danno with bad intentions. The terrified hotel manager quickly became horrified as he entered his best room.

"Oh, Danno. What am I going to do here now?" he asked.

"Can someone take Mrs. Garland home?" Danno asked. "It's okay, I'll be home in a couple of minutes." Danno kissed his shaking wife on the forehead and handed her over to two pairs of open arms. "Stay with her till I get home," Danno ordered his wife's escorts.

"My room is ruined, Danno," the manager said.

Danno ushered him to a private spot. "I'll pay you for the room, of course, the damage, and any business you're going to lose this week while it gets fixed."

"What happened?" the manager asked.

Ricky walked back into the room, shaking his head at Danno. This wasn't over and he wanted his boss to know it. The rest of Danno's wrestlers moved in together.

"You better leave," Danno said to the bewildered manager.

Proctor, the Jap, the Ugly Handsome One, and the Afro all came around the corner. Proctor's face was contorted with anger and drink. "You think I'm going to leave 'cause you told me to, Danno?" Proctor shouted as he entered the room.

The New York circle of wrestlers walked forward to protect their boss.

Danno walked in between both groups and pulled a small pistol from his inside pocket. He aimed it at Proctor's forehead. Everyone froze.

"I will blow the top of your fucking head clean off, Proctor," Danno said.

Proctor stopped. Even Danno's cluster was shocked and uncomfortable at his reaction.

Ricky carefully walked forward. "Boss?"

Danno never took his eyes off Proctor. "Business is business, but you went too far. You apologize for manhandling my wife or you're dying right here."

Proctor quickly sobered up. "You better be ready to use that, Danno."

"I fucking am."

Ricky put a calming hand on Danno's shoulder. Danno shrugged him off. "Apologize."

Proctor looked Danno's Boys in the eyes and smiled. "No."

Danno dropped Proctor to his knees with a direct kick in the balls. He clicked back the hammer and squeezed the handle of the gun as he pressed the barrel into Proctor's closed eye. "I've spent decades keeping her away from animals like you." Danno jabbed the gun into Proctor's mouth. "Do you fucking hear me, you cunt?"

"Boss," Ricky pleaded.

"Answer me, Proctor."

"Boss?" Ricky said.

"Fucking answer me," Danno shouted.

Ricky again interjected. "Boss, the cops are coming."

Danno tuned back into the room. He could hear the sirens in the background. "We're going to do this very same thing again, very fucking soon." Danno said as he wiped the sweat from his brow with his gun hand.

Proctor stayed locked on Danno. Pee Chu and Barry grabbed Proctor under the arms and dragged him from the room. Danno pocketed his gun.

"That fucking asshole," Pee Chu said to his boss as they hurried along the hallway.

"Danno has got the balls for this after all," Proctor said, laughing and limping uncomfortably down the hallway.

A rolled-up dish cloth never tastes good, especially when you're choking on your own blood at the same time. Lenny wondered if they used this cloth for mopping up dog piss. Sure tasted that way.

"Don't blow that nose, Lenny," Danno warned.

Lenny nodded from his sitting position on Danno's kitchen countertop. He had been placed there by his slightly wobbly boss, like a child with a grazed knee.

"You blow that and your eyes will close instantly. You'll be fucked. Uglier than usual."

Ricky Plick decapitated a few beers and laid one down beside "Doctor" Danno Garland, who was looking up Lenny's nose, guided by the light of a match. Ricky stuck another beer in Lenny's hand. "For after," Ricky said.

"After what?" Lenny mumbled through the cloth.

Danno blew out the match. "There's only one thing for a break like that."

"What's that?"

Danno quickly vise-gripped Lenny's nose and yanked it downward. Lenny howled in pain as a mixture of crunch and pop sounded inside his own head.

"It's done," Danno informed him. "You're in a bad way, kid. Your face looks like the inside of a surgical bucket. Luscious Lenny Long."

Ricky nodded. "Yeah, Luscious. Nice job, boss."

Lenny gingerly slid down from the counter and looked at himself in the mirror. His nose was deformed, but better than the last time he checked. His eyes were meaty and swollen and he was missing bits of his front teeth. "Proctor's got a head like a fucking anvil."

"Things got out of hand." Danno held up his drink and waited for his two guests to follow. "I'll sort things out with him tomorrow." They all three clinked and downed a mouthful of cold beer.

"I think I have some TV breakfasts in here. Have you seen these things? Shit in a dish. Should be lovely at this hour of the night," Danno said, leaning into his fridge.

"How is Mrs. Garland, boss?" Ricky asked.

Danno opened the microwave and threw the food in. "Two valium and some fresh sheets. I might not see her till next Friday."

Danno approached Lenny and put his arm around him. "You did a stupid fucking thing tonight, Lenny. I appreciate it."

"No problem, boss."

"People who put themselves out like that get rewarded in a very special way," Danno said as he pressed CANCEL and took the TV breakfast from the microwave. "People who put themselves out like that get the egg," he said as he opened the tray. "And I won't hear nothing about it." Danno took out the runny egg and put it in Lenny's hand.

"I don't think it's done, boss," Lenny replied.

"Done enough," Danno said as he tucked in to his lukewarm sausage.

"*I'm* done," Ricky said.

"I've seen women who can drink more than you, Ricky," Danno replied.

"No, I mean done. I'm retiring."

Danno dropped his fork and choked down his half warm, half chewed lump of meat.

Ricky continued, "I couldn't find a good time to tell you. Things are happening fast for you these days."

Danno wiped his hands on Lenny's shirt. "Done?"

"Yeah. My back is . . . you know."

"Fuck me."

"Yeah."

"Done?" Danno asked one last time to make absolutely sure.

Ricky nodded.

"You're my number one, Ricky," Danno said. "I mean, I knew you were hurting but . . ." Danno hugged Ricky.

Lenny could feel the closeness between Danno and Ricky. "I'd like to get involved more in the business," Lenny threw into the conversation.

Danno and Ricky both laughed simultaneously at Lenny's request.

Lenny was a little offended. "What?"

Both men clinked their glasses and laughed harder.

"What? What did I say?" Lenny asked.

Lenny's reaction to their reaction made them laugh even louder.

"You don't think I'm tough enough?" Lenny said.

"I know you're not," Ricky replied.

Lenny got more and more hurt at the way they viewed him. "Why not?" he asked as he blew his nose in the dish cloth.

"Don't . . ." Ricky said, trying to stop Lenny.

Lenny's eyes immediately swelled shut. "What the fuck happened?"

Danno's laughs went silent as he struggled to breathe.

"I can't fucking see," Lenny said.

Ricky collapsed into a seat, holding his belly. "You never blow out of a broken nose . . ."

"What, am I blind?" Lenny asked. His serious, worried tone made Danno and Ricky slap each other's legs with hilarity.

Danno suddenly stopped dead.

"What the fuck?" he said.

He walked the hallway to his front window and saw an orange reflection from outside dance on the glass as he approached.

"You alright?" Ricky asked.

"What's wrong?" Lenny wondered.

"Boss?" Ricky said.

Danno looked out his window. "Call the fucking fire department," he shouted back to Ricky as he ripped open his front door.

"What?" Ricky replied.

Danno stood on his top step and watched his new Cadillac burn.

Ricky followed Danno to the front door and Lenny latched onto him as a guide. Ricky looked, entranced, at the fire rising in Danno's driveway. The flames were blooming and swelling around the Cadillac's immaculate white interior. The red paint on the outside was ruined and bubbling. Ricky snapped to and grabbed Danno before he got too close to the car.

Danno struggled. "Get off me, Ricky. Get off me."

Ricky collapsed back into the hallway with Danno in his arms. The car was gone. Destroyed.

"This thing might blow. Isn't that what cars do?" Lenny said and asked at the same time.

"Annie," Danno shouted. "Annie!"

Danno shrugged free from Ricky and ran as fast as he could up his stairs. The car began to groan with the sounds of expanding metal. Ricky scrambled to his feet and pushed Lenny back toward the kitchen.

"Danno," Ricky roared at the top of his voice. "Stay down."

Ricky covered Lenny on the floor. Upstairs, Danno sat in the far corner of their room, with his groggy wife wrapped in his arms.

The blast from the gas tank shot straight up and its impact shattered all of the front windows in Danno's house. Annie jumped with fright. Danno held her close as she began to come around.

"It's okay," he whispered in her ear.

"What's happening?" she weakly asked.

Danno, sweating and out of breath, kissed her on her forehead.

Downstairs, Ricky edged toward the open front door. Lenny sat in awe of the destruction. "Holy fuck." Even though he could only make out watery shapes and colors, it was still mightily impressive.

Ricky shouted up the stairs, "You guys okay up there?"

Danno shouted down that they were fine.

Ricky watched over the flames as the neighbors of the Garlands came out and gathered at a distance. Lights were switching on in the houses across the road. In the middle of the chaos, Ricky could hear the wheels of another car squeal away from the scene.

CHAPTER EIGHT

"They look better than my real ones, don't you think?"

Bree was unpacking in the room across the hall.

"Honey?" Lenny said as he held his lips open and looked in the mirror. "They look really good, don't they?"

Bree walked into their bathroom and looked. "Can you get some stuff from the car now?"

Lenny walked down the hall with his lips peeled back and his teeth clenched. "It feels funny to have proper teeth again."

"They're not."

"Not what?"

"Proper teeth. Yours were proper teeth."

"Do you know how much these cost?" Lenny stopped and turned back toward his wife's voice.

"No. But I'm sure Danno told you over and over before he got them for you." Bree stood in the hallway and kicked off her shoes. Lenny had seen this look before. "Can we not talk about him?" Bree slipped into the room that would be their new bedroom.

Lenny hurried like a child chasing the ice cream truck. It had been a long time.

"We don't have nothing to lie on, and the floorboards don't look that comfortable," Bree said.

"I swear to God, I will find a sheep or a blanket or something to lie on if you let me have sex with you right now."

"Deal." Bree undid the buttons on her frayed bell-bottom jeans and waved Lenny out of the room to begin scavenging through the few boxes and bags they owned.

Lenny recklessly trampled from room to room. He stumbled down the raw board stairs and rummaged through the boxes stacked in the hallway, tossing family treasures and memorabilia aside.

A glint of broken glass caught his eye by the door. The once-coveted picture of Our Lady lay smashed in a makeshift bin in the corner. Lenny had found it under their bed in the move. Bree used to pay more attention to that image than she did to him sometimes.

All that had changed after the funeral. Lenny had never heard her mention her faith or God since.

"You find anything? It's getting cold up here," Bree shouted down the stairs.

"No, it's not. Do some jumping-jacks," he replied.

Lenny dug deeper and pulled out an old winter coat. Perfect. He backed up and jumped the stairs three steps at a time. Before he cornered into the bedroom, he slowed down and took a breath.

There she was, the woman he loved, waiting naked in the corner of the room. She shielded herself from the chill in the room by gently rubbing both her arms.

"Is that it? Is that what you got? A coat?"

"What's wrong with that?" Lenny said, tearing off his clothes like a child at the beach.

"A coat?"

"It's soft."

"You used to wear it fishing, Lenny."

"Please, honey. I have to go soon. Don't leave me hanging."

Bree looked down at Lenny. "You're not."

Lenny tried his best to pull a large red chair from the back of their car. He was wearing Bree's floral dressing gown and struggling to dislodge the seat and keep himself decent at the same time.

Bree peered out the top window. "Should I come down and help you?"

"No. Stay there, the way you are. I'll just be a sec."

Lenny dragged and pulled the seat to the door. Neighbors and cars passed as his gown came undone under the struggle. Everything was on show, but Lenny no longer cared. He was getting that seat into the house before their son came home from school, no matter what.

Lenny maneuvered the seat into the hallway, peeled off the little material still on him, and slammed the door. "Come down here, woman."

Eleven minutes later, and Bree sat, naked, on the red puffy chair in their hallway. Lenny was placid and relaxed, lying on the floor by her feet. He playfully nibbled on her toe as she swung her leg, in contentment, past his face.

"Stop," she said.

"What?"

"Feet are disgusting."

"Tasty feet."

Lenny again began to nibble.

"Stop."

Lenny stopped, but his legs weren't recharged enough to actually get up and function yet, so he stayed where he was.

"Is the door locked?" she asked.

"I think so."

"What would you do if your mother walked in now?"

"Die. And vomit," Lenny said.

"You'd die first, and then vomit?"

"I'd die first, then vomit, and then shit myself."

"You're disgusting. I'd say, 'How do you do Mrs. Long? Turned into a fine boy, hasn't he?'"

"And I'm disgusting?"

"I'd say, 'Show your mother the trick you showed me a few minutes ago.'"

"Stop." Lenny scraped over a stranded newspaper with his foot. The cover had a picture of Danno's burned-out car and a caption that read: SPORTING DECENCY UP IN SMOKE.

"Did you see this?" Lenny asked as he leafed through the inside.

Bree slid down onto the floor beside her husband. "Yeah. You better not get wrapped up in that madness."

"Danno thinks that someone leaked it to the papers. I heard him saying that there's information in that piece that people couldn't possibly know." Lenny opened to the article and showed Bree the accompanying photo of two wrestlers working in the ring. "Will you make me a costume?" he asked.

"No," she replied.

"Why not?"

"'Cause you're not seven."

Lenny continued to scan the magazine. "What would my gimmick be?"

"Your what?"

"Gimmick. My thing. What makes me different from everyone else. Every wrestler or manager has a gimmick. Some wrestlers have bull horns or bowler hats or feather boas."

"How about you're the only who doesn't wear clothes?" she said.

"Perfect."

Lenny got up and danced naked around their hallway. "I could dazzle my opponent with my gorgeousness and then hit him in the head with my giant, virile testicle."

"Left or right?"

"Left is bigger."

"Is it?"

Lenny seemed surprised that Bree didn't know that fact. "Yeah."

"Let me see." Bree put out her hand.

The inspection was interrupted by their front door handle being pulled down forcefully. The door lock did its job.

"Fuck," Bree said as she ran up the stairs. Lenny was already at the end of their hallway, hiding in the kitchen.

"It's your mom," Bree informed Lenny. "Do your trick."

CHAPTER NINE

"Your body is still growing. I'm sure you know that. Trouble is, it looks to me, anyway, that your major organs are still growing too. This is going to lead to a race of sorts, where your organs will outgrow, in terms of speed, the skeletal structure that holds them."

Christopher Reagan, known to the outside world as Babu, sat opposite the best doctor that a world heavyweight champion could buy. This wasn't how he wanted to spend his day off from being the most hated wrestler in America.

"What does that mean, doc?"

"I'm not sure. I've never seen this in person before, Christopher. However, all signs point to—"

"I want to know what to expect."

"It's hard to say for sure," the doctor said as he pored over his notes. He seemed like a man who hadn't studied for his test and was now just winging it.

"Well, fucking guess," Babu said as he swung his huge hand down onto the doctor's desk, the force of which made the doctor very anxious.

Babu immediately took a breath. "Sorry. I just need to know what I'm dealing with."

"I know this must be tough for you to understand."

"It sounds like it's tough for you to understand."

"I've never seen it before, if that's what you're saying."

"What do your books say? What do I have coming to me? I want to hear it. No sugarcoating, either."

"Okay," the doctor said slowly. "Several complications, most likely. Heart, lungs, and severe difficulty in movement." He stopped and looked up to double check that his patient really wanted to know.

He did.

"Maybe disfigurement of your skull . . . forehead and lower jaw could continue to grow disproportionately. I'm sorry. What I do know is that I'm the wrong person for you. There are huge gains being made in this field in—"

"How long till I . . . you know?"

"Again, it's hard to—"

"How long?"

"In my brief research, heart failure seems to be common. Some males in their mid-to-late forties."

Babu grabbed his trench coat, slipped it on, and buttoned it to the neck. He then put on a pair of sunglasses and a peaked baseball cap. "Thanks." He wrapped a garment around his head and walked down the corridor, ignoring the usual double-takes and staring.

"Wait," the doctor called after him. Babu never looked back.

A couple of hours later, Babu drunkenly tried to turn the key in his apartment.

"Surprise!" roared the whole wrestling company as he walked through the door. Danno stood front and center with a cake shaped like a wrestling ring in his hands. There were two fat candles in the middle of the ring. One was shaped like a 4 and the other like a 5.

"Congratulations," Danno whispered in his champ's ear. "We love ya."

December 22, 1969 — Four Weeks Later.
New York.

Melvin Pritchard loved the sport of boxing. He tried, when he was a boy, to become something in the ring—but he just didn't have it. He wasn't a violent man in any sense of the word, but he loved boxing. The majesty of it. The strategy. The competition. When he got married and opened his practice, he volunteered to work the corner for all the up-and-coming local kids. Dr. Pritchard was always there in their ear, calming them down, walking them through what was unfolding in the match. He was a student of the game and tried his best to pass that on to any young mind that would take it.

He put his own two sons in the ring as soon as they could stand unaided. Their whole relationship was based on the theory of a great fight. They would talk about it at dinner and practice it before bed. Melvin spent more time with his sons than any other father in New York. He did it because they were linked by more than duty.

When his sons got older and moved away, Melvin found that he didn't have much else in common with them. He didn't like using telephones, and they didn't seem to keep up with the boxing world once they were married and working. Melvin just carried on finding new people to teach and train. It was what he did his whole life. And what he hoped to do even more now that he had been instated as chairman of the New York State Athletic Commission.

He was effectively responsible for the laws and policies of the boxing world in New York. Well, boxing and wrestling, which had attached to it its embarrassing cousin, professional wrestling.

"Come in, Danno," Melvin offered as he held open his office door.

Danno entered the office with his hat in his hand and took a seat at Melvin's direction.

"Where's Mort?" Danno asked.

Melvin took his seat. "Are you a religious man, Danno?"

"Suppose I am."

"Then he's resting peacefully."

"And what if I wasn't?"

"Well, then he mercifully died after three weeks of intense pain due to a cancerous system that took over most of his vital organs."

Danno tried to remember how to cross himself the right way. He failed.

"What can I do for you . . . ?" Danno purposefully left his request open so Melvin would step in with his name. He didn't. He instead opened the brown file in front of him.

"I was sorry to read about your car," Melvin said.

"Not as sorry as I was," Danno replied.

"Any clue as to what happened?" Melvin asked.

"No. But it wasn't anything as dramatic or sinister as the paper made out. Some kids, maybe."

"Do you mind if I read from my notes here?" Melvin asked as he thumbed through the file's contents. "There's a world of interesting reading in here."

"Whatever you like," Danno replied.

Melvin cleared his throat. "It seems that our two sides have crossed many times over the years, Danno. Can I call you Danno?"

Danno nodded and opened his jacket button.

Melvin continued, "April 1910. A Federal court convicts John C. Maybray, Joe Carroll, Bert Warner, and other wrestlers and promoters of using the US mail to illegally rig the results of wrestling matches." Melvin continued to read. "I'm sorry; it's just I'm new to this job and I was going through the business of the commission here and some of these . . ." Melvin followed a passage with his finger. "1934. January. The New York State Athletic Commission investigates 'secret agreements' and 'title juggling' in wrestling at a January 9 hearing. After the witnesses testify, the New York State

Athletic Commission says, in a statement: 'We have heard all the testimony. We have sent it out to be translated into English. When that is done, we will consider it.'"

Danno knocked Melvin's desk in the hope of lifting his eyes from his file. "Is there something *I* can do for you?"

"Ronnie Milner, John Hurley, Jopper London . . ." Melvin recited from memory. "And Terry Garland. Isn't that your father?"

"He is. Was. And I can't be responsible for what he did or didn't do in the past."

Melvin sat back into his chair. "Am I supposed to believe that what you promote, Mr. Garland, is legitimately sporting?"

"Is this an official meeting?"

"Not yet."

"Well then, I'll see you when it becomes such." Danno settled his hat back onto his head as he stood. "You have a look at the cover of this week's *Sports Illustrated*, and check out my world heavyweight champion. Then tell me if we're legit or not."

"Danno?"

Danno stopped and turned back.

"I don't want anything other than an honest answer. Then we go quietly from there," Melvin said.

Danno leaned back toward Melvin. "We go wherever the fuck I say we go. You understand?" Danno pointed to the mounted picture of boxer, Jinky Keeves, behind Melvin's head. "You ask me if we're legitimate. I will put up ten thousand dollars that *five* of your boxers couldn't last ten minutes with any *one* of my guys."

Melvin cut Danno off. "That's not what I asked you. Your wrestlers may well be legitimate—but is your business?"

"We are one hundred percent more honest than fucking boxing," Danno replied as he turned and exited Melvin's office.

CHAPTER TEN

January 4, 1970.
New York.

Bree wasn't sure. Well, she was, but wanted to make sure she was sure. She placed the two-for-one box back on the shelf and looked around for an exit.

Sometimes the pain was sharp, and sometimes it was dull. She took a second to assess what was happening to her. She knew she had been overly jumpy this time around and she wanted to lessen any stress at this stage. The aisle in front of her was empty, its floor well polished. It ran, uninterrupted, to the exit if she needed it.

She took a second to decide if she needed it.

She needed it.

"Luke?" she called as she walked down the aisle to the door. "We gotta go."

The sound of her car engine at high speed scared Bree as she drove, but there was no way she was going to the hospital alone again this time. She could make it to the Garden in twenty minutes if she maintained the high speed. She didn't like to drive into the city, and certainly not at night, but she didn't feel like she had any choice.

It was the first Sunday of the new year and that meant Lenny was working in town and working Madison Square Garden.

All he talked about over Christmas was the hundred times he had been there as a fan and all the matches he had seen. About how the Sugarstick had walked down the aisle and the women's screams had deafened him.

This was his first show on the other side of the railing, and he couldn't wait.

The traffic on the bridge moved to pull her into Manhattan. One way or the other, all of this was happening to her and she had very little control over any of it. There was no way she would be in the city, at this time, if she didn't absolutely feel she had to.

Every traffic light sent her heart racing, hoping she could just keep moving through the decaying city.

"What's wrong with those people, Mommy?" her son asked her from the back seat. Bree wasn't sure what he saw, but she could bet that it wasn't any good.

"Close your eyes and go to sleep for me, baby. We're nearly there." She could see a light hanging red in front of them. She slowed down and tried to keep the car moving toward it without stopping.

"That man is waving to you," Luke told his mother.

Bree floored the pedal and gambled on the changing light. She narrowly made it. "Jesus," she quietly chastised herself. Her contractions were getting more intense and closer together.

"Where's Daddy?" Luke asked, getting a little jumpy from his mother's rashness.

"He's at work. We're going to find him," Bree replied, trying not to contort her face in pain.

"Are you okay, Mommy?"

"Just a cramp in my leg, little dude."

The young passenger was easily distracted from his mother's weirdness by the sights and sounds of the city. They turned left onto

West 33rd. Bree craned her neck, searching the cylindrical fortress that was the Garden, looking for the entrance. She saw a bunch of people that had to be wrestling fans, so she quickly followed them in her car.

"Excuse me," Bree said out her rolled-down window. "Is this a wrestling—are you going to a wrestling event?"

The group *whoohooooo*ed at her and kept on their march.

Bree again tried to get their attention. "Sorry, excuse me?" she said to the disinterested pool of people. "Hello?"

The pain was getting more pointed and impatient. She pressed her car horn to its limit. "I need my husband," she shouted at the top of her lungs.

The group stopped dead for a second. And then they moved on into the building, laughing at the sweaty, crazy lady in the car.

Lenny slept on the other side of the road with a newspaper over his face and his feet on the dashboard of Danno's otherwise empty car. He heard the commotion, but hearing car horns in Manhattan was like hearing birds in an aviary. The noise just usually wasn't this insistent and prolonged. He removed his paper mask and looked to see what nut job was causing a scene at the Garden this time.

"Bree?"

Bree continued to hold her hand on the car horn. Her son put his hands over his ears at his mother's request. Lenny left his car and hurried across the road. He knocked on his wife's passenger window, but Bree couldn't hear him. Lenny opened the door and entered the car. Bree only saw a figure in her car from the corner of her eye. She jumped with fright and lashed out. "Lenny, you nearly gave me a—"

Bree stopped and looked down at her belly.

"What's wrong, what are you doing here?"

"I'm having the baby," she said.

"Now?"

Bree grabbed her sides and sucked in the pain. "Yes, now. You need to drive."

Bree could now see the panic in her husband's face.

"What are you waiting for?" she asked.

"What?"

"Now." Bree's voice rose to a painful moan.

"Okay," Lenny said.

"Hey, Daddy," Luke said from the backseat.

Lenny turned to his boy. "Hey, little man. I didn't see you there."

"We need to go," Bree said.

"Okay. I just have to go inside and—"

"Are you serious?" Bree shouted.

"What?"

"Unless you have to go inside to get me a hospital you better not finish that sentence."

"No, I was just going to—"

"Fucking drive, Lenny!"

Bree opened her door and crab-walked around the car. Lenny pulled himself over into the driver's seat. They both took up their new positions and Lenny paused to pull his stubborn seatbelt down into the locked position. It stuck a few times but he was insistent. He also continuously looked past his struggling wife and into the entrance for somebody or something. He checked the mirrors. He put the car into drive and took off at a mile an hour from Madison Square Garden.

"You better hurry up or I'm going to kill you, Lenny."

"Sorry."

January 6, 1970—Two Days Later.
Memphis.

"Can we have two of everything, please?" Danno asked from the booth of Huey Burger in Midtown, Memphis, Tennessee.

They were in a hurry and Danno was rich. He'd been the promoter of the world heavyweight champion now for over a year and the money was beginning to seriously roll in.

Ricky, dressed uncomfortably in a suit and tie, sat opposite, writing something on the back of a napkin. "You sure you want to do this, boss?" Ricky asked.

Danno nodded and sprawled his arms confidently across the back of his seat.

Ricky still wasn't ready to commit this plan to paper. "Just think about it again. This has never been done before."

"I've thought about it enough." Danno pulled a walkie-talkie from his pocket and pushed the button. "Ten-four, Rubber Ducky. Come in."

"Here. Over," Lenny replied from his walkie-talkie outside.

"No, I mean come in here. The restaurant," Danno said.

Danno waved through the window at Lenny, who was watching them intently from the car.

"Into the restaurant? Over," Lenny asked.

"Yes. Over," Danno replied.

Lenny excitedly jumped out of the car and made his way through the parking lot.

"Lenny's got another baby now. Did you know?" Danno said.

"We need to talk alone, boss. This fucking guy is everywhere," Ricky said about Lenny.

Danno thought for a second and could see Ricky's point. He put up his hand to stop Lenny opening the door to enter. "Abort. Over."

"Awww. Over." Lenny disappointedly turned and headed back to the car.

"We'll get him a bag to go," Danno reasoned to himself.

Ricky studied his scribbled notes and focused back in on the business. "Well, Proctor is giving a hundred bucks a match down there—"

Danno interrupted, "Give his men two hundred for the night, and two fifty a week for two months if they agree to not work in that time period."

Ricky looked up from his plan and smiled. "You're going to pay them to not work?"

"If he's got no wrestlers, he's got no cards. Two months of no shows should be a big loss of earnings to the prick, don't you think? How much do you think a Cadillac Coupe DeVille costs?"

Ricky continued to write. Danno pulled himself closer and leaned into the table. "How much has he offered you? Proctor, I mean."

Ricky stopped writing again and dropped his pencil. "A hundred grand."

Danno smiled. "He likes his hundreds, this man. When?"

"I'm with you, just like your father before you," Ricky said.

"I know. When did he offer you to jump down to his territory?"

"Last time was a couple of days ago. I didn't say nothing 'cause there's nothing to talk about."

"I'll give you a hundred and ten—"

Ricky flapped his hands at Danno to stop talking about such undignified matters. "I'm happy with what we agreed when I started in the office."

"Let me finish, Ricky. A hundred and ten. The ten is so you can pay for the program." Danno picked up the menu for another look, just in case.

Ricky was taken totally by surprise. "What program?"

"I know what's going on in your life. You need to stop. If the Boys hear about what you're doing, then they'll cut you out. I can't have that in the locker room."

Ricky thought about trying to deny it again.

"Have we got a deal?" his boss asked.

Ricky reluctantly nodded and Danno shook his hand from behind the oversized menu. "Look at the size of that burger. Can we get Luscious Lenny in here now?"

Danno slid over the fake leather seat and knocked on the window. He again spoke into the walkie-talkie. "Din-din is a go. Over."

Lenny looked up. "You mean it? Over."

"Yes. Over."

"Well, it was kind of humiliating the last time, so I just wanted to check. Over."

Danno knocked on the window again and reassured Lenny with a more enthusiastic wave. Lenny again popped out of the car and rushed to the restaurant.

Danno laughed at Lenny's commitment to burger bars. "He fucking loves them. We can name every good burger joint along the East Coast between us."

Ricky began to quickly hide the notes from the table.

"It's okay. Lenny knows how to keep kayfabe."

That was a word that was used around Lenny a lot. Kayfabe. Over the years, Lenny grew to understand it to mean "shut the fuck up, here comes someone from outside this business," and it usually meant him. Anytime Ricky said "kayfabe" around Lenny, the conversation changed.

Danno slapped Lenny in the back of the neck. "He looks like a man who can hold his water."

"Yes, sir," Lenny, buoyed up at the mark of respect from his boss.

Ricky wiped his crumpled notes back into shape. He reluctantly began, "Okay. We're going—"

Danno cut across Ricky and spoke to Lenny. "I ordered one of everything."

"I'm starving. Looks good in here," Lenny said, answering his boss, but also holding his attention fully with Ricky.

"Can I . . . ?" Ricky wanted to know that he wasn't about to talk to himself.

"Sorry," Danno said.

"Okay," Ricky continued. "Proctor's planning a big card down there at the end of the year. If you still want to do this, we can arrange a card—"

"A loaded card? Better than his?" Danno asked.

Ricky nodded. "Yeah. We'll get everyone in."

Danno added. "I don't want us to do anything until he's paid for the building and advertised his matches. Then we pay his Boys to jump over to us and run on the same night."

"What's this?" Lenny asked.

"We're going to Florida." Danno answered. "What do you think of that?"

Lenny wanted to take his time and let his response sound measured and assured. "Great," he said.

"Maybe you can take that family of yours to Cypress Gardens while we're down there," Danno said.

"Love to." Lenny cut back in before his floor to speak was gone. "Proctor won't be too happy about that though, will he? You guys never run on each other's turf."

"You think?" Ricky said.

"Fuck him," Danno said with a look of disgust at the mere mention of his name. "You know what they call this in our business, Lenny? A fucking receipt. You hit me and I owe you one back. So here's your fucking receipt."

Lenny was starting to feel good about creeping into the inner circle. "And what about the business meeting you had today? What was that?"

Danno turned to Lenny with a very serious look on his face. "What was it?"

Ricky shook his head at the thought of his boss letting the cat out of the bag.

"Something big," Danno said. "Something really fucking big."

January 9, 1970 — Three Days Later.
New York.

Nothing was more secure than James Henry Long in his mother's arms. Nothing. Night after night, day after day, she watched him nonstop, held him all the time. She didn't want to say it, but she was afraid she might lose this new baby too.

"Do I look decked out? 'Cause I don't want to look like I made too much of an effort," Lenny said to his wife after his mirror rendered an inconclusive vote.

"You look like a man, Lenny."

"Look like a man," Lenny repeated. He paused and thought about his wife's comment. "I don't know what to think about that statement, darling."

"Handsome," she said.

Lenny walked over to his newborn son and kissed him on his tiny wrinkled forehead. "I keep thinking of little . . ." Lenny stood quickly and tried to flush out his thoughts. This was a happy day. A celebration of his new son.

"Me too," Bree said with tears in her eyes.

"Dad?" Luke called from his room. "Can I kick the dog?"

"Why?"

"'Cause he's an asshole."

Lenny again turned for his wife's opinion. "What did he say?"

"He said the dog's an asshole," she said.

Lenny paused. "And is he?"

Bree nodded.

"Can I?" his five-year-old son asked again.

"No. Put him out in the yard or something."

"I can't."

"Why not?"

"'Cause I . . ." Luke tried to think of some good reason as to why he couldn't put his dog out.

"'Cause you're too lazy," Lenny said.

"He's not too lazy," Bree answered for her son.

"He's not lazy?" Lenny replied. "This morning I saw him eat his cereal raw because the fridge was at the other side of the kitchen."

"How is cereal raw?" Bree asked.

"You know what I mean. Un-milked."

"He doesn't like the fridge."

Bree's answer stumped Lenny for second. "He doesn't like the fridge?"

"No," his wife said very matter-of-factly.

"Why not?" Lenny asked.

"'Cause a slice of bacon fell on him a couple of days ago."

Lenny paused for a third time and tried to absorb the quirks of his family.

"Bacon?" Lenny asked.

"Yeah. He thought it was a snake," Bree replied.

"He thought bacon was a snake? It's not even . . . they don't even look like each other."

Luke appeared in his parents' doorway. "Can you put him out, Dad? I just want to play a game and he's licking me in my ear."

"He's being nice," Lenny said.

"He's being an—"

"That's enough, son." Lenny scooped up his little boy and walked over to his bedroom. Brownie, the one-eyed family dog, was sitting on the bed and wagging his tail.

"He looks like a good dog to me," Lenny said.

Luke leaned toward his father's ear and whispered, "He's missing an eye and he looks like he has a hairy eye and he has no eye."

"Where did your mother find him?"

"Outside the store 'cause no one loved him and he's ugly 'cause he has one eye with hair growing in it."

Bree walked to Lenny and her son and hugged them both with the baby in her arms. "It's nice that you have a day off, Lenny."

Lenny thought so too.

After some careful logistics, Lenny managed to fill the family car with all that belonged to him. There was snot and bottles and bags and toys and strollers and diapers and milk and extra layers and suntan lotion—in January. There were lots of white clothes and the smell of freshly washed hair. And that baby smell. The nice one.

"Hey, Luscious," Ricky called from his car on the street outside Lenny's house.

"Luscious?" Bree asked.

"It's nothing," Lenny said as he walked from his driveway at speed to stop Ricky saying anything else that could get him in trouble.

"The boss needs to know where the church is," Ricky said.

Lenny whispered as he walked to Ricky's car. "It's nothing the boss needs to trouble himself with. It's fine. It's a small, family thing."

"The boss told us all to be there. So where's 'there'?" Rick asked.

Lenny looked back to see Bree trying to figure out what the holdup was. "No, really . . . tell the boss that everything is . . ."

"Lenny? Do you want to tell him that he's not invited?"

Bree noticed the parking lot of the church was unusually busy with gaudy muscle cars and packs of motorcycles. She was a little suspicious, although a quick glance at her husband's poker face gave her nothing further to go on. She had been giving God the cold shoulder since last year. And even though she felt she was dead right in this argument, she wanted to hedge her bets and have her new baby christened.

Lenny, ever the gentleman, opened the large, heavy wooden door and slipped into the church, leaving his wife and children struggling to follow him before the door banged closed.

They didn't make it.

Lenny looked around. They were all there. The whole New York territory.

Jesus fucking Christ.

"Lenny?" Bree said from the other side of the door. "What are you doing? Open the door."

Her questioning alerted the congregation to their arrival. Lenny despondently opened the door. "I'm sorry," he mouthed to his wife.

Bree walked in and saw the picture before her. "Holy fuck," was all she could say.

One of the waiting attendees whistled at their arrival, which sparked a massive ovation and a crying baby.

"I'm sorry. I'm sorry. I didn't have any choice. I'm sorry," Lenny said under the deafening applause.

Bree pressed her newborn's head as close to her chest as she could. Her five-year-old hugged her leg. The Long family walked down the aisle toward a perplexed-looking priest through a forest of applause and backslaps. Lenny felt great that he meant so much to his wrestling family. Bree didn't, and neither did her terrified children.

"Honey, this is Danno. My boss."

Danno put out his arms for Bree to fill.

"Hello," she countered with a handshake. "Nice to finally meet you."

The church was now empty and the awkwardness of Danno and Bree's exchange had nowhere to hide.

"Beautiful service," Danno said as he pulled back the blue blanket to look at the baby's face. "We wouldn't have missed it for the world."

"Okay, thanks for coming," Bree said as she moved her family to the door.

"Wait a minute. Where are you going, Lenny?"

Lenny stopped. "Nowhere, sir. Just for a little to eat."

Danno reached into his pocket and pulled out a wadded-up bundle of notes. "There will be nothing little about today." Danno peeled off the top five or six hundred-dollar bills and planted them in Lenny's pocket. "Go and get a cake and we'll meet you in Casper's."

Bree retrieved the money and politely handed it back. "You're very kind, but we were just going to keep it simple on account of the noise and . . ."

Danno nodded. "Of course."

"I could get something small," Lenny meekly chimed in. "It would only be for a couple of hours, wouldn't it?"

"Absolutely. Nice to meet you," Danno said to Bree.

"We'll be straight there, boss," Lenny said.

"Lovely child." Danno turned and walked away with a whistle.

Lenny could feel the heat of his wife's rage on the tip of his nose. "What could I say?"

"How much time do you people have to be together? Huh? And what's with the orders on your day off? 'Get the fucking cake'?"

Lenny slipped out a nervous laugh.

"What's funny?" she asked.

"Bree," Lenny said, stopping his wife's rant. "How many drivers do you think get this kind of attention from their boss?"

"Exactly." Bree grabbed Luke by the arm and walked down the long aisle toward the door.

CHAPTER ELEVEN

March 25, 1970 — Two and a Half Months Later.
New York.

Melvin turned his car into Danno's driveway. The large estate in front of him was busy with storage trucks and workmen who were lifting furniture into the house. He slowly approached, then stopped and slipped his car into park.

Danno Garland's new house was big and square and had rows of square windows. It sat on five acres and had a driveway that grew wider as you approached the front of the house. It was a farmhouse with barns and un-city-like structures in the back with nosy horses at the sides.

Melvin checked his mirror before opening his door and taking in the scene in front of him. It seemed like wrestling paid a hell of lot more than the State Athletic Commission did.

The idyllic setting was punctured when Melvin saw Danno come charging from his front door. "What do you want?" Danno said like he was talking to a sworn enemy.

Maybe he was.

Melvin stood still at his car. "I've been trying to reach you for several days, Mr. Garland."

"So you come to my house?" Danno walked straight into Melvin's face. "Get the fuck out of here."

Melvin stepped back until he pressed into his own car. "You should hear this, Danno."

"Dan?" called Mrs. Garland from a window on the second floor. "Is everything okay down there?"

Danno stepped back and assured his wife with a smile that everything was fine.

"I didn't think coming to your home on a workday would cause you such distress. I have truly tried every other form of contact that I know to reach you," Melvin said.

"What is it?"

Melvin drew Danno's attention to all the movers, who had stopped working. "Would you like to talk someplace else?"

"No." Danno turned to the stopped workmen. "Is there something I can do for you people?"

Work quickly resumed and Danno focused back on Melvin. "Well?"

"There's a senator by the name of Hilary J. Tenenbaum from New York. Are you aware of him?"

"Why?"

"'Cause he's about to hold hearings. He wants to introduce a bill to ban professional wrestling in the state of New York."

Danno gave Melvin a silent, disinterested look.

"Did you hear me, Mr. Garland?"

"Let me tell you something, Mr. Pritchard. You people have no problem taking your cut from my business. You can pretend to be horrified by us when the papers ask or when someone is running for government. But I have yet to receive a returned check in all the years I have been kicking up to your people. You understand me?"

Melvin turned back to his car. "This guy is serious."

"You can try me. Let's see how far you get."

May 19, 1970 — Two Months Later.
New York.

Danno, Lenny, and Ricky stood at the end of Danno's driveway. Lenny was dressed like a circus clown. Danno's house and gardens were garnished with balloons and streamers, and a wrestling ring was set up in the front.

"What time did they say, Lenny?" Danno asked.

"Four, boss," Lenny replied.

Danno noticed the great indifference in Ricky's face. "We are going to win this war in the papers."

Ricky silently walked away.

A car pulled past the gates and entered the bottom of the driveway. "You ready?"

"Yes, sir," Lenny answered.

Danno took up his position on the other side of the driveway. "Remember, don't shake their hands or anything 'cause you don't know what they've got."

Lenny nodded.

Oscar Dewsbury pulled the car up beside his boss. Three young boys' heads excitedly stuck out the back window.

"What the fuck?" Danno said.

Oscar Dewsbury moved his large body from the driver's seat and began to explain before his boss lost his temper. "Now, the hospital wouldn't gimme none," he said in his Southern accent.

"Did you tell them what it was for?" Danno asked.

"I sure did. They said they didn't much care."

"So who the fuck owns these?" Danno asked.

Oscar turned around and smiled and waved at the children in the back. "Well, they came from the orphanage. Father Vincini gave them to me for a couple of hours."

"Are any of them sick?"

Oscar shook his head. "Not that he was aware of. Although the smallest one has a slight stutter."

Danno could hardly contain his rage. "What the fuck am I sup-posed to do with three normal orphans?"

"I'm sorry, boss, but I didn't want to come back empty-handed."

Danno and Lenny sat at the top of Danno's front steps.

"Did any of the other bosses send presents or donations for the kids?" Danno asked.

Lenny shook his head. "They probably forgot or something."

They both watched the orphans running around having fun. The WRESTLE FOR REALLY SICK CHILDREN banner above the wrestling ring in the garden flapped in the wind.

"What time are the press getting here?" Danno asked.

Lenny looked at his watch. "In about twenty minutes, boss."

Danno took a deep breath in through his nose and let it flap his lips on the way out. "This place was supposed to be packed with polio and head bandages. Hundreds of them. I thought a hospital would be delighted to get rid of the kids for a few hours."

Danno turned to see Ricky watching them from the side of the garden and shaking his head at him in disgust.

"Any of your kids got anything?" Danno asked.

"No. Thankfully," Lenny replied.

"How are you with scissors?" Danno asked.

Danno sat one of the kids down on the closed toilet seat lid. Lenny was kneeling beside him with a pair of scissors and a razor while Oscar was blocking the doorway.

Danno pointed to Oscar. "You see this man?" he asked the terrified child. "You see his bald head? That's groovy, or whatever you say."

The child didn't move.

Danno mimed a scissors cutting with his fingers. "Okay?"

The child didn't move.

"He said, 'okay,'" Danno whispered.

"No he didn't," Lenny replied.

Danno grabbed the scissors from Lenny and cut a chunk from the child's hair.

"I don't like him," the child whispered, looking at Oscar.

"Huh?" Danno replied, pretending not to hear.

"I like my hair," the child said.

Danno continued to cut. "You like beer?"

"My hair," the child said more forcefully.

Danno stopped. "I'm sorry. I thought you said you wanted it like this. I was just trying to help you."

The little boy slid himself from the toilet and walked to the mirror. He was stunned by his lopsided new haircut.

Danno handed him a hundred-dollar bill. "We'll have to fix it now, son." Danno said, acting remorseful. "Couldn't possibly leave it like that."

The completely bald orphan sat beside Danno's knee and licked a giant lollipop. A middle-aged brunette reporter sat across from them and scribbled down her notes.

"How often do you come here?" she asked in a sympathetic voice.

"He finds it tiring to talk most times," Danno interjected.

"I see," she said.

"So . . ." Danno stopped.

"Pamela," the reporter supplied, smiling.

"Pamela, of course. You can see that professional wrestling is a big advocate for really sick children like Junior here."

"His name is Junior?"

"It is to me, because he feels like family right here in my home."

Danno took out his handkerchief and wiped "Junior's" forehead with it. "This is what I would rather be doing than having to answer nonsense questions from a senator who is struggling to make something of himself for the next election."

The reporter leaned forward toward Danno. "Senator Tenenbaum says that he and the American people have the right to know if your company is deceiving them out of their hard-earned cash, Mr. Garland."

"Pamela, you're in my home. I have nothing to hide." Danno shimmied himself to the edge of his seat and clasped the reporter's writing hand. "Let me show you something."

Danno and Pamela walked down Danno's large hallway. "I just wanted to take you away from there, because we're trying to keep Junior's spirits up and I know he's hard to look at."

"Excuse me?"

"I know." Danno passed Pamela into the waiting charge of Lenny in his clown suit at the front door. "I hope to see you before you leave."

"But I—"

"This is Lenny and he'll show you to your car."

Lenny quickly escorted the confused woman out of the house. Danno turned to see Ricky standing at the end of his hall with another man he didn't recognize.

Ricky walked toward his boss and introduced the stranger when he saw the coast was clear.

"This is Mickey Jack Crisp and he says he's been hired in the past by Proctor King. You should hear what he has to say."

CHAPTER TWELVE

July 11, 1970 — Two Months Later.
Florida.

Most of the heel dressing room was preparing in a strangely quiet way. Usually, when all the "bad" guys get together, you can't see the walls through the smoke or the floor through cans, fast-food wrappers, and playing cards.

This event was different. It had gotten off on the wrong foot.

One of wrestling's cardinal sins was entering a dressing room and not shaking all the hands that were in it. This was where most of the greenhorns got their asses whooped in the beginning. It didn't matter if you'd just left your fellow wrestlers in the hotel lobby five minutes before—when you walk into that dressing room full of those same people, you shake everyone's hand again.

That was the way the old-timers showed respect to each other, so that was the way it stayed.

However, this particular event wasn't one dressing room of wrestlers. It was two. Danno had brought his New York wrestlers down to Proctor's territory. That was bad enough. But he had paid Proctor's wrestlers to work for him, too.

That's where the handshake problem had started. The Floridian wrestlers didn't know if protocol was appropriate here. They would take Danno's money and help him fuck over Proctor, but they wouldn't shake the enemies' hands while doing it. It was the principle of the thing.

The guests from New York weren't happy about that at all.

"Hey you, asshole," Wild Ted Berry called across the room. "You and I doing business tonight?" The big stubble-covered Texan awaited a reply.

"Me?" Flawless Franco asked in reply.

"Yeah." Ted stood up to reveal his pre-match ritual of nudity, chewing tobacco, and cowboy boots. "You and me."

Franco nodded as he unlaced his dress shoes. "Sure. I'll work with you out there."

"Okay. Let's go out there and give these sunburned bitches a hell of a match. What's your name, sweetheart?"

Franco stopped suddenly with his shoe in his hand. "Sweetheart?"

"Yeah, something wrong with that?"

Franco stood up. He fell many inches short of Wild Ted. "Don't disrespect me in my own locker room, man."

All the New York wrestlers on Wild Ted's side of the locker room stood, which made all the Floridian wrestlers on Franco's side stand too.

"Did anyone tell all you marks that this is a fucking work in here? Relax, ladies," Wild Ted said, dismissively turning his back on Franco and his gang.

"It's a work out there," Franco replied, thumbing toward the arena. "Back here it's nothing but real."

Wild Ted tried to be respectful, but just couldn't. "'Back here it's nothing but real'?" Ted's crew began to laugh. "That's a terrible line."

"What?" Franco wanted to know. "What?"

The New York crew continued to laugh. "Back . . . here . . . it's . . . nothing . . . but . . ."

"Fuck you," Franco shouted.

"Is this guy not letting this go, or is it just me?" Wild Ted asked Oscar Dewsbury, who was getting ready beside him.

"I think he's making something of nothing," Oscar answered. "He's a bit rude, I think."

Ted walked to the middle of the locker room. "Yeah, I think he's a bit fucking rude too."

At the end of the hall, Danno watched Ricky write out all the night's matches in "the book" from his makeshift office.

"You been to that program yet?" Danno asked.

Ricky wasn't comfortable with Danno's persistence. He certainly wasn't comfortable being questioned in front of Lenny.

Danno leaned forward into Ricky's eyeline. "Hello?"

"I made an appointment. Going soon," Ricky mumbled.

"Do you need to make an appointment to go to one of those meetings nowadays?" Danno asked, looking for Lenny to weigh in.

"I'll go and let the Boys know what they're doing," Ricky said as he stood and left the room.

Danno lit a cigar and unsuccessfully attempted to throw his leg onto the corner of his table.

Fuck.

Danno knew Lenny saw him miss. Now they were both embarrassed.

Danno quickly tried again and fell short again.

"Fucking bitch." Danno stood and tossed over the table. "I have this new underwear restricting my legs from doing things they are used to," Danno said, bouncing his cigar off the fallen table in anger.

The cigar rolled to a stop under the changing room benches.

Danno thought about kneeling, but he wasn't sure his knees could take him back up in good enough time. Lenny wanted to help but was still pretending that he hadn't seen anything in the last minute or two.

Danno angrily swallowed his pride. "Can you get me that?"

Lenny hurried over and retrieved Danno's cigar from the floor. He prayed that act would kill the uncomfortable feeling in the room. He was wrong.

"I've gotten a little bigger since we got the belt," Danno said, biting the wet end from the cigar.

Lenny just wanted to jump out the fucking window in response. "You're just, eh . . . heavyset, boss. Manly."

Danno spat the bite of cigar in the bin. "I can't fucking tie my shoes no more, Lenny."

Lenny liked Danno. He thought he was great at his job, nice to work for. A mentor. What he liked most was Danno's pride and manhood. Both of which jumped out the window before Lenny could.

"Mrs. Garland got me a fucking stick thing with a slope. It goes on your ankle. Under it. Slides your foot in to the shoe."

"You just need a few back stretches. It's not 'cause you're fat or anything," Lenny said. "It's stress."

Danno knew somewhere that was bullshit. Still, he wanted to believe it. "You think it's just stiffness in my back? I feel strong, you know. In general," Danno said, tucking his shirt tight into his trousers and holding in his stomach.

"Muscle comes in different shapes. It's probably your big shoulders that are stopping you from getting down there quicker. You should stretch them, too."

Danno slowly rotated his shoulder in practice. "Yeah, fuck it. Just 'cause you're a big man doesn't mean you're unhealthy."

Ricky walked back into the doorway. "It's getting close to showtime. We should take some time to . . ." Ricky waited for Danno to follow his point.

"Yeah, oh yeah. Lenny, go wait in the car," Danno said.

"I know what's going on," Lenny said.

Ricky walked into the room, toward Lenny. "Yeah?" Ricky asked. "What's that?"

Lenny looked to Danno to step in and speak up for him. He didn't. "You're going over 'the book' to see who . . ."

"Who what?" Ricky asked.

"Who . . . goes over," Lenny replied. "Who wins the matches."

Ricky lit up Lenny's face with an open-hand slap that knocked him off his feet and into the metal lockers behind him. "What did you say?"

"Danno?" Lenny pleaded from the floor. "Tell him I . . ."

Danno closed his door. Ricky stooped over Lenny with a closed fist. "What did you say? I asked you."

Lenny tried to pull himself into the corner of the room. Ricky stopped him.

"What did you say?" Ricky shouted.

"Nothing," Lenny replied.

Ricky walloped Lenny again. "What?"

Lenny tried to cover up. "Nothing. I don't know anything."

Ricky pulled Lenny from the wall by his hair and dragged him to the door. Lenny struggled and kicked, but Ricky was too strong.

"You think this isn't real?" Ricky calmly said.

"Enough," Danno said.

Ricky shot Danno a look of pure disappointment.

"Gimme a minute," Danno said to Ricky. "You go and sort out the business and I'll find you in a second."

Ricky didn't move.

"Do it, Ricky," Danno ordered.

Ricky reluctantly let go of a terrified Lenny. "You better not talk about nothing when you leave here, Lenny," Ricky warned as he left the office.

Lenny was shaking.

"You're lucky he didn't break some bones," Danno said.

"What—"

"Shut up and listen, Lenny."

Lenny swallowed his next five sentences and wiped his eyes. Danno pulled up a seat and perched himself on the edge. "You

don't know fucking anything about anything around here. I promise you that."

"I won't say anything."

Danno could feel himself getting annoyed. "There's nothing to
say. Things around here and in this business are in a very tight spot
at the moment . . ."

"I know, boss."

"No, you fucking don't. Did you learn anything in here? You're a
driver. You worry about the car. That's it."

"I'm sorry. I won't open my mouth no more."

"I want you to go home." Danno grabbed his jacket and forced his
arms into the sleeves.

"You're firing me?"

"You don't smarten yourself up to this business, Lenny. You have
to be broken in by someone who's inside already. That's the way
things work."

Danno left.

Ginny Ortiz stood at the curtain and took in the crowd noise. He
wasn't happy Danno had paid the Floridian wrestlers more than he
was getting. All the years he worked for Danno, and Danno's father,
and some fucking jabroni loser was getting more than him on their
first night in.

What made Ginny even more irritable was the fact that he wasn't
confident he could make it through the ropes. But he hadn't missed
a match in his twenty-five years. Never missed a match and never
injured anyone he was working with.

That was about to change.

He desperately tried to slide his right elbow pad onto his arm, but
his left hand was numb and trembling. He'd been this way for the
last six months. Numbness, then pins and needles up and down his
arm. But he had always found a room or a dark corner by the curtain
to steady himself and get his head right.

Even Ginny knew that this was more than psychological now.

Wrestlers always had to pretend that they were more hurt than they were when they were in the ring, but they had to pretend to be less hurt than they actually were when they were in the dressing room. They could never be just how they were. If you asked for time off, you'd never get your spot back again. Owners hated weakness in their talent. If you don't wrestle, you don't get paid.

Simple.

That was why Ginny was trying in vain to simply put on an elbow pad. Wrestling was the only job he was ever good at; at fifty-one years of age, there wasn't much else he could expect to do.

"You let me get my shit in and then you make the comeback. Kick me in the nuts cause you're the heel. Then I'm going to give you my finish for the one-two-three. Okay?" the Folsom Nightmare said as he walked up the raw brick hallway.

Folsom's opponent didn't answer.

Ginny turned around to see Beguiling Barry Banner walking nonchalantly behind the Nightmare.

"You hear me?" Folsom asked. "I've come down from a civilized state to this place to slap you around."

Barry just chewed his gum and kept pace.

Ginny shook the sensation from his hand and tried, despairingly, to pull his elbow pad up before they got to him.

Folsom stopped suddenly and turned to his Floridian opponent. "You better say something to me that has the words 'yes' and 'sir' in it, or I'm going to beat your fucking ass right here in your hallway."

Barry tried to breeze his way past, but Folsom stopped him again. "You know why they call me 'The Folsom Nightmare'?"

"No idea."

The Folsom Nightmare grabbed Barry by the throat. "You want me to eat your fucking cheek meat?"

Even Ginny took a second to shake his head and laugh at that one. Barry slapped Folsom's hand away. "That made no sense."

"Neither does your mother," Folsom shouted.

Ginny dropped his pad and kicked it under the long black curtain. He tried to get something flowing by continually pumping his fist down by his side.

"You next, Ginny? I thought we were up," Folsom asked.

Ginny shook his head. "Sorry, I thought I was."

Ginny walked past both wrestlers toward the dressing rooms.

The Folsom Nightmare could see that his stablemate was acting kind of strange. Maybe it was the ungodly heat and humidity.

"This place is such a fucking dump, huh, Ginny?" Folsom shouted up the hallway.

Ginny didn't turn around or answer.

"How you doing?" Ricky asked Ginny as they passed in the hallway.

Ginny couldn't look him in the eye. "I'm good."

Ricky took a quick look around and leaned into Ginny. "How's your arm?"

Ginny took a second to think about it. He knew at least there was one guy he didn't have to bullshit. "Worse. It's getting worse."

"You have to tell Danno," Ricky said.

Ginny shook his head and walked on.

Danno heard the whispering. The questions. The comments made in the halls when it got out that he was running in Florida. Everyone in his office acted impressed and everyone in his locker room told him that it was a stroke of genius.

Then he left and they said what was really on their minds.

How could he possibly know what a crowd down there wants? They won't know any of the wrestlers from New York because they don't get our TV in Florida.

The biggest stars in Madison Square Garden would be absolute nobodies down south. That was the way the territories and the regional TV worked. The TV broadcasts that made these men stars were only shown in their specific markets. Without TV, no one knew who they were.

But Danno knew what Florida crowds wanted. Or at least he was willing to bet he was close. They wanted what every crowd wants: something new and exciting.

What he created in Florida was something that wasn't done that often in wrestling, and certainly not on purpose—this event was a home team versus the invaders. Wrestling just didn't have that. Usually a territory boss held the contracts of everyone that was on the card, so there was never an "us versus them" situation. That was why wrestling had always gone for the "good guy" versus the "bad guy" to create conflict for the spectators to get invested in.

That was what Ali did with Foreman, McCarthy did with the Russians, and every religion did with every other religion since the beginning of time.

Danno was tired of the good-guy-versus-bad-guy set up. And based on the sheer passion in the crowd, all his wrestlers in the dressing room, who had questioned his thinking, started to wonder if maybe Danno was right, after all.

This night there was absolutely no need for any of that kind of buildup or storyline to explain why these two wrestlers in the ring didn't like each other. They were simply from different places. People always hate people who aren't *their* people.

The Florida wrestlers were worshipped and the New York wrestlers were hated. Even the lower-card wrestlers, who usually got no reaction week to week when they worked for Proctor, were treated as heroes when they walked through that curtain for this event.

You could smell the money in the air.

"Where is he?" Ricky quietly asked Danno at the curtain.

Even though this huge gamble was paying off in every way, Danno was distant and removed.

"Boss?"

"Huh?"

"Where's Lenny?" Ricky asked.

"I need a new driver," Danno replied as he turned from the curtain. Ricky followed him. "What about Ginny?"

Danno stopped. "Ginny?"

"Yeah, why not?"

"'Cause he's a wrestler. Wrestlers don't drive for a living."

"Ginny is about as smartened up as anyone when it comes to this business. You wouldn't have to talk in rhymes all the time when you're on your way to somewhere. You could trust him with anything he hears. He'd be perfect."

"Is this him talking or you, Ricky?"

Ricky thought about his next sentence. "I know what it's like to get older in this business."

"And you're coming to me 'cause you're concerned for him?"

Ricky nodded, reluctantly.

"How nice." Danno turned and walked away. "If both of you go to a meeting, then I'll let him drive if he wants to."

Back in the ring, the Folsom Nightmare from New York picked Beguiling Barry Banner from Florida up by the hair. The crowd dutifully fired insults and boos in Folsom's direction. Back in New York, Folsom was usually the good guy. He was enjoying the hatred and taking it as a job well done.

He covertly leaned into Barry's ear and called for "a kick in the nuts."

Barry obliged and dropped him for real. Folsom hit the mat with just about all the pain he could take. And, like most nut shots, it only got worse in the moments after.

"What the fuck, man," Folsom shouted as Barry began to stomp on his chest in the corner.

Barry drove a hard knee into Folsom's head.

This was what the good trainers prepared you for before they broke you into the business. A shoot. A situation where you were going to have to be able to look after yourself for real in the ring. Unfortunately, Folsom had had a terrible trainer and was just trying to figure out what was happening.

Ricky could see Barry was taking liberties with his wrestler from the curtain. "What's he doing?"

The Flawless Franco walked away from the curtain without saying a word. Something wasn't right.

Even though Barry was laying them in, Folsom continued to do his job, which was to sell the ferocity of the moves to the audience. There wasn't that much acting going on. Barry's amateur wrestling background made him a legit badass. He wrapped himself around Folsom's neck and locked his hands. Folsom tried to breathe, but he could tell, as Barry began to apply pressure, that he was quickly blacking out.

The audience rose to its feet and wildly endorsed the unconscious body in the ring. Barry flipped Folsom over onto his stomach and made his way down to Folsom's feet.

Ricky knew. He hadn't seen it in years, but he knew. Barry mugged for the crowd who were demanding carnage.

"He's going to break it," Ricky shouted down toward the dressing room before he ran as fast as he could to the ring.

Barry dropped his knee straight down onto Folsom's heel and snapped it in half.

Folsom screamed in agony.

Ricky dove under the bottom rope and only managed to half connect his fist against Barry's head before the blow took Barry through the ropes and hard against the retaining railing.

The crowd littered the ring with their trash and booed ferociously. Ricky had just ruined the best action they had ever seen in a Floridian ring. Just vicious action. And the New York wrestler was hobbled.

It was magnificent.

Folsom, disoriented and in complete shock, began to try to walk. He stumbled at his first step and fell into the bottom rope. His foot was cocked almost ninety degrees to the side from his ankle. The locker room emptied and Barry ran through the crowd and stumbled past an unkempt former boxing talent called Mickey Jack Crisp as he left the building.

CHAPTER THIRTEEN

November 2, 1970 — Four Months Later.
Los Angeles.

The heat was sticky and unwelcome in a room without windows. Added to that was a cigar puffing contest, a broken fan, and enough tension to start a war.

"Nice room, Niko," Tanner Blackwell, from the Carolina territory, said sarcastically as he took his seat.

Niko replied with his middle finger. "Okay, welcome to Los Angeles. It's my pleasure to have you all in my territory. Eh, let's get straight to it. Danno declined to be chair, so Joe Lapine gets the job based on seniority."

The owners doled out a respectful but brief round of applause for Joe Lapine, from Memphis, as he stood. The chair of the National Wrestling Council was a powerful and important job. The position called for tact, diplomacy, and a lot of babysitting the other bosses.

Joe's first point of business was to give his condolences to the widow of the former chairman on behalf of the Council.

"Thank you all for making me feel welcome since I took over from my husband," Ade replied for the record.

At this stage, everyone was fed up with looking somber for that old bastard, but they trotted out the sorry-for-your-trouble face one more time. They knew it was all hollow formality and bullshit. Most of the room resented Ade even being there because one, her husband was such a prick to them for so long, and two, she happened to possess a vagina.

Joe ran his gaze around the table and noticed there was an empty seat. "Before we get on to business, where's Curt?" Joe asked the room as chairman. "Is he traveling late?"

Most of the owners looked puzzled or unaware of his whereabouts. Niko cleared his throat. "From what I understand, Curt Magee is gone."

Danno looked at Proctor for a reaction.

"Gone where?" Joe asked. "Don't fucking say heaven."

Niko wiped the sweat from his wrinkled brow. "There was a dispute in Texas with the local TV station there, something to do with ownership. Apparently they shut the station down and Curt couldn't hang on any longer while they figured it out."

There was general shock and empathy around the table—except from Proctor and Danno. It was hard to know if either had heard a word since they entered the room.

"A fifty-year territory—gone, like that," Niko continued with a click of his fingers.

"What happened?" Ade Schiller asked, concerned about making the same mistake in her greenness.

Niko scoffed at even being asked to explain.

"A bit of respect to a fellow owner, Niko," Joe said.

"You're probably going to find this out sooner rather than later, sweetheart, but there's really only two things that keep this business alive." Niko extended his thumb as a visual aid. "One, wrestlers that people want to see." He then duly extended his pointing finger. "And two, the TV to put them on. 'Cause honey, without TV, we're all a bunch of broke, angry men shouting at each other in an empty hall. We wouldn't last two months."

Ade nodded like she had known this all along. "Yeah. My own gates are starting to fall off."

She hoped her comment would spur on pearls of wisdom from her "colleagues."

"I noticed," Jose Rios, from Mexico, muttered as he looked at the cash returns to the Council. "'Fall off' is a polite term to use."

"Maybe you could have a little pink cake sale to raise some cash over there?" Niko mumbled back across the table to Ade.

"So Curt defaults Texas back to us? To the Council?" Ade asked.

"No, the territory is his. He can sell it to who he likes. They just have to kick back up to us if they want to run down there," Joe replied.

"Why are we here, Joe?" Proctor wanted to know. "I'm dying in here and we're talking about nothing."

"Let's get to our main business, shall we?" Joe asked the room for a consensus.

Danno and Proctor both nodded. Everyone seemed in agreement.

"Well, there has been serious concern, I think that's fair?" Joe stopped and took the temperature of his fellow owners. "Between us, with regard to the ongoing tension between two of our members."

"Just get to it," Danno said.

"Okay. We feel that this escalating . . . let's just say relationship between you two is going to end up costing us all money. Some of the rumors going around about the stuff that's happening to you two is a little shocking, to tell you the truth."

Danno stood up and pointed to Proctor. "I will not work with that man ever again."

Never in the history of the NWC had there been such a statement.

"Excuse me, Danno?" Joe interrupted. "But with all due respect, you have the belt. We took a vote to give it to you on your word that you would share the champion with us all equally."

Danno never took his eyes off Proctor. "And have I been good to my word?"

"Yes, but—" Joe said.

"I'm done here," Danno replied. He left the room in silence.

Ricky waited like an expectant father in the stairwell. Danno walked hurriedly down from the meeting.

"How did it go?" Ricky asked.

"Bought us some more time," Danno said.

"For what?" Ricky wanted to know.

Danno burst out the door.

November 10, 1970—Eight Days Later.
Boston.

Another raw brick hallway. Another show finished. Two more before the wrestlers could go home for a day. Then another twenty-day loop around the East Coast. The day off would do everyone good, except for the ones who had to do media. There had been a lot more of that lately—wrestling was a hot topic again—papers, magazines, radio.

Times like this were the wrestler's equivalent of making hay while the sun shone. The crowds were huge, which meant the payoffs were bigger than usual. A smart wrestler could retire to a nice small business off the back of a run like this.

That was why the injuries would have to be unbearable to get one of them to come off the road.

Ginny stood chewing some tobacco by the pay phone at the end of the hallway. Chewing some Beech-Nut at the end of the night was Ginny's nightcap. He'd given up drinking many years ago. He had to make up a story about there being a hole in his stomach and doctors telling him that he would die outright if he continued.

Truth was, he wasn't able to handle it. Some people were allergic to seafood; Ginny was allergic to alcohol.

Other wrestlers limped past him or delicately iced up their joints on the way to their cars. Pain or no pain, the cash payoffs were burning a hole in their newly bought polyester pants. They were rich on the road, but they'd be broke by the time they got home to their struggling families. It was the wrestler's curse. No one thought the well would dry up in the good times.

Or else they never thought they'd have to come off the road.

Ginny crushed a quarter into his hand. The hand that still worked. He was in agony, but the other passing wrestlers would never know. Most of the time the act didn't stop when they left the ring.

"Where are the rats, Ginny?" a fresh-faced farm boy wrestler from Oklahoma asked. Ginny didn't like the term "ring rats." He hated when the Boys talked about their conquests like that.

"What's wrong with calling them ladies?" Ginny asked.

The young wrestler frowned at the old-timer. "'Cause they're fucking rats, Ginny. They come to the shows to be fucked by the stars."

Ginny could see how statements like that seemed forced in the young guys. That was the way the road worked on you. Made you do things and say things that you never would at home. Give a man a roll of cash and no way home and it wouldn't take long to see the worst of him.

"We're going to Dreamer's Bar," the young Oklahoman offered to Ginny as he left. "Good match tonight."

The exodus from the locker room to the exit slowed to a stop. Ginny kept chewing and smiling, just in case there was a straggler still in the showers.

His whole body filled with an anxiety that wouldn't let him wait one more second before he sank the quarter into the phone.

Back in a small, tidy apartment in New York, Ricky picked up. "Hello?"

"It's me," Ginny whispered.

"Are you okay?" Ricky asked, sensing immediately something was wrong. He knew Ginny long enough to know that he hated using phones. "Ginny? What's wrong? You okay?"

Ginny paused and looked down at his dead arm. "I was fucking working with this greenhorn and he dropped me . . ."

"Jesus."

Ginny took a cautious look down the hallway. "Thing is, my arm is . . . I might need to take a week or two."

Ricky began to plan the shortest route in his head. "I'll be there in a little while."

"No. I'm fine. I need you to call Danno about that job. I'll take the driver's job. Just for a while till I get fixed or whatever."

Ricky was a little taken aback by Ginny's turnaround. "Okay."

"Okay. Thanks." Ginny hung up.

Ricky remembered what Danno's terms were.

November 11, 1970 — The Next Day.
New York.

"Sir?" asked the pretty secretary from around the waiting-room door. "Are you ready to change?"

Ricky thought about it for a second. He noticed the various Stations of the Cross that were hung around the room. The good Lord himself was there to witness his lie. "Sure."

"Good. The first step is admitting that you have a depraved hunger inside you."

Well, that was a bit harsh.

"Is the meeting through here?" Ricky wondered as he followed the brightly dressed woman down a small corridor.

"You have to do your interview first."

"Interview?"

The secretary nodded as she opened the door. "We need to see just how far your deviance has sunk. Have a nice day."

Ricky sat in the beige room and counted the lamps. There were a lot. And candles. And crucifixes. Nine lamps, floor and table top, about fifteen candles, and lots of crosses.

Fuck you, Danno. You fat piece of shit.

The door opened beyond the large desk and a very young-looking, thin, well-groomed man threaded through the doorframe and walked into the room.

Ricky stood and offered his hand. The man walked around the outstretched greeting and hugged Ricky really tightly for a really long time.

"Bless you, my son," the man whispered closely into Ricky's ear.

The man finally broke the embrace and offered his guest to take a seat. "My name is Rufus Shimmin."

"Shimmin?"

"Yes, Shimmin. Like swimming without the 'w' and the 'g.' Shimmin. And put in an 'h,' obviously."

Ricky nervously sat himself back down. "Okay."

Rufus confidently threw himself into his big chair behind the desk. "And you are?"

"Rick—"

Rufus cut Ricky off. "Apart from a sinner, I mean."

"Kevin . . . Myers."

Rufus put his feet onto the desk. Even the bottoms of his shoes were immaculately kept.

"Okay, *Kevin*," Rufus began mockingly. "Let's see if we can't get you back on the road to salvation." He reached under his desk and positioned a Super 8 camera facing Ricky.

"What are you doing there?" Ricky asked, leaning out of shot.

"I like to study my sessions later," Rufus answered.

Ricky shuffled his seat to the right of the lens. "Turn it off."

"Excuse me?"

"Turn it off."

Rufus dropped his feet from his desk and disappointedly pushed the camera away from Ricky. "It's a policy here, Mr. Myers."

"I came here for a group. One group. That's it. You give me a piece of paper or something to say that's what happened and I'll be on my way."

Rufus was shocked at Ricky's demands. "I can't do that."

"Why not?"

Rufus left his chair and positioned himself on the corner of his desk. "Because you can't walk out of here the same way you walked in. It's our promise."

Ricky was unsure of what to do next. He had pictured a group in a circle telling stories. Some place he could go but not take part.

Rufus playfully tapped Ricky's knee with his foot. "How often do you have thoughts of that nature?"

Ricky began to feel hugely uncomfortable. "What nature?"

"Well, you're a big man, Mr. Myers. I'm sure it's hard to contain all the urges that must run through a body like that."

Ricky stood up. "How about I smack your jaw?"

"Pray with me."

Ricky grabbed Rufus by the face. "We're done here," he said as he grabbed a business card from the desk.

The secretary burst in the door. "Leave him alone," she shouted.

Ricky looked around the room for peepholes. "What the fuck is wrong with you people?"

"You have a chance to change, Mr. Myers," Rufus shouted after Ricky.

Ricky got into his car outside the white building. Ginny was sitting in the passenger seat cradling his arm. "Well?"

Ricky didn't want to answer; he wanted to go back into that building and kick the shit out of Swimming or whatever his fucking name was.

"It's going to be okay," Ricky said as he leaned over and kissed Ginny.

"Didn't work, then?" Ginny asked with a smile.

Ricky angrily started the car. "How's your arm?" He pulled into traffic without really looking.

"The same," Ginny said.

Ricky slammed on the brake. "Fuck them. I want to do something."

A couple of cars behind started to honk.

"Like what?" Ginny asked.

"I don't know. You want to go dancing or something? Let's get on a plane and go somewhere for a few days."

"Move, asshole," shouted a voice from behind.

"We have groceries in the trunk. We don't want the ice cream to go all funny." Ginny said.

Ricky calmed down a little. "You're right." He pressed on the gas and headed down the road.

CHAPTER FOURTEEN

January 6, 1971 — Seven Weeks Later.
Los Angeles.

"No fucking way. Let some of those pieces of shit come down here and try and take the belt off me," Babu said as he put his foot through the greenroom door.

"Take it easy," Danno pleaded. "Don't get us thrown out of here. I've already made the deal."

"You're going to just hand Proctor the heavyweight title?" Babu asked.

They both heard footsteps approaching.

"Kayfabe," Danno said.

A young intern peeked warily into the room through where the door used to be. "They're ready for you, Mr. . . . ." The intern checked his clipboard. "Babu?"

The giant nodded and the intern walked quickly away. Babu ushered Danno into the corner of the room. "What the fuck am I doing here?" he whispered.

"You're going to be great. It will play to your strengths."

"I'm mute, remember."

"What does that matter?"

"It's a fucking *talk show*."

"It's a talk show *sketch*. National TV. You know how long it's been since our business has been allowed on national TV?" Danno said.

Danno signaled for Babu to follow him into the bathroom where they could talk openly. "I would never position you to look foolish or weak. Never. You're my champion. It's my job to make you look strong."

Danno locked the bathroom door behind them for extra peace of mind. The space remaining in there was tight. Very tight. Danno was pressed uncomfortably close to Babu's huge chest. He knew what was really bothering his champion.

"Why are you telling me to lose to these assholes?" Babu asked.

"It's business, Chrissy. That's all," Danno explained to the frustrated giant. "We've made our money for now. We play this right and give the belt to Proctor and we'll get it back again."

"Fuck the business for a minute, Danno. What about them disrespecting your wife, ruining your anniversary, nearly killing the two of you with the car exploding outside your house? They retired Folsom. He'll be lucky if he can walk without a cane for the rest of his life. You should have blown Proctor's fucking head off when you had the chance."

Danno looked up to placate Babu. "We can't forget the business, Chrissy. That's not what we do."

"There's no ticket sales in this."

"You're wrong."

"I'm not dropping the belt to those animals in Florida, Danno. Not after everything they've done to you and this company. Fuck them. All of them."

Babu smashed the stall door open with his hand. "I take pride in that belt. I work hard and always give the people a good show for their money. *They* won't do that."

Danno followed Babu back out into the empty greenroom. "Proctor is a better worker than you think. He'll do business the right way when the time comes."

Babu checked that the hallway outside was empty before speaking. "Well, he's not getting the belt. I still have respect enough to not let him walk all over you, even if you don't."

Babu walked toward the set.

Danno could feel the squeeze of the seat around his hips. He tried to maneuver himself to find a little comfort while the lights were dimmed. At the top of the studio, he could see people making their way back to their seats after the bathroom break. To his left was the vacated desk of the host, Jonny LaFleur. Over to his right, he could see Babu stepping out of his ape's costume. The sketch was over and now it was up to Danno to try to change the perception of the business for a national audience.

Jonny came flying back into his seat. He didn't make small talk or even look at Danno while a bevy of people huddled around him to touch him up, wipe him down, and tuck him in.

LaFleur was a man of a certain age who seemed to be desperately trying to cling on to times long past. He was caked in makeup, had unusually white false teeth, and possessed one of the worst hairpieces of all time.

In his own eyes, he was gorgeous.

"And we're coming back," a voice shouted from the darkness. The large APPLAUSE sign flashed. The audience clapped accordingly. The lights cranked up and Danno's eyes struggled to adjust.

The voice from the darkness started again. "And five . . . four . . . three . . ."

"Welcome back, everyone, to *Talk More with Jonny LaFleur*. My guest at this time is . . ." Jonny picked up the blue card in front of him and looked at Danno for the first time. "Danno Garland, who is a professional wrestling champion." Jonny stopped himself and looked to the crowd. "No, that can't be right."

Danno tried to pull his jacket closed over his belly and cleared his throat. "I'm an owner of a wrestling company. The best in the US, in fact."

"Oh, really? That makes more sense." Jonny threw his eyes to heaven and the audience played along with a laugh. "No offense."

Danno took a drink of water. "None taken."

"So, tell me, Danno. What is the perception of professional wrestling out there at the moment?"

"I think it's great. We're on magazines and shows like this now, which kinda speaks for itself a little bit—"

"Our musical act cancelled."

A drum beat off stage at the quip.

Danno continued with a fake smile. "Well, maybe so, but we appreciate the chance to come and talk to America about what we do."

"Okay, we'll get to that some more in a second. We just saw your champion in our skit before the break . . ." Jonny leaned into Danno. "He's a big fella, is he not?"

Finally, Jonny had teed up a question Danno could get some mileage from. "You're right. That's the heavyweight champion of the world. And I say 'world' because we found him in South Africa, of all places."

"Which part?"

Danno paused. "The most dangerous part."

Some of the audience laughed but Danno was starting to get a better sense of what he was dealing with.

"Okay," Jonny said, backing off a little. "I don't know much about what you people do. If you were a wrestler, what kind of wrestler would you be?"

"Me?"

Jonny disinterestedly nodded.

"Well, Jonny. As you can see, I probably wouldn't be the most agile wrestler, or the fastest, but I would try to be the most cunning, maybe."

"Smarts help you in there?" Jonny asked, half reading something else on his desk.

"Smarts help you everywhere, don't they? But in wrestling, in my business, you can strong-arm yourself into getting what you want, or you can plan your way there. Either way, you have to work with what the good Lord gave you. So that's the kind of wrestler I would be. Smart."

The host mimed himself sleeping as Danno finished. The audience again laughed a little. "My people tell me that all the news is about the owners of the different wrestling . . . places. What do you call it?"

"Yeah, there are other companies out there, but only one has the real world heavyweight champion."

LaFleur threw his talking points over his shoulder. "They tell me, though, that the only real fighting that goes on is between all you old guys behind the scenes. Is that true?"

Danno was growing more aware about how uncomfortable he was looking and just how comfortable old Jonny was looking. "I didn't know this was going to be an undercover piece, Jonny. Don't you have any knock-knock jokes?"

"So this is fake, though, right?" Jonny said as he reached into his pocket for his cigarettes.

"Excuse me?" Danno was no longer concerned about Jonny LaFleur, or his questioning. He knew the second those words left LaFleur's lips that they wouldn't be the only two people on set anymore.

Jonny repackaged his question as he lit up. "Fake? No?"

The crowd chuckled along. Right on cue, Babu appeared in the wing and walked right into the shot. He stood over the host with that look on his face.

"No," Danno warned his champion.

Every wrestler was drilled on protecting the business. No one dared call what these men did to feed their children fake. There were too many bum necks, torn muscles, divorced couples, and broken-down old-timers to call it that. Babu could never step into the dressing room again if he didn't do something.

Jonny laughed. "Is this part of the double act you two have going?"

Danno knew that there was only so much that even he could do for Jonny in a situation like this. "I just wouldn't continue to talk like that if I were you. Seriously."

"Right," Jonny replied sarcastically.

"I mean it," Danno warned. "This is the most dangerous man on the planet."

"Is that right?" Jonny rose from his chair and mockingly punched Babu in the chest. "I mean, this guy is huge, but he might as well be punching a kitten for all the damage he does."

Jonny sat back down and shuffled his cards for the next segment. He looked to his producers off camera. "Maybe next week we could get some ballet dancers on here?"

Babu grabbed Jonny around the throat and lifted him clean out of his chair. The audience gasped. Danno struggled free from his chair. "No, let him go," he shouted to Babu.

Babu walloped the host's head and LaFleur slid unconscious to the floor. Audience members cried out and the producers of the show ran around signaling in the dark.

Babu calmly walked into the wings and Danno followed him. He waited until they had passed all the terrified staff backstage before whisper-shouting, "What the fuck, Chrissy?"

Babu didn't answer.

Danno grabbed him by the shoulder and they both stopped in the empty hallway. "Do you know how much that's going to cost me?"

"I guess we'll have to keep the belt to pay for it then, boss."

January 7, 1971 — The Next Day.
New York.

Danno waited in the hangar. His chartered jet stood ready and open to bring him to Texas whenever he wanted to leave. "Can we get a second?" Danno tapped the driver's seat in front of him and Ginny snapped back from his daydream.

"Of course," Ginny said as he left the car.

"I don't want no pillow talk or whatever the fuck it is you people do," Danno warned Ricky.

Ricky produced Rufus Shimmin's card from his pocket. "It's over, I'm done."

"I'm too busy to call you a liar, Ricky."

"God made me like pussy now."

"Listen to me," Danno said with authority. "I have other matters more important than your strange faggy stuff. I want you to lay out a schedule that's going to take the champ out of here for a while. Send him to the other territories, but get him back to us for our big shows. Then, Japan, South America . . . there's even interest in taking him to Africa."

This was a highly unusual request on Danno's part.

"Okay," Ricky replied without any questions.

"Keep him out of New York; keep him earning, but keep him the fuck away from any media."

Babu's TV performance was going to cost Danno at least a million and also a brighter spotlight from the government.

"I don't know how long we have this belt for, but I'm going to lose a couple of years' earnings because of last night. Fucking asshole," Danno said before he left the car.

Ricky got out the other side. "You want me to go to Texas with you?"

"No. I'd like to meet with him one on one. Besides, I need you up here handling the champ's business."

Danno threw the end of his cigar on the hangar floor and walked to his waiting jet.

March 13, 1971 — Two Months Later.
New York.

Lenny struggled with his tie in the mirror. Downstairs, the dog was barking and Luke was screaming *"Bang! Bang!"* at some invisible enemy. The blender was at high pitch, mangling his breakfast shake.

Lenny wanted fucking bacon.

Piece of shit tie. Fucking stupid house.

The only one who seemed quiet and at peace was James Henry in the cot beside him.

"Hey," Bree called from the kitchen. "You okay?"

"I'm fine," Lenny replied. "I can feel a tap dance of pure joy coming on. You want to come up and watch?"

"Does it end with you jumping out the window and killing yourself?" Bree asked.

"It fucking might," Lenny replied.

"Good." Bree switched the blender back on. She stopped it again with a thought. "What do you think about opening our own business?"

"Doing what?"

"I don't know yet. I've always wanted to be my own boss."

"But honey, you're the boss of this house." Lenny could tell that Bree wasn't happy with that one. "The boss of my heart?"

"Are you trying to be an asshole, Lenny?"

At the breakfast table, Luke wanted his father to put up his hands and surrender.

"Where's your mom?" Lenny asked, choking down the green sludge that was left for him in the long glass.

"She's, she's changing James Henry's diaper, Dad. Now freeze."

Lenny half-heartedly put up one hand and tried to hold his paper with the other.

"Dad, put two of them up," Luke said.

Lenny dropped his paper and turned to his son and his plastic space gun. "You want to play something?"

Luke nodded.

"Put the gun down," Lenny said.

Luke did as he was told. Lenny quickly peeked out the kitchen door to see if his wife was a safe enough distance away. "Now, your mother wouldn't want me to show you this stuff."

Luke was instantly in. If he wasn't meant to do it, he wanted to do it even more. "What is it, Dad?"

Lenny broke out his pathetic double bicep pose. "Wrestling." He then threw a slow-motion air punch at his son and added a crunching sound effect at the end.

Luke didn't move.

"You have to sell the move, son. And work the crowd. Do you know what that is?"

Luke shook his head.

"Working the crowd means you make them believe you're injured. It's the most important thing in all of wrestling. If the audience doesn't believe you, then they don't care. Ready?"

Lenny threw another punch, but Luke didn't budge. "Okay, okay." Lenny did a few jumping jacks to limber up. "You do it to Daddy and I'll show you."

Luke wasn't sure. "What if I hurt you?"

"It's okay. Your old man can handle himself."

Luke aped his father's punch and landed a soft, slow blow into Lenny's stomach. Lenny dramatically fell to his knees and acted winded. Luke excitedly got the game.

"Good. Now finish me off," Lenny said.

Luke swung another air punch and Lenny fell over onto his back. "Now pin me, son."

Luke didn't understand what that meant.

"Jesus." Lenny rose up, grabbed his boy, and draped him over his own fallen body. "Count to three," Lenny said.

Luke began to count. "One, two . . ."

Lenny kicked out and was feeling it now. He began to comment on their match. "He just kicked out, ladies and gentlemen. Luscious Lenny Long is unstoppable."

Luke stood up and tried to figure out why his father didn't let him win. Lenny scooped Luke into the air and laid him flat on his little back.

"He's slammed him hard to the mat. It looks like Luscious is going for his finisher." Lenny grabbed his son's arm. Luke tried to stop him, but Lenny yanked it away from his body. "He's going to lock up that arm, and retain his championship."

Lenny stopped and noticed that his son was desperately trying to stop himself from crying. "What is it?" Lenny asked with dread. He looked around to make sure they were both still on their own. "Buddy?"

Luke nursed the arm that his father had just pulled on. His eyes closed and his mouth opened wide. He was crying but there was no sound. Yet.

"I'm sorry. Luke? Buddy?"

And soon followed the siren of a child's wailing.

Lenny reached into his pocket and pulled out a ten-dollar bill. "Here. Look. Luke? Here, you have this. Big pocket money this week."

His boy was inconsolable and his volume was growing louder. "You're really working your old man now, Luke. I totally believe that you're hurt. Good job. Do you hear me? Good job selling, little man."

Luke only got worse. The tears poured down his cheeks as he held his little arm close to his body. Lenny panicked at the thoughts of having to explain what happened to Bree, so he picked up his lunch bag and quickly left the house.

Lenny stood at the counter of his father's small, empty grocery shop. His stomach rumbled a little. He opened up his brown paper lunch bag and sank his hand in to get his tomato and rye. His fingers encountered the usual squishy parcel, but also something else.

Lenny opened the bag and took out a ball of material with a note attached. It read: "Sorry you're so down," in Bree's handwriting.

Lenny held up the material and his bewilderment started to come into focus.

"She did it," he muttered.

Lenny rushed over to the shop door and whipped the sign around to CLOSED.

A couple of minutes later and Luscious Lenny Long was standing in full wrestling gear at the back of the shop. It was an outfit worthy of the Luscious moniker. A ladies' pink swimming outfit had been carefully cut into pink trunks and the torso was cut in the shape of a heart from pelvis to neck.

There was even a pink headband to give him some real heat with the audience. Lenny posed in a musty corner shop in Long Island and let the world's cameras take his picture.

CHAPTER FIFTEEN

September 27, 1971.
New York.

The yellow cab screeched to a halt outside the large gray walls of Attica Correctional Facility.

Over the previous few weeks, stories of vicious killings, beatings, and torture had crept out over its walls. Thirty-nine people had been killed in an attempt by soldiers and prison guards to reclaim the prison from the inmates. Twenty-nine prisoners and ten officers who had been taken hostage were killed in the end. Weeks later, the remaining inmates were being stripped and beaten on a daily basis for their part in the uprising. Attica Correctional Facility was the most dangerous and volatile prison in America.

Gilbert stared at the intimidating gray structure from the cab's window.

"Thanks, Sheiky," Gilbert said to the driver as he took a neat roll of small bills from the crack of his ass.

The disgusted driver thought hard about taking the cash, but times were tough and it was a huge fare. He had driven the silent man for hours to get to this destination before noon. Even with traffic and sparse directions, he had made it on time. Ass crack or no ass crack, money was money.

Gilbert slid into his jacket and pointed to the bag beside him on the back seat. "Now, you take this to the address on that piece of paper I gave you," he said as he peeled off another twenty. "It's not a head or a gun or anything. Just some everyday things that I want to meet me there when I arrive. When you get there and the woman there checks that all my shit is present and correct, she has another hundred for you. Okay?"

The cab driver nodded.

"Good." Gilbert got out and watched the cab as it drove away.

A car horn sounded across the lot to grab Gilbert's attention.

"Hurry, you fucking lemon," a voice shouted.

Gilbert began to trot toward where he thought the voice came from. Proctor King stood, one leg in his waiting car and the other on the cold ground.

"Hey, Pop," Gilbert said as he slowed down. "How you doing?"

"Hurry the fuck up," Proctor ordered as he looked around to see if anyone could see them.

"Nice to see you, too." Gilbert kissed his father on the forehead and held him at arm's length to get a good look at him.

"You want to take a fucking picture?" Proctor asked, stuffing Gilbert in the back seat.

In the stationary car, both men watched each other in the rearview mirror.

"You look good, Pop."

"Did anyone see you arriving?" Proctor asked.

"No. Fuck. Do you think I'm fucking stupid or something? Jesus."

"You're lucky they aren't here yet," Proctor said.

"Fucking Raghead driving me. We killed the wrong Indians."

Proctor turned around to see his son. "You look good too."

"Thanks, Pop."

"What?" Proctor said.

"I said that's—"

Proctor tapped his right ear. "Lean in between the seats, into my right ear. Fucking deaf."

Gilbert leaned in and opened his mouth to speak, but his father elbowed him hard in the face before he could utter a word.

"What the fuck? What did you do that for?" Gilbert asked.

Proctor adjusted the mirror to see what damage was done. "Look where you were supposed to be for the last few years," Proctor said with a nod toward Attica. "Pure hell in there and you're sitting back there like you've been to the spa for a couple of years."

"Your elbow bone . . . what's that called?" Gilbert asked.

"An elbow."

"Yeah, it hit me in the eyeball."

Proctor could see a car arriving in the distance. "That's them. Go."

Gilbert opened the car door and snuck out. He tiptoed between the parked cars and carefully made his way up to the main gate of the prison to stoop out of sight.

Proctor walked out into the road and flapped his arms to distract the occupants of the oncoming car.

"You're late," Proctor said into the rolled-down window as the car slowed. Beguiling Barry Banner was driving with Flawless Franco in the passenger seat and Pee Chu Ming sitting beside a big-boobed blonde in the back.

"Sorry, boss. I thought you said twelve," Barry said, looking at his watch.

"We got him a coming-out present, boss," Pee Chu giggled from the back.

"Hi, Lizzie," Proctor said.

"Hi, Proctor," the big-boobed blonde replied. "We've been driving forever to get here."

"Just make Gilbert King happy when you see him come out of that hell hole," Pee Chu warned Lizzie.

Flawless Franco suddenly remembered himself and jumped out of the car. "Sorry. Sit in there, boss."

Gilbert whistled from the gate and walked toward the full car.

"Is that him?" Pee Chu asked. "That's fucking him," he confirmed for himself. "Gilbert King, everybody."

Barry beat his hand on the car horn and whooped it up through his open window. Proctor walked slowly to his son like he hadn't seen him in years and held out his arms. Gilbert King hugged his father and leaned toward his ear. "What's the name of this place again?" he whispered.

"Fucking Attica, you retard," Proctor whisper-shouted.

"I just want you to know that your personal insults to me have an effect. Alright?"

Both men turned to the waiting troop with their arms around each other. The car emptied and the traveling wrestlers rushed their newly freed champ-in-waiting.

"I hope those fucks didn't go too rough on you in there, man," Pee Chu said, checking the swelling under Gilbert's eye.

"I've already forgotten what that place was like," Gilbert replied. "All I can say is the guy who did this to my eye is the world's largest cock-sucking fuckface penis-loving gay friend to all the gay people. And I could beat his ass any day I choose."

Everyone nodded with understanding.

"You got no bag, Kid?" Franco asked.

"What are you trying to say?" Proctor interjected.

The blood drained from Franco's face. "Nothing, boss."

"Fuck that place. I'm all about where we're going now." Gilbert said, roiling up his troops.

Proctor pulled the excitement level down with a grunt and said calmly, "We're going to get our heavyweight title. That's where we're going. There's business to be figured out."

Proctor walked to his car and motioned for Gilbert to follow him. "We've got a long drive ahead of us."

The others looked suddenly deflated.

"We drove for a day already, Kid," Pee Chu said. "We even got you a take out," he said as he pushed Lizzie forward.

Gilbert waited for Proctor to walk out of earshot. "Go into the city. Where will I meet you guys?"

November 29, 1971 — Two Months Later.
Boston.

Danno stood silently against the old blue lunch car where he'd bought his burger an hour ago. It was closed now and the parking lot he waited in was dark and empty. Perfect in one way, unnerving in another.

The smoke from Ginny's cigarette curled out through the slightly opened back window. Danno took a few short steps back toward his car and peeked in the back to see the waiting stacks of cash.

Ginny was counting slowly. Danno could see him moving his lips in jumps of one as he planted every hundred-dollar note, one on top of the other. They'd just finished another sold-out show. Boston was a gold mine. So was New York. When Danno thought about it, the whole northeast coast was growing rapidly. In two short years, his company could run three shows a night in three different areas.

He hardly knew what else to do with the money that was coming in. The stacks of cash beside Ginny just reminded him of how far they had come. And of how reluctant he was getting to lose it.

"Who are we down here to see, boss?" Ginny asked out the window.

"What?" Danno pretended not to hear to give himself an extra couple of seconds to cook up a lie.

"Who are we waiting on?"

It was late and Danno was too tired to be clever. "It's nothing, I just like the burgers down here."

Ginny continued the count. Danno blew his nose and wiped the drops of sauce from his shirt. "Fuck."

A car pulled into the corner of the lot and sounded its horn. Ginny knew something wasn't right. He carefully placed the money back into the waiting bags and reached under the back seat for the strategically placed bat.

Danno walked slowly and warily toward the waiting car. "Gimme a sec."

Danno and Proctor sat in the front of Proctor's car. Neither man looked at each other.

"He got out today," Proctor said.

Danno's heart sank. Ever since the deal was struck, he was dreading hearing those words.

"You hear me?" Proctor asked.

"We had a deal, Proctor. That's my word you got," Danno replied.

Proctor reached across an already jumpy Danno and cracked open his glove box. Danno began to slide his hand into his inside pocket until he saw it was only a hip flask of whiskey that Proctor was reaching for.

"You want some?" he asked Danno just before he took a swig himself.

Danno shook his head.

"Did you make the money you wanted?" Proctor asked.

"I did okay."

Proctor struggled to remove his jacket in the confined space of the car. "I hear you're running triple shots now? That must be a hill of cash."

Danno ignored this line of questioning and changed direction to future business. "I want the change to mean something. When your boy takes the title, I want the world to be watching."

"Of course, that's what we agreed, didn't we?"

Danno stopped Proctor with his hand. "I want it to happen on my turf, is what I'm saying."

Proctor laughed. "What?"

"You heard me. It needs to happen in New York."

It wasn't as easy for Proctor to get a read on Danno as it used to be.

"Why would I allow that to happen?" Proctor asked.

Danno turned to Proctor. "Because I fucking said so. Because that's where the money is. And because I'm only interested in the business of this thing."

"You saying I'm not?"

Danno turned his stare back out the windshield. "I'm saying that you coming to my town and beating my champion looks good for you. So much so, that we're going to split it eighty-twenty my way."

Proctor wiped the sides of both of his lips and took another swig from his silver hip flask. He knew that Danno had made New York a gold mine. Much bigger than he could offer at the moment. "Fifty-fifty. No more and no less."

Danno stood firm. "Eighty-twenty or you can come up to my city and try and take the belt off him yourself."

Proctor just wanted his son to have heavyweight title. In truth, it didn't matter to Proctor if Danno got one hundred percent. But fuck him, the fat piece of shit.

"Seventy-thirty, Danno," Proctor said.

Danno buttoned up his top button to leave. "I'm going to give you one more chance. And then I'm closing the door."

Proctor struggled to keep himself in check. Where was all this attitude coming from all of a sudden? "Deal," he muttered.

He reached into his back seat and bundled an old-school black leather doctor's bag onto Danno's lap. Proctor opened it to show Danno that there was money inside. A lot of money.

"At least one of us can stick to their word. That's your last two hundred, you fat prick," Proctor said as he squashed the bag into Danno's stomach.

Danno sat calmly and counted the money.

"When?" Proctor asked.

Danno dislodged himself from his seat and closed the door behind him. Proctor leaned over and rolled down the window.

"When are we doing this?" Proctor shouted after him.

"I haven't decided yet." Danno answered without even turning around.

Proctor punched his steering wheel. "Answer me, Danno."

Danno stopped and turned back. "You went too far with all of this. I'll call you when I'm ready to talk to you again. Apart from that, you fuck yourself."

Ginny got out of the car with his bat by his side to let Proctor know he was watching. Danno gave him the bag and lowered himself into the car. Proctor's car screamed onto the street.

Later that night, Danno's phone rang beside his bed, startling him. Ever since Danno got knee deep in with Proctor, he found himself being startled more often than a person should be, and receiving more calls in the night than a person should.

"Hello?"

"Boss, it's Ginny," the Folsom Nightmare said in a concerned voice.

"What? Is that you, Folsom?" Danno switched on the bedside lamp and put on his reading glasses for no discernible reason.

"Yes, sir." Folsom took a deep breath and continued. "He's been turned over in the car. He's in the hospital, boss."

Danno had only been asleep an hour or two. He was totally muddled as to what was going on. "What happened? Hello?"

Folsom said, "We think he dropped you off and then on his way home he got . . ."

Danno turned around to see his wife oblivious and undisturbed. "Come get me."

"My bum leg . . . I can't drive. But there's a car on the way."

Danno went to hang up but caught himself just before he did. "Did . . . is he alright?"

"They tell me he's pretty bad."

Danno slowly hung up. He took a couple of seconds to try to form his thoughts in the night's silence.

How can you fucking sleep through that?

Annie hadn't even moved beside him in the bed. Her smaller and smaller participation in their lives was really starting to grind on him. Danno angrily roared into her ear. "What?" she asked in a groggy drone. "Is there . . . is it something?"

"No," Danno answered, acting all confused as to why she was even awake.

"Oh, okay." Annie began to slide back into sleep.

The pills were a great help at the start. Now they were just taking over.

"Go back to sleep," Danno said as he walked out of the room with his clothes draped over his shoulder.

Annie went back to sleep. Danno carefully walked past every dark corner of his huge house until he got to his front door.

"Who are you, anyway?" Danno asked his young—very young—driver.

"I'm Folsom's kid," the nervous voice from the front replied. "He can't drive too good for a while."

Danno's life had changed so much that he didn't even feel all that comfortable in a car with someone he didn't know. "Just take it slow, son."

"My old man told me to get you down there quickly, sir."

"What's Folsom doing sending you? Where's Oscar Dewsbury?"

"My old man said he hasn't seen Oscar in days. Can't find him anywhere."

The battered lime-green 1960 Rambler clipped the side mirror of a parked truck as they took another hairpin corner. Danno tried to stabilize himself by lodging his hands into the ceiling and his feet underneath the seat in front of him.

"No, I overrule your old man and I say we're slowing down."

"He told me he would whip my ass if I didn't get you there as quickly as I could, sir. My daddy don't lie about them things," the young man replied, flooring the pedal.

Danno's power and money meant nothing in contrast to an ass-whoopin'.

The hospital sat on the right as Danno and the boy driver came to a screeching halt.

Danno ejected himself quickly from the back. "Jesus Christ."

"Will you tell my daddy that I did a good job, mister?"

Danno peeled off a hundred and handed it to the boy. "Tell him I could do with him back at work."

Danno looked up to see Ricky waiting at the hospital entrance, staring squarely in the car's direction. Danno waved to catch his attention, but Ricky didn't acknowledge him. Danno was sure Ricky saw him all right. He just wasn't responding.

"Can I leave now, or do you want to me take you someplace else after you're done here?" the boy driver asked.

"I'm . . . you can go."

Danno walked up the steps of the hospital and his ride pulled off at top speed behind him. Every step he took, he found it harder to look Ricky in the face for some reason.

"How is he?" Danno asked as he got closer.

"He's lucky to be alive," Ricky replied. "They fucking ran him off the road and took the money."

Danno walked to the hospital entrance. Ricky walked the opposite way.

"Where is he?" Danno asked.

"They're doing something with him."

Ricky just needed to get out of there before he said something that would make everything worse.

Danno walked after Ricky, but Ricky kept a noticeable pace in front.

"Wait."

Ricky stopped but didn't turn around.

"Are all the Boys here?" Danno asked.

Ricky shook his head. "I asked them to go." Ricky took a half-empty pack of cigarettes from his pocket and lit one up.

"Was Oscar Dewsbury with them?" Danno asked.

Ricky shook his head again.

Danno focused on the task at hand. "What happened?"

Ricky quickly blew the smoke out of his way. "I thought you might know."

"Know what?" Danno said.

Ricky looked his boss straight in the eyes. "You need to tell me what's going on, Danno. No more fucking me around."

Danno and Ricky sat on the bench outside the hospital with cups of steaming coffee in their hands. Both men were silent, but one of them was seething. Danno struggled with where to start and Ricky had nothing to say until he heard what the angle was. He had known for a long time that something wasn't right, but it had never affected him before. Wondering what was going on wasn't part of his job.

"Now, if we're going to do this, I want to be honest with you. I'm too tired for lying and you're too hurt. Okay?" Danno said, stirring his drink with a stick. "I won't dress none of this up. Not even the bad stuff that makes me look like an asshole."

Ricky was ready for some honesty. "What is it?"

Danno had one last chew on whether revealing the angle was a good idea or not. How much money would telling Ricky end up costing him? Danno quickly weighed it up and knew he could trust Ricky. He leaned in closer. "It's a work," he whispered.

Of all the things Ricky thought he might hear, that wasn't one of them. "A work?" Ricky caught himself and lowered his voice. "A work?"

"Well, that's the way it started," Danno said.

Danno's immediate honesty took Ricky by surprise. "What's a work?" Ricky asked.

"This thing." Danno took a cautious sip from his cup. "I wanted to make it as real as possible. The idea was that situations would be set up to start the feud. At the start Proctor didn't have a challenger ready to face the giant because his boy was inside. So to get people talking and interested in a match, we had to use what we had—which was each other."

"You were working your own company?"

Danno nodded. "We knew the parameters. Public places. Like get-togethers were okay to work the angle. Like my anniversary. If he showed up, we would work some more. Create some more bad blood to get people talking. If he showed, we worked, if he didn't, we didn't."

"He gave you permission to put a loaded gun in his mouth?" Rick asked.

"Nope. But I didn't give him permission to touch my wife, either." Danno poured his coffee into a potted plant beside him and dropped the cup on the ground. "It was a great idea that's turned fucking sour. Like a play fight that turns serious. He'd push me a little harder than we'd agreed, then I'd do it to him. In the end, we forgot we were supposed to be playing. It turned into this—people in the fucking hospital. Real stuff."

Ricky paused and ran over all the situations that could have been a work. All the celebrations that Danno attended. His insistence on having wrestlers around. His insistence on having Lenny around. All the pieces were starting to form a picture.

"You knew the wrestlers would leak what they saw or heard," Ricky said.

Danno nodded. "The territory system is dying, Ricky. National promotion is the key to us making it. The only way we do that is with TV and mainstream interest. And I had to make it look like I had no control over it. I did at the start. Now I've quite clearly lost the run of this in the middle, but I've still got the belt. The finish to all of this is my call—whether he likes it or not. I'm looking at the biggest match in our history. In our territory. Shea Stadium. We say how the end of this angle plays out."

"Do you think Proctor did this?" Ricky asked, struggling to hold his temper.

Danno thought about it. "Maybe."

Ricky looked at Danno. He could hardly speak, he was so angry.

"So what do we do?"

"What do you mean?"

Ricky stood up. He wasn't an easy man to handle if he left his reasoning behind. "What are we going to do to this fuck?"

Danno was confused by the question. "What we always do—make money."

Ricky shook his head. "That's not what I'm looking for, Danno. What I'm asking is: how do we retaliate?"

Danno smiled. "Can't we do both?"

Danno slipped a newspaper clipping into Ricky's hand.

CHAPTER SIXTEEN

December 1, 1971 — Two Days Later.
New York.

Danno patiently watched the brown phone that sat on the hardwood desk in his newly refurbished office. Ricky sat in the visitor's chair and observed all the differences—all the new money in the New York Booking Agency office.

New money that seemed to be passing him by.

"You sure this call was this morning?" Danno asked.

Ricky nodded. "That's the word we got back."

"Okay." Danno waited for the phone to ring. "You hungry?"

Ricky had enough of the waiting around. "Let's just go down there and break this fucking guy's head, boss."

Danno shook his head. "I have no interest in losing money from this, Ricky. All due respect to the personal aspect of it, but you're going to have to start sounding like a man who trusts I have this one."

Danno secretly willed the phone to ring. Before Ricky had even arrived, he checked to make sure the line was working at least fifteen times. He was spending more and more time acting cool when he didn't know what the fuck he was going to do next.

"How's Ginny today?" Danno asked absently.

"Same."

The word was the call was going to be this morning. Danno hoped so, because he knew if Ricky didn't see something was being done, he was way more likely to go off page and do something stupid in Florida himself.

"It wasn't an approximate thing? Like, roughly this morning?" Danno asked.

Ricky shook his head. "No, it was exact. Like, definitely today. This morning."

The phone rang. Danno fixed his appearance as if the caller on the other end could see into his office.

"You going to answer that?" Ricky nervously asked.

"Two more rings."

The phone rang once. They both moved closer and waited for it to ring again. Danno had rehearsed his routine in the shower fifty times since he got word it was going to happen today. One more ring and it was show time.

The phone stopped. Danno looked at the silent phone, bewildered.

"Julie?" he roared out the door.

"Yes, boss?" answered a female voice from outside.

The phone began to ring again. Danno immediately picked it up. "Hello?"

"Hello, Mr. Garland. It's Melvin Pritchard here."

Danno gave Ricky the thumbs up and settled back into his leather seat. "You were the last man on the planet I expected to hear from today, Mr. Pritchard."

"Well, I won't keep you."

"No, you're right—you won't."

Danno could see Ricky settle a little easier into his seat.

Melvin continued. "Out of respect for you, sir, I would like to inform you that the date has been set for the Senate Task Force hearings. The bill is on whether to ban professional wrestling in the state of New York or not."

Danno twisted his pen between his teeth and prepared a notepad. "Dates, committees—don't make much difference to me one way or the other, Mr. Pritchard."

"However, I would like you to know that the date is set for October 5, 1972—and will be chaired and presided over by Senator Hilary J. Tenenbaum, who will be representing the state of New York."

Danno scribbled down the date and slid the pad to Ricky. "Can I ask you one question in relation to this matter?"

"Of course," Melvin said.

"Is it him or you running the show in relation to this matter?"

"It's the senator, with my full support as chairman of the Athletic—"

Danno hung up and dialed another number. Proctor answered immediately, "Hello?"

Danno smiled. "How did you know I was going to be calling you this morning?"

"I didn't," Proctor lied.

Danno was feeling in full control, like a master pulling the levers. "Listen carefully. We're going to have our match on September 30, 1972. Just under a year from now."

Proctor didn't answer. In fact, Danno wasn't even sure he still had a line. "You still there?"

"Yeah, I'm here," Proctor muttered into the phone.

"You heard me, you prick. September 30, Shea Stadium. New York City."

Proctor very calmly responded, "You don't want to leave me waiting that long, Danno. It's like you're trying to get out of this or something."

"It's already a done deal." Danno hung up.

Ricky was slightly shocked, but majorly impressed. "You're going to Shea a week before the hearings?"

Danno didn't want to answer Ricky directly, so he just smiled knowingly and nodded. He was all for letting Ricky in, but only some of the way, until he figured out how all this was going to go down.

"Proctor sounded pretty hot," Ricky said.

"If you think that's bad, wait till you hear him when he finds out he's not getting the belt."

Ricky could hardly contain the feeling that some measure of justice was about to be served. "You're not giving him the strap?"

Danno again played safe and shook his head. "Now, you go and do your bit and I'll figure out what other pieces we need to pull this off."

Ricky stood up and smiled proudly at Danno. "Yes, boss."

December 26, 1971 — Twenty-Five Days Later.
New York.

"Dad, look at me," Luke called to his father as he ran around in a circle for the fiftieth time.

Lenny's family room was usually a sanctuary to him when he came off the road. The couch was fat and comfortable, the stream of hot meals was consistent. He *usually* loved being home. Just not full time.

"Dad?"

Lenny loved his son, but watching him run in a circle and think it was impressive just made Lenny want to smash his own face through the glass coffee table.

"Dad? Look."

Lenny tried to smile. He just couldn't. "That's great, champ."

Luke picked up his coat and put it on backward to cover his face. "Dad. Look at me." Luke ran around in a circle again. "Look, Dad."

Lenny rose and walked into the kitchen. The cupboards were full of Christmas treats. He could still hear his son in the other room. "Look. Look, Dad."

Dear God in heaven. Please fucking kill me right now.

"Dad?" Luke came running into the kitchen.

Lenny could feel himself reaching the boiling point.

"Dad?"

"What?" Lenny snapped.

His son was taken aback. "There's someone at the door."

Lenny felt like a shit-for-brains—or worse, like his own father. "I'm sorry." He patted his little boy on his head and went to see a large man's silhouette behind his front door screen.

"Hello?" Lenny said as he approached.

"Lenny?" Danno replied. "That you?"

Lenny stopped suddenly when he placed the voice. He thought about running. He didn't know why. Maybe Danno was here because something leaked out. Lenny turned to see his son looking at him.

Lenny walked forward and opened the door. Danno stood with his cap in his hand.

"Hey, boss." Lenny was surprised by the strength of the sunshine outside. It had been a while since he and the sun saw each other; its brightness was blinding.

"Come in," Lenny offered.

Danno politely shook his head. "I called to the house you were living in last time when . . . Anyway, the lady there told me where to find you."

"That's my mom."

Danno seemed preoccupied.

"Are you sure you don't want to come in?" Lenny asked.

"If it's all the same, I'll manage here," Danno said.

Bree pulled into their driveway with their youngest son in the backseat. Her impending entry into the conversation seemed to make Danno even shiftier. "Would you like to get a sandwich or something?" Danno asked.

"Sure. I'll just . . . one sec." Lenny breezed past Danno and briskly walked to their car.

"What does he want?" Bree whispered as she took the shopping from the trunk.

Lenny shrugged and took James Henry in his arms.

"Tell him you don't want to work there, Lenny. Tell him we're going to set up our own business."

"Doing what?" Lenny asked.

Bree couldn't answer yet. She'd been narrowing down some new ideas but didn't have anything concrete.

Lenny took their son into the house. Bree followed with some bags.

"Hello, missus," Danno said to Bree as she passed.

"Fuck you," she replied and disappeared into the house, closing the door with a bang behind her.

Lenny quickly opened the door a crack and slid out. "Women's troubles."

"You should get her some valium. It worked like a treat for Mrs. Garland."

Lenny nodded.

"Do you want to drive?" Danno asked, holding out his keys.

"Yes," Lenny said, maybe a little too emphatically.

"I just meant to the sandwich place or whatever."

Lenny was immediately crushed and also embarrassed by his eagerness. "Yeah, that's what I meant."

Lenny walked ahead down his driveway and cursed his desperation in his head.

"Lenny?"

"Yeah?" Lenny answered, not ready to turn around.

"Lenny?"

Lenny stopped and turned.

"I came here to offer you your old job back. I was just going to do it in a burger joint or something."

"No, thanks," Bree said from the open window upstairs.

Lenny looked up but couldn't see where his wife was eavesdropping from. "You came to ask me back, boss?"

"Yeah," Danno said.

Lenny didn't even need to think. "Deal."

Danno was a little surprised by how easy the offer went. "Okay."

"Except," Lenny continued, "I want in."

Danno wondered if he was going to be negotiating with both Lenny and Bree. "Can we . . . ?" Danno moved away from the house down to the end of the pathway. Lenny followed him.

"In what?" Danno wondered.

"In. I want in. You know. In. I want to get in there with the wrestlers. Referee or something."

Danno thought about it. "Oh, you want *in*?"

Lenny nodded. He wanted his boss to see maturity in his response. Danno took out a cigar, chomped, and spat out the end. He watched Lenny closely and waited to see if he would fill the quiet with something further.

"You know the guy that took over from you nearly got killed? No one else in my crew wants to do it. That's why I'm here," Danno said.

"I'll take it."

Danno lit and puffed. "You sure?"

"I am—*if* you break me in."

Danno could see a change in Lenny. A change he liked. If he'd only shown these balls before, he would have been smartened up to the business before now. "I'm in the middle of something now that's going to take all my time. But you have my word, when this piece of business concludes, you will be one of my top guys."

Lenny didn't hesitate. "Deal." Danno Garland's word was money in the bank to Lenny. They both shook hands at the end of Lenny's pathway.

December 27, 1971 — The Next Day.
New Orleans.

Lenny and Ricky sat up at the bar, waiting in silence. Ricky had the newspaper clipping that Danno had given him outside the hospital.

Lenny could see the piece of paper had a picture on it. A picture that Ricky continually referenced whenever a new male customer walked in.

"Who we waiting on?" Lenny asked.

Ricky didn't answer. He instead pulled his baseball cap down farther like he was going deeper undercover. Anytime Ricky moved his hands, Lenny was expecting a slap in the chops. He tried to act like it was nothing, but his wife knew different. It was not very manly, but Lenny had had a hard time leaving the house after Ricky slapped him around. Bree knew it. And Lenny knew that she knew it.

No matter how small or skinny or out of the fighting world you're supposed to be, every man struggles to live with himself after a beating.

"Move," Ricky gruffly ordered, trying to look over Lenny's shoulder.

Lenny submissively leaned into the bar. He was only drinking soda. He wanted to make sure he called home on time. The first full day back at work and he wanted to show Bree that things had changed since the last time.

Ricky's patience with Lenny grew thin. "Here," he said, moving from his seat. "You sit there."

Lenny and Ricky swapped.

Lenny wanted to break the silence between them. "I heard about what happened to Folsom in Florida," Lenny said. "How is he?"

Ricky took his eye off the door for a second to think about answering Lenny. "He lost his place. He had to move his family back to his folks' place in Atlanta."

"That's awful."

"His ankle was shattered. And if you can't work in that ring, you can't earn. Simple as that."

"And Ginny?" Lenny asked.

The door of the bar opened and Ricky's attention was drawn to the man who entered and sat at the bar. Ricky covertly checked the picture from the newspaper clipping and looked pleased.

The man at the corner of the bar was small in stature and seemed gentle enough in the way he tried to seek the bartender's attention. He wore a large cross around his neck and a name-tag on his chest. He waved away the lingering bar smoke from his face when he thought no one was looking.

"Who's that?" Lenny leaned in and asked.

"I have to apologize to you, Lenny," Rick replied. "I'm not the sort of man that whips on another man like I did with you."

Lenny was surprised at the response. "It's . . . I . . . deserved it. Big mouth."

Ricky slid his arm under the bar for Lenny to shake. "The boss says you're good, then I trust him."

Lenny was relieved and overwhelmed. "Thank you, Ricky."

The men shook hands.

Lenny said, "I've been thinking about that day—"

"Wait here," Rick said. He strolled down along the bar. The man at the corner noticed Ricky's approach and watched him warily.

"How you doing?" Ricky asked him.

The man looked way more nervous than just a regular guy with nothing on his mind.

Ricky put out his hand. "Ricky Plick."

"Sean . . ."

"Peak, right?" Ricky said.

Sean seemed bewildered as to how a stranger would know that.

"It's on your chest. Can I buy you a drink, Sean?" Ricky asked.

Sean didn't seem so keen. Ricky huddled up beside him anyway and caught the bartender's eye. He ordered two bottles of beer and lit himself a cigarette.

"Do you want me to put that on your room, sir?" the bartender asked.

Both Ricky and Sean answered "Yes" at the same time.

"Are you staying here too?" Ricky asked Sean.

"It's just a conference." Sean nervously asked, "Do I know you?"

Ricky swiveled his seat around, "Not yet."

CHAPTER SEVENTEEN

Lenny inched Ade Schiller through the traffic leaving JFK International. "How was your flight, Mrs. Schiller?"

Ade was freshening up her face in the back of the car and reading the giant billboard to her right. "*The Great White Way to New York.* Is that what they say now?"

"Mr. Garland is really looking forward to your company tomorrow after you get settled," Lenny said.

"How is Mr. Moneybags? I hear he's having to deal with a lot of shit from that asshole, Proctor."

Lenny concentrated on finding the smallest opportunity between the Buick and the Mack truck in front of him. "I wouldn't know about those things, I'm afraid. The word is, though, that Proctor hasn't even been heard from since the boss gave him what-for about the match at Shea."

"Really?" Ade seemed intrigued.

"No one has heard a single word," Lenny said.

This update seemed to make Ade very happy. "Really," she said again.

Lenny popped the cigarette lighter and handed it back to Ade, who duly lit up.

"How did Danno know I was coming out here?" she asked.

Lenny shrugged at his boss's mystical ways. In truth, it was more than likely a wrestler from her territory said something in passing about them not working this week 'cause their boss was coming to New York. This, of course, would have been overheard by his tag-team partner, who was a brother of the ring announcer in LA, who met with Ricky last week to see about working some towns with them while his brother finished up a messy divorce in Jersey.

Telephone. Telegram. Tell-a-wrestler.

Danno reached into the safe in his bedroom behind the large painting of his father. He quietly unloaded some stacks of cash into a waiting knapsack. Time was ticking and he needed to get out of his house without alerting Annie.

He counted the money and threw in another two thousand just to be sure. With every passing day, he could see his old man coming through in him. Their faces were practically the same. The older Danno got, the bigger his nose grew and the less his hair did. The painting of his old man was starting to look more and more like a mirror. There was no way that Danno was going to end up the same way he did, though. Not if he could help it. He threw the bag of money over his shoulder and tiptoed to the window to see if Annie was out front.

"Dan?" Annie was standing behind him in the bedroom doorway.

Danno thought about dropping the knapsack and sliding it under the bed, but it was too late to hide it. "Do you always creep around like a cat in this house?"

"Where are you going?" she asked him.

Danno walked past his wife and continued for the stairs. "Out."

"What's in the bag?" she asked.

Danno walked to the stairs.

"Is all of this nearly over?" she asked.

Her words were so soft that it made him stop and turn back. He hadn't looked her in the face in a long time. She walked toward him and he dropped his bag and put out his arms. Her standing on the landing with him down a step made them equal. She hugged him tight and he could feel the embrace of someone who worried about him. That feeling was something he had forgotten.

"It's nearly over," he said.

"And are we going to win?"

Danno nodded on her shoulder. "Yeah," he said softly into her ear. He wasn't sure, but he didn't want to worry her any more.

Annie broke from his embrace and fixed his tie. "You should let me in, Dan. I'm not one of the Boys."

"I know." Danno checked his watch again. "Can I bring you out for a late lunch? I'd like to do that. I have to go on business for a few days and I'd like to spend some time in your company before I go."

It was on the tip of Annie's tongue to decline. She wasn't feeling that attractive or energetic. She found it harder and harder to want to leave the house. It was guilt that was holding her. Shame.

"Will you come with me?" Danno asked. "I want to be seen out with my beautiful wife."

Danno and Annie sat at the best table in New York. Ricky Plick, a struggling Ginny Ortiz, Wild Ted Berry, and midget wrestler Tiny Thunder joined them.

"And then I said to him, if it tastes good on one end, it can't taste bad at the other," Wild Ted finished with a laugh. The whole table laughed along with him. Except Annie.

"Sorry, Mrs. Garland," Wild Ted said when he noticed her discomfort. "I should remember my manners more around a lady."

"What? No. I've got a few shit jokes of my own," Annie replied. "Well, now we're all uncomfortable," she continued after several long seconds of shocked silence.

"I guess we are," Danno said, letting his troops know that it was okay to laugh. Ricky got up and excused himself from the table and walked to the hallway by the restrooms. He dialed the pay phone.

"Hello?" Lenny said, swinging in Danno's office chair.

"It's me. Did you get Ade to the hotel okay?" Ricky asked.

"Yeah, of course," Lenny answered a bit more seriously.

"Okay, listen. The boss wants you to go to his place now and collect a knapsack that's at the top of his stairs."

"Well, I . . ."

Ricky leaned back and looked to make sure the full party was still at the table. "This is important. He might need access to some cash in a hurry, soon. So, get the money and put it somewhere safe until he needs it."

Lenny wasn't comfortable with two sides of this job. He didn't want to enter his boss's place when no one was there, and he certainly didn't want to be responsible for that amount of cash.

"You're looking for a leg up in the business? Well, this is the start," Ricky said.

He was right. "Okay, I can do that. I'll hide it in my garage or—"

Ricky hung up.

June 25, 1972 — Six Weeks Later.
New York.

Proctor sat in the bush and giggled to himself like a child about to pull a prank. He watched Danno pull himself from his car and waited for the perfect moment to startle him.

"Nice house," Proctor shouted as he jumped into sight.

Danno dropped his keys from fright. "What the fuck, Proctor?"

Proctor laughed at getting his desired result. "Here, let me get those for you," he said as he bent in front of Danno to retrieve the keys.

Danno did all he could to stop himself taking out his gun and blowing the back of Proctor's head off as he stooped.

"Why all the hostility, Danno?" Proctor wondered as he slid the keys back into Danno's pocket.

"What are you doing here?"

"Just came to clean up some garbage talk out there."

"And what would that be?" Danno asked.

Proctor stood directly in front of Danno. "Is it true that you're not going to drop the belt to my boy at Shea? I mean, I waited all this time for you to pay me back and now I hear you're going to fucking weasel me out of the payoff."

Danno was very careful to frame his next words. Not because he didn't think he was right to do whatever he wanted to Proctor after all Proctor had done to his crew—but because this situation felt all wrong. It was pitch dark, in his own driveway, at three in the morning. Anyone would have to measure their answer.

"Fuck you," Danno said as he continued toward his house. At each step he prayed that he would make another as he walked with his back to Proctor.

Proctor said, "Well, it's not going to happen that way, Danno."

Danno was afraid to turn back around. "Why is that?" he asked as he continued to walk.

"Because I have your guy," Proctor replied.

Danno immediately thought of the giant and how unhappy he was with all of this. Had he jumped?

Proctor continued, "Oscar Dewsbury jumped to Florida. He's working for me now."

Danno stopped, confused. There was no logic in Proctor's reply. Oscar was never more than a mid-card act for Danno. He was handy to run errands and drive Danno around from time to time, but was never going to make money. Oscar was the reason he was so confident?

"What?" Danno slowly turned to see that Proctor was right behind him.

"I didn't think you were going to actually pull out of our deal. I wanted to ask your big fucking fat face myself. And even after I got you all this." Proctor shook his head in disgust and looked around at Danno's mansion.

"Your guy didn't get to Merv. You think I don't know that? Huh? You did nothing to get me this," Danno said.

Proctor smiled. "Whatever it is you're planning to fuck me over with, you stop it now. You drop the belt to my boy or Oscar tells the good people from the government anything they want to know at those hearings." Proctor got in Danno's face to emphasize his point. "I'll make sure he points directly at you and tells them how crooked you are. You hear me? You drop the belt."

"Do you really think testimony by someone on the inside of the business isn't going to spread your way eventually?" Danno weakly countered.

Proctor laughed. "We do things the old-fashioned way in Florida, Danno. The last thing I have to be worried about is a politician from New York."

Proctor began to leave. He whistled cheerfully like a man out for a stroll. "Do the right thing. You made your money. It would be a shame to lose all this at your stage in life."

Danno watched as Proctor sauntered off into the darkness. He could feel his stomach sink and his chest thump. He wanted to tear down his own door to get into the safety of his house, but he couldn't look weak or rushed.

He turned slowly, struggling to breathe, unlocked his front door, and closed it gently behind him. On his own, in his house, with no one looking, Danno was convinced that he wasn't cut out for this. It was all the second-guessing, worrying, outthinking, attacks from all sides. He wasn't even enjoying what he had. The house, the cars, the money. They weren't worth it in light of what he was facing.

This whole sorry fucking mess was doing strange things to him.

"Hello?" he shouted from the hallway. "You there, Annie?" Danno didn't really expect an answer. A bomb would have a hard time moving his wife from her sleep.

"Annie?"

Danno's chest began to tighten and it became hard for him to call her. It felt like a car was parked on his chest and he was unable to control the flow of air leaving his body.

"Annie," he said, his voice getting weaker. "Annie, wake up." Danno threw his back against the door and slid to the floor. He ripped at the buttons in his shirt. He didn't have the breath to call her anymore. All that went through his head as he fought for his life was that Proctor got to kill him after all.

July 14, 1972 — About Three Weeks Later.
New York.

Lenny's phone rang beside his bed. Bree immediately sprang up with her husband. Lenny dove for the phone. "Hello?"

Danno hadn't been seen much publicly in the previous few weeks. Ricky did everything he could to make contact with the boss. Lenny went over every day, only for Mrs. Garland to tell him that her husband wasn't feeling well and that she'd get Danno to call him.

Tonight, he finally did.

"Hello?" Lenny whispered as he peered around Danno's unlocked front door. There was no answer, so Lenny entered and quietly tiptoed into the hallway. "Hello?" Out of the corner of his eye, he saw Danno sitting on the edge of a seat in a room off the hallway. "Boss?"

Danno looked distraught. His whole body was sickly pale and his skin showed glimmers of sweat under the light. "Thanks for coming," Danno said in a hushed voice.

"Are you okay, boss?"

Danno sat in thought like a now-sober man looking back on his behavior from the night before. "You want something from the fridge or something?"

Lenny shook his head and entered the room.

"I'm a little fucking embarrassed for you to see me like this," Danno said.

"No, no, no," Lenny said, waving his hands in protest. "I'm glad you called me. I wanna help."

Lenny sat on the edge of the seat opposite his boss. Danno sat up in his own seat and leaned forward. Danno followed Lenny's eyes as they looked toward the gun in Danno's hand.

"I don't think I could shoot one of these if my life depended on it," Danno said. "I came into this world without the killer instinct, and I'd dearly love to leave it the same way. But I've got to grab this situation by the neck or it's going to kill me." Danno wiped the tiredness from his eyes. "Something happened in this business with my old man. He got in his Caddy one day and never came home. He got caught in the middle, pulling all the strings. But me, I'm going to be killed by the planning of it all. Not even a fucking bullet or a knife. I'm going to roll over and choke like a fucking woman at the thought of it. Huh. No wonder he didn't give me the business."

Lenny said, "Something happen, boss?"

Danno's face turned from maudlin to sober. "I'm trusting you to look after this house and my wife in it until we get this deal done, Lenny." Danno had a wild look in his eye. "Every night, whether I'm here or not. And I don't want her to know you're around. It would only make her more nervous. Be discreet, but be here. You hear me?"

Danno walked to the door with his gun in his hand.

"Where are you going?" Lenny asked.

"To find my balls."

CHAPTER EIGHTEEN

July 15, 1972—The Next Day.
New York.

Danno rang Ricky and gave him some instructions, telling him there were a couple of people who needed visiting. Danno hung up before Ricky could ask any follow-up questions. In the beginning, Danno had purposefully surrounded himself with big mouths and loose lips. He had needed all his secrets out there. That was part of the plan. But now that he needed some real work done, he called on the few people he could trust.

Ricky called Lenny and filled him in. Oscar Dewsbury had jumped ship from Danno to Proctor's territory. Ordinarily this wouldn't have meant much, if anything at all. But Proctor didn't want Oscar for his tepid wrestling skills. He wanted Oscar as a pawn to send into Danno's Senate hearings if he needed to. Danno and Ricky both knew that Oscar was the kind to do it, and Proctor was the kind who would pay handsomely to have it done.

So no more messing around.

Within thirty minutes, Lenny was tearing up the stairs of an apartment block. It wasn't often that Ricky cut him in on what was happening, so Lenny wanted to make sure that he did a good job. He could visualize his rise through the ranks if he could deliver Oscar back to Danno on a platter. Maybe the boss would even let Lenny be in front of a crowd. Just one time. Just for one minute.

Even more exciting to Lenny was the fact that he knew where Oscar was, when no one else knew where to begin. Oscar Dewsbury was an unusually private person. So much so that even the Boys—who lived in each other's pockets—didn't know where he lived. Most of the time the single wrestlers would bunk together in the same apartment complex and share all the bills, but Oscar never spoke of any wife or kids or of where he lived. Lenny had driven Oscar up and down a lot of roads. He always bought Lenny's wife's sandwiches, too. It seemed the thing Oscar loved best besides eating was talking about eating. Big, fat Oscar loved planning and scheming his food days on those long journeys from town to town.

He once told Lenny that he loved the Thai place that just opened under his apartment. He promised to take Lenny there when they came off the road. Pongsri. Oscar said it was the best food in the whole of New York.

And there was only one restaurant in the city with that name.

Lenny hung around outside the restaurant and asked questions like Popeye Doyle. Oscar wasn't an inconspicuous type of man; within three people, Lenny was able to find out exactly where he lived.

Lenny stood at apartment 17-C and knocked lightly but repeatedly. It was a strategy that was paying little reward after twenty-four minutes. Lenny stood back, checked to make sure he couldn't be fingered for the job by any witnesses, then drove his foot into Oscar's door.

Pain shot from his heel to his hip and dropped him to the ground. The steel-reinforced door didn't even vibrate.

"You alright there, son?" an old lady asked from the open sliver of her door.

Something dragged Lenny's eyes down from her cloudy gray eyes and white-mustached lip. The old lady held a small handgun down low and pointed right at his heart.

"I'll ask you again—you alright?" she said.

Lenny slowly got to his feet. "I'm looking for a friend of mine. His name is Oscar Dewsbury. Big, fat man with a bald head."

"What do you want with Oscar?"

Lenny blurted out a mangled sentence. "He owes me some money, not a lot, it's a friendly amount."

"He don't live there anymore." The old lady withdrew her gun and closed the door.

"Wait," Lenny called after her.

It was too late; the old lady was gone.

Lenny thought he'd be the one who cracked the case for the boss. He'd seen himself dragging Oscar up Danno's driveway and standing triumphantly on his neck like a big-game hunter with his catch. Unable to just leave empty-handed, he knocked on the old lady's door. "I'm sorry, it's me. Do you know where he went?"

There was a pause before the old lady spoke. "I have my gun pressed about three feet up from the ground. Does that sound like somewhere you might be standing?"

Lenny quickly moved away from her door. "Please, can you tell me if you know where he's gone?"

"Florida," she shouted. "Now get the fuck away from my door."

As Lenny walked away from Oscar's apartment building, Ricky waited outside the office of Senator Hilary J. Tenenbaum. He didn't know what he was going to do when he saw him, he just knew that he had to see him. Bribing a senator wasn't something he had prepared for at any stage in his life, but that's what the boss wanted him to try.

Georgia.

Danno choked the wheel like a man possessed. He didn't drive himself much anymore, but this was something he had to do alone. All that open time in the car gave him a clearer sense of what he was doing and, more importantly, why he was doing it. He tore along at a speed that was outside of his character. But Danno just wasn't himself.

New York.

"Senator?" Ricky called after the suited man rushing off down the packed New York street.

Senator Tenenbaum didn't even look around. "My office is open for another twenty-five minutes if you'd like to make an appointment."

"Just a minute of your time, please."

The well-dressed senator stood at the side of the road and held out his arm to wave down a cab. "I'm late for an appointment."

"Danno Garland wants you to reconsider the hearings, Senator."

Tenenbaum turned around with a puzzled look on his face. "Why does that name ring a bell?"

"The task force on professional wrestling?"

The senator nodded, the light coming on in his head. "Well, you tell Mr. Garland that I expect to see him and his people come and give their side of the story in a few months' time."

Ricky approached carefully as a cab pulled up. He had his left hand on an envelope full of cash and his right hand on a forty-five Colt. "I am one of those people."

Senator Tenenbaum looked warily at Ricky for the first time and opened the cab door quickly. "Well then, I'll see you there, too."

The cab door slammed closed and the senator took off into traffic.

Ricky was too honest to use his left hand and too scared to use his right.

July 16, 1972—The Next Day.
Florida.

The scorching heat took Danno's breath away as he stepped out of his car. The humidity wrapped itself around his face like a hot towel fired from a cannon. New York got sticky, but this kind of heat was a whole other world.

He walked to the restaurant door and barreled past the front-of-house staff. At the end of the dining room, he could see Proctor at a table with several other guests. As Danno got closer, he could see Joe Lapine, interim chair of the NWC; Tanner Blackwell, the owner of the Carolinas; and another man he didn't recognize, all laughing and enjoying a good breakfast.

Proctor spotted Danno and flinched before he could steady himself. Danno stopped at the foot of the table and silently stared at Proctor. Joe and Tanner began to feel like cheating spouses who had just been caught on camera.

"I believe you know everyone here, Danno, except my son, Gilbert—the next heavyweight champion of the world," Proctor confidently said.

Gilbert King stood up to shake Danno's hand. Danno ignored him.

"He *is* going to be the next champion, isn't he, Danno?" Proctor said.

Danno licked his lips and drank Gilbert's drink. He delivered his next words slowly. "Enjoy this feeling Proctor, 'cause I'm going to fuck you as hard as I possibly can after these hearings are over."

Danno turned back the way he came. He slapped open the restaurant doors, slipped on his sunglasses, walked to the parking lot, and pointed his car back toward New York.

He had said what he needed to say, in the way he needed to say it.

July 17, 1962—The Next Day.
New York.

It was only a barn, but this was where the money was sown to someday grow again. Thirty-two athletic greenhorns doing sit-ups and Hindu squats till they puked. They were tough guys and football players, strongmen and nightclub bouncers. Maybe one or two would make it through the training camp and go on to make money as a professional wrestler. Most would simply be broken, humiliated, and sent packing to tell all their friends just how real wrestling was. Even in training the new guys, no one was smartened up until just before their first match. That meant they trained for real competition. That got painful very quickly. All the old-timers delighted in making the greenhorns squeal and quit as soon as possible. This was where the next generation would learn to love the business and, more importantly, protect it.

Ricky was standing behind the small glass window in the kitchen, watching Ginny in the ring. The ring was set up across the other side of the warehouse and Ginny was taking a group of rookies through their paces—though now he had a tendency to lose his thoughts. In wrestling, that was the final nail. If you couldn't remember where you were supposed to be in there, then someone was getting hurt. That had been happening to Ginny a lot since the crash. It broke Ricky's heart to see him like that.

Danno came in and rooted in the brown bag for his sandwich.

"How did the meeting with Ade go last night?" Ricky asked.

Danno walked to the window and looked out at the new recruits in action. "She's having a terrible time getting the crowds in now. The honeymoon is over."

"Did she find Merv's money yet?"

"I don't think so. She said something about tearing her house down to find it."

"That's great for our future," Ricky replied.

Danno nodded. "It could be. If the government leaves us in business."

"Fuck them. We'll figure out a way around them," Ricky said.

Babu struggled to enter the warehouse through the small door. All the trainees stopped what they were doing, one by one, when they saw the champ walking past. He was even bigger close up.

"Back to work, you fucking marks," Ginny shouted as he shook the ring ropes in frustration.

Ricky gathered his notes and followed Danno upstairs.

Danno, Ricky, and Babu sat at an old table at the end of a dusty old room above the warehouse. There was a silence that sprang from sheer tiredness and resignation. It had been a long four years, and each was coming to the end of it with little energy left.

"Are we going to do business?" Babu asked.

"Yeah," Danno answered.

"We're dropping the belt?" Babu asked, looking for absolute clarification.

Danno and Ricky both nodded.

"Just checking," Babu said.

Danno threw down his sandwich—his thoughts were putting an actual bad taste in his mouth. His whole world was haunted by the idea of Proctor being handed the belt after all he had done, and then, a week later, some asshole senator would try to put him out of business.

For the first time, Babu was accepting of Danno's position. He knew his boss was fighting two wars at the same time. "I'm not going to lie to you; I had a fucking blast with that belt. Made a lot of money, too. It's going to kill me to see them walk out of there with it in their hands."

"I wish I coulda had a run with it," Ricky said enviously. He wasn't the only one. Very few people got the belt. Those who did went down in history.

"And not only were you a great champ," Ricky said, looking at Babu, "but you were a fantastic draw, just like the boss said you would be."

Danno opened his sandwich to show his brain there was nothing poisonous between the bread. Even though his stomach was sick at the thought of Proctor taking his belt, Danno ate.

Ricky said to Danno, "When Proctor's lame son bombs as champion, the other bosses are going to be crying for you to get the belt again. We just need to do this the right way and leave it clean enough for us to get it again."

Danno nodded.

"Tickets are nearly gone. Shea Stadium is going to be an easy sell-out," Ricky said with a proud smile. "Most of the other bosses have been calling the office to congratulate you, boss."

"I must confess, I have been calling the box office a hundred times a day to see if we're sold out," Babu said.

Danno looked shocked that Babu would take such a risk.

"What are they going to do, recognize my voice?" Babu asked.

"True," Danno admitted.

"You call the box office?" Ricky said, smiling.

"I sometimes pretend I'm an old Jewish lady, sometimes a Chinaman," Babu said.

"Fucking mark." Ricky laughed.

"I was listening to the news on the way over, they're coming from everywhere to see this," Babu said. "Some of the news shows are even talking about it. They're expecting war to break out between the two bosses before the night is over."

Danno wiped his mouth and threw down his sandwich again in defeat. "Well, they're all going to be very disappointed. There's no way anything is going to happen between me and Proctor. This night is all about what happens in the ring. Me and Proctor are done."

CHAPTER NINETEEN

September 14, 1972 — Two Months Later.
New York.

They met in the gray parking lot of a dealership in Queens after three weeks apart. Bree Long did her best to stop herself from crying, or fighting, or whatever else was on her mind. This was where she would get to talk to her husband. To tell him how things were at home. Swap pictures of their kids. This was their meeting place. In a parking lot. In Queens. After three weeks apart.

Lenny could see his wife walking toward him. She was beautiful. He loved her completely. But she was tired, he could tell. Even after weeks apart she couldn't bring her eyes up from the ground to meet his, because she didn't know if she would laugh or cry. She didn't know if her looking at him would tell her for sure that they were over. So she looked at the ground. And he watched her.

"You want to take a look around the back?" she asked.

"No, thanks," Lenny replied. He was already standing in front of the van he wanted. A brand-new VW Kombi van. This was the van he was going to drive the world heavyweight champion to Shea Stadium in.

Bree walked up to her husband and stood between him and the van. "I'm trying real hard here, Lenny."

"What?"

"Can I help you, sir?" the fresh-faced salesman asked as he bounced across the lot.

"Can we get another minute?" Bree interrupted.

Lenny walked from the van to give Bree some space. "What is it?"

Bree couldn't quite pull her sentence together in her head. She stared at him, dumbfounded. "Are you a fucking retard, Lenny? Is that what you are? A spastic?"

"What?" Lenny replied, absolutely taken aback.

Bree was trying to remove her flailing hair from her mouth. "You don't see anything wrong with this?"

"With what?" he asked.

"This. Us. We meet on a lot? You haven't been home for weeks. You're okay with this?"

Lenny's confusion just grew. "What? I'm working."

"You say 'what' one more time and I'm going to beat you to death with a car, Lenny."

"I don't understand what's happening. I thought today was going to be a happy day."

"A fucking happy day?" Bree repeated with dismay. "You finally call to let me know you're still alive, you ask me to meet you at a car lot? In Queens? Does this equal happiness to you?"

Bree waited to see a light bulb or a sudden realization hit Lenny, but there was nothing brewing. "This fucking business you're in . . ."

"I work hard. I make money. We have things," Lenny said.

"You missed both your sons' birthdays this year," Bree said walking away. "I'm not living this life with you anymore."

Lenny hurried after her. "What does that mean?"

Bree stopped. "We're at home, Lenny. It doesn't have to be this way. We could be doing our own thing. I have ideas I want to show you. Ways we can make our own money."

Lenny lied. "All I'm getting here, Bree, is a better way of driving my family around."

"Do you want to come with me, or do you want to buy something to impress those fucking wrestlers when you drive them around?"

Bree waited, but only long enough to see that Lenny wasn't coming with her.

CHAPTER TWENTY

September 29, 1972 — About Two Weeks Later.
New York.

It was warm enough to sit out on Danno's porch. Ricky was ready, Lenny was ready, but Danno was quiet. His mind was racing for one last rally, one slender hope of retaining the belt and shutting down the hearings. He had let Proctor get away with so much because he thought he could stiff him in the end, come out with all the money and the belt to the cheers from his Boys.

Now, Proctor did all he did and still got the prize at the end. That realization was driving Danno crazy.

"The ring crew goes into the stadium today," Ricky said, trying to sound optimistic. "The place is going to look big time. They've got this machine now; blows smoke, but it's not smoke."

Ricky's enthusiasm petered out when he noticed Danno wasn't really following him.

"Cool," Ricky said in response to himself.

"What is it, then?" Lenny asked.

"What?" Ricky replied.

"The smoke. If it's not smoke, then what is it?"

"It's . . . a smoke-like . . . cloud," Ricky replied.

Lenny was interested now. "Of smoke?"

"The fucking air or whatever. It's a machine that makes the air look like smoke. Who gives a shit, Lenny?"

Danno turned to Ricky and said, "You call Proctor, and tell that prick I'm still in charge until tomorrow night."

Ricky nodded. "Of course."

"This is still my match and I say how it ends. If he doesn't like it, he can kiss my ass." Danno threw the last dregs of his coffee out into the driveway and walked to his door.

Ricky said, "Boss?"

Danno stopped, but couldn't even bring himself to look back. "Yeah?"

"The first chance we get, we level this guy."

Danno paused and Ricky waited for an answer, or some sign of fight. But Danno just walked silently into the shaded darkness of his house. When he was far enough out of sight, he took the letter from his top pocket: "You are invited to attend the Task Force on Professional Wrestling one week from today."

Danno crumpled the letter and flung it into an open doorway on his way to the kitchen.

September 30, 1972 — The Next Day.
New York.

It was cold, but it was beautiful and dark, quiet more than anything. Just a few of the ring crew were tightening the buckles and sliding under the ring with wires and cables. No one knew that Danno was in the last row of the nosebleeds. A venue like this was why he had wanted the business from his father. The energy of thousands of people being entertained and enthralled by two men in a fifteen-foot-by-fifteen-foot ring was the ultimate for Danno. He had been a fan long before he was an owner.

"Cold, isn't it?" Annie said as she approached her husband along the back row.

He was caught unaware. "What are you doing here?"

Annie sat in the seat next to her husband. "Lenny told me you were here. The poor man needs to go home to his own house, Dan."

"Did he?"

Annie shook her head and linked Danno's arm. "He's outside," she said, resting her head on his shoulder.

The hugeness and the stillness of the place reeled Annie in straight away. "It's going to be one for the ages."

Danno afforded himself a little smile. She was right. It *was* going to be one for the ages. This was the match and the venue that people would still be talking about in fifty years' time.

"Remember when we hired that bear to wrestle some of the guys 'cause we thought it would sell a few tickets?"

Danno laughed. Somewhere in the back of his brain was a locked closet full of his rookie failures. "And the poor mime I hired to wrestle himself in a sixty-minute draw?"

"We were really broke back then," Annie said.

Danno hugged Annie closer. "Some people would say we were happier, though. Not fucking me. We were miserable."

"Yep."

Danno surveyed the stadium once more and drank it all in.

"Are we going to lose?" Annie asked.

She never got into finishes before. She never really got into anything to do with the business side of wrestling before. Danno felt strange breaking kayfabe, even with his own wife.

"Yeah. We're going to lose tomorrow," he said.

"Well then, you were the best of them, Dan. You made the people believe again."

Danno chuckled. "That's 'cause it was real. I'm like the magician who actually set himself on fire to make everyone believe that magic is real."

"Well, what's the alternative?" Annie asked, looking up at her husband's strained face. "What else can you do?"

Danno felt a rush of openness make its way to his mouth. "I want it both ways, Annie. I want to stay on top, but I don't want to get my hands dirty doing it."

Annie wanted to ask what dirty hands meant, but she thought she already knew. Danno wasn't made for that side of the business. The dirty side.

"You've done it. You've made your mark. Let someone else have the stress of it all. There's no need to get your hands dirty."

Danno kissed Annie on top of her head and patted her lap to move. They both got up from their seats.

"I'm not ready to hand it over," Danno said as he steered Annie to the exit. "But I will."

A coffee-fueled Lenny walked quietly into the back room of a low-ceiling amusement arcade. There was a ring set up in the middle of the room where Babu, Proctor, and Gilbert were standing. Gilbert had on his red wrestling trunks and boots. He was the heavyweight champion in waiting and he was not in shape.

The door closing behind Lenny alerted the room to a visitor.

"Sorry, Danno sent me down," Lenny said to the pissed-off looking trio in the ring.

"Kayfabe," Gilbert said under his breath.

Lenny was offended by the comment. "The boss sent me down. I'm not some mark who ambled in off the street. Kayfabe my ass."

Proctor laughed disbelievingly. "Do you hear this prick?" he said as he got out of the ring and walked to Lenny. "Aren't you the little lady I floored at Danno's anniversary party a couple of years ago?"

Lenny wanted to back out of the room, but stood his ground. "Danno wants you two out of here," he said, looking over Proctor's shoulder to Babu. "The boss wants the champ rested."

Proctor grabbed Lenny by the jaw and made him focus on his face. "We're not done here. Get the fuck out of the building before I open you up."

Lenny again looked for Babu's direction. Babu nodded. Lenny slapped away Proctor's hand and walked back out the door. He was emboldened by Danno's new faith in him. He was also terrified of getting hit.

"That guy is a little cunt," Proctor announced as he got back in the ring. "Let's get back to work."

"Babs, you want to go with that finish instead?" Gilbert asked Babu.

"No. And if you abbreviate my name again, I'm going to break you in half," Babu said.

Proctor and Gilbert were getting exhausted. For the last two days they had laid out a hundred different finishes to the giant champion. Every one of them he rejected just to fuck with them.

"Well, what do *you* want to do?" Proctor asked.

"Get a shower," Babu said as he threw his leg over the top rope and left the ring. "We're on in about seven hours. We'll figure it out when we get in the ring."

Ricky came in with a coffee for Babu. "Go and get yourself some rest, champ."

Babu left the room.

"None for us, Ricky?" Proctor asked.

"I wouldn't drink your fucking coffee anyway," Gilbert said. "So you can shove it up your ass."

Gilbert bumped past Ricky on his way out the door.

"Good job raising that one," Ricky said to Proctor. "He's adorable."

Proctor smiled and gathered his things from the bench.

"The boss don't want you here later," Ricky said.

Proctor stopped and quickly shifted from anger to reason. "Why not?"

"He said you're not welcome and he can't guarantee your safety from the Boys if they hear you're in the building."

"Does that include you, too?" Proctor asked.

"Yeah." Ricky wanted to hurt Proctor as bad as he possibly could, but everything had to wait until the time was right.

"I thought this was all about the money, Ricky? That's what we all live and die for," Proctor said.

"And?"

Proctor knew he was going to be all at sea without a solid number two to take care of the details. Someone who had just been through it. Someone who had helped steer the shit hole that was New York into becoming a money machine.

"If you want to jump to Florida and make some real money, I won't hold any grudges about what's happened in the past. You'll come in with a clean slate. Three hundred and fifty a year. You'd run the show. I'd call you every now and then from a beach. We wouldn't have to even look at each other."

Ricky had ample time to leave the room, but he didn't. His old-school money attitude was just right for such an offer.

"If we're all here to make money, then I don't think you're going to get more than that sticking with Danno. Not now he's on the way down again. Chances are, he won't even stick around the business himself. What do you do when he jets off to his retirement? Has he left you enough to live on? Fatso is going to be looked after, no matter what happens with the government next week."

Ricky knew the belt was leaving, which meant his money would drop considerably. If Ginny was out, he was out. What was he going to do for a living if they did ban pro wrestling in New York?

"If I hear from you before I get to Florida tomorrow, I'll know you're in. If I don't, I'll know you stayed on the sinking ship."

Proctor left.

CHAPTER TWENTY-ONE

September 30, 1972 — Show Time.
New York.

This was the most important call Lenny had ever received in his wrestling life. He still had the phone in his hand. The message was simple: "Bring the champ. Everyone is in."

He caught a glimpse of himself in the hotel mirror, dressed in his new three-piece polyester plaid suit. He was big time. This night was big time. But Lenny really just wanted to go home. He really wanted to pick up the phone and beg Bree to let him come home.

But he didn't. He stood in the lobby of the hotel and thought about it. But he did nothing.

"Lenny?" Gilbert King shouted from behind. Lenny thought for sure that he was hearing things.

"Lenny?" Gilbert shouted again.

Lenny looked around to see the man who tonight would be crowned the new champion of the world, in his wrestling gear, with a cooler full of beer in his hand. He had the elevator door held open with his foot. There was blood on his chest and he looked like he was drunk, stoned, or both.

"I'm not doing it," Gilbert said, his voice shaking slightly. "So fuck you." He removed his foot from the elevator doors to let them close.

Lenny watched in quiet disbelief as the elevator pinged number after number before stopping at the fifth floor.

What the fuck was that?

Lenny pushed open the only door ajar on the fifth floor. He recognized Pee Chu Ming, who was passed out on the floor by the bed. "He was supposed to get me to Shea," Gilbert said from the bathroom.

"What? What's happening? You should have been gone an hour ago," Lenny said.

"What time is it?" Gilbert asked, stumbling toward Lenny. He dropped a prescription bottle on the tiled bathroom floor.

"Is he . . . what's wrong with him?" Lenny asked about Pee Chu.

Gilbert slapped Lenny in the face. "Tell me I'm awesome."

Lenny stumbled back.

"Tell me I'm awesome, motherfucker!" Gilbert jumped on the bed and bounced up and down before leaping onto Lenny, driving them both into the dressing table.

Gilbert got up and high-fived himself. "I'm fucking awesome. I'm going to be the best fucking champion of all time."

Lenny was still a confused mess on the floor. "You have to go. They're waiting for you."

Gilbert started stomping his bare foot down on the side of Lenny's head. "Let them wait. Let them all wait for the champion."

From the floor, Lenny could see Babu's unmistakable feet approaching him and Gilbert. Gilbert's ranting stopped dead when Babu grabbed him by the back of the neck and flung him effortlessly toward the door. Gilbert didn't even open his mouth to protest. Babu then scowled at Lenny and signaled for him to get up.

"I was coming to get you. I swear I was," Lenny said as he bolted for the exit.

Gilbert grabbed his cooler and both he and Lenny left the room, one much more quietly than the other. Babu listened to Pee Chu's mouth to make sure he was breathing. His eyes were open, but he wasn't able to speak. The giant turned him onto his side and jammed a pillow against his back to make sure he couldn't roll back. He looked into Pee Chu's eyes and could see there was someone home. He just needed time to ride it out.

Lenny slid open the door on the VW Kombi van in the underground parking lot. Babu hurried in and sat on the floor and covered his head with a towel while Gilbert stumbled in, clinging to his cooler.

Lenny waited for Gilbert to put the box down before he swiped it from the back and slammed the door shut. A single bottle of beer fell out and rolled under the seats.

"Hey, motherfucker," Gilbert protested as he stood up in the van.

"You've had enough," Lenny said through the window.

Lenny walked around to get in the driver's seat. Babu quickly slapped Gilbert in the balls, which dropped him to his knees. "You get your head right for doing business or I'm going to kill you right here. Do you hear me?"

Gilbert nodded. Babu slapped him hard across the face to sober him up.

Lenny started the engine. "We're going to be cutting it tight."

Gilbert, from his kneeling position, spotted the loose beer bottle and fetched it from under the seat. Lenny sped out of the lot and began the short journey to the stadium.

"I wasn't inside," Gilbert mumbled ashamedly.

"What?" Lenny said, unable to hear from the front.

Gilbert was more interested in coming clean to Babu in the back. "I was in rehab. A few actually. One in Omaha, which kicked me out after a couple of weeks. Two in Los Angeles, and one upstate on a farm. I wasn't in prison."

Gilbert looked at his unopened drink. "This time, I'd been sober for over four months, so my old man called me back."

Babu started to say something but stopped. He gestured for Gilbert to give him the bottle. Gilbert thought hard about it. Lenny was struggling to drive and see what was happening at the same time. He veered suddenly to the right to avoid running into the back of a bus. Gilbert flew into Babu's lap with the precipitous jolt. "Watch where you're going, asshole," Gilbert shouted.

"Sorry," Lenny shouted.

Gilbert popped up and lunged for Lenny. He grabbed him around the neck from behind and the van started to career all over the road.

"Say I'm awesome, fuckstick. Say it," Gilbert shouted into Lenny's ear.

Lenny couldn't talk even if he wanted to—Gilbert was choking the life out of him. He could feel a darkness coming in from his peripheral vision. His fingers began to slip from the wheel.

"Say I'm awesome, motherf—" Gilbert was yanked away from finishing his sentence by Babu, who knocked him silly with another slap.

Lenny carefully pulled over and steadied himself. "What the fuck is wrong with you, you fucking fuckface motherfucker?" he said. Even through his anger, he could see that Babu had enough. It was time to get to the fucking stadium.

Lenny settled himself and moved steadily back into the flow of traffic. Gilbert rolled into a ball and hugged his last remaining unopened drink. Babu slid back down into his sitting position on the floor. They all rode along silently. The arena was drawing closer and the tension of delivering the match began to rise.

"I need to pee," Gilbert announced desperately.

Lenny kept driving. He was sure that Danno and the crew were already asking where he was. "We'll be there in less than five minutes."

Lenny took 72nd and Roosevelt and saw the long, dark road open up in front of him. Gilbert began to hop around in the van. "I need to pee, I said," he shouted.

Babu needed his own space. He had never been this late to a building before and he had his pre-match rituals that he needed to get done. Looking at Gilbert was just pushing him closer to violence, and if there was violence in the back of the VW, there would be no match. He angrily pulled his towel over his face and closed his eyes and tried to zone out.

"Did you hear me?" Gilbert shouted at Lenny.

Lenny put his foot down to the floor and switched on the radio. No one was going to say that he couldn't get his job done. Both champion and challenger would arrive in good time, and surely, he figured, he would get the credit for getting Gilbert there too.

"I fucking said I need to piss," Gilbert screamed and threw his bottle at Lenny.

With a dead clunk, the unopened bottle bounced off the back of Lenny's head and knocked him out cold. The van shaved the sides off a couple of parked cars before it slammed off the side of an exterior wall and shot Lenny and the cooler out through the windshield. Gilbert ended up being launched from the back to the front of the van and Babu was slammed head first off the ceiling as the van turned over and smashed into the leg of the railway bridge.

All three men were out. All that could be heard was the singing of the radio.

"Are you coming out to have a look?" Ricky asked Danno as they stood by the entrance to the Shea Stadium field.

"Maybe later," Danno said.

"It's something the old-timers who did this before you could only dream of, boss. There are people out there who have crossed the country, left other territories to come to yours."

The wild cheers grew larger as the bell rang for the finish of the first match.

"Listen to that," Ricky said in awe. "They fucking sound happy to me."

"Is the champ around?" Danno wondered.

"He's probably waiting in the locker room with the Boys."

Ricky put out his hand for Danno to shake. "I was going to wait until later."

"What?" Danno asked as he shook Ricky's hand.

Ricky had a huge grin on his face. "You beat the Beatles' record here. Sixty-five thousand four hundred and seventeen tickets sold."

Danno was impressed, but didn't really feel like celebrating. "That's great."

"I'll see you out there," Ricky said as he left.

Babu crawled from the van. He could hear the sirens growing closer. Lenny was passed out close to the van with a cowboy boot on the ground behind him. Gilbert was barely conscious on the sidewalk at the other side of the road. Babu looked for any witnesses as he lifted Gilbert over his shoulder and ran as fast as he could away from the oncoming sirens.

Protect the business at all costs. That was what mattered more than anything here. If they were seen together, questions would be asked as to why two men who were about to go to war were giving each other a lift to the battlefield. There was already too much of a light on the business. So Babu ran and laid Gilbert in the first alley he could find that was just far enough away and laid him down on the trash bags as the cops rapidly approached. Babu then found a phone booth and rang the Shea Stadium box office. It was the only number he knew, having dialed it a hundred times to see if they were sold out.

Well, they were sold out, but Babu knew he wouldn't get to see it.

"Tell Danno Garland that Chrissy said the match is off. Little Proctor is hurt bad. It's important that he gets this message. Do you hear me?"

The woman on the other end of the line promised she did.

CHAPTER TWENTY-TWO

Danno stood in the empty hallway in Shea Stadium. He was strad-
dling the line between internal panic and external patience with a
disoriented Lenny on the other end of the line.

"I can't remember, sir. The van crashed. It looks like we hit a couple
of cars and rolled into the bridge. And now I can't find Gilbert King."

"He's missing?"

"I was talking to him, trying to pull him out. I can't remember. I
think I have a concussion. Things—"

"Is he in the van?"

"I don't think so. I thought I—"

"Lenny, is your fucking van invisible?"

"No, sir."

"Is it so far away or so damaged in the crash that you can't look
into its windows?"

"No, sir."

"So. Is. Gilbert. Fucking. King. In. The. Van?"

"No, sir."

"Perfect." Danno thumped the receiver against the chipped walls
in the bowels of Shea Stadium.

"I'm sorry. I was knocked stupid myself, and I can't even really
remember what happened. I would do anything to make this right,
boss. You know that."

"Are you still on the phone?"

"Yes, sir."

"Fucking find him. Do you hear me? You've got ten minutes to get them both here, otherwise do you know what will happen? The—"

The phone abruptly disconnected. Danno was stunned. *What the fuck is going on?* he wondered to himself. "Hello?" he called down the dead line in disbelief. "Hello?"

Danno beat the phone against the wall several times in sheer frustration. Now he wanted someone to be watching so he could lay into them for just being there.

"Ricky?" Danno cried down the hallway. "Ricky?"

The bell time was drawing closer. Danno paced as Ricky sat quietly.

"I need to send a car out there now, boss. If the main event doesn't go ahead there is going—" Ricky stopped short when he realized the obviousness of his statement.

"We need to wait," Danno said.

"If we don't act now, then the whole house comes down."

"Wait," Danno repeated.

"There are sixty-five thousand people out there . . ."

Danno stopped. "Hit me."

Ricky had waited a long time to hear those words, ever since Danno backed off on Proctor after Ginny got turned over. But now Danno was giving him permission. "What?"

Danno walked over to Ricky and held his shoulders. He was wild-eyed, but smiling slightly. "You have to hit me out there. We need as many people as possible to see it."

Ricky had no idea what Danno was talking about.

"This main event isn't going to happen now, for whatever reason. We have to think past it. You have to hit me out there in front of the locker room," Danno said.

Danno grabbed Ricky and walked him to the door.

"What are you doing?" Ricky asked.

"I'm not sure, but I know this is where to start."

"Get someone to see if they can find out where they are," Danno snapped.

"Alright, there's no way to sugarcoat this; our main event isn't going to happen."

The waiting collective dropped their heads in unison. A few deeper voices in the middle somberly cursed their luck.

"We still getting paid, boss?" a brave but anonymous voice asked from the back. Danno ignored it.

"It's time to make a call on the finish. We're going for a big shmoz, clusterfuck finish with everyone in the ring. Everyone who isn't booted up—get so," Danno ordered the waiting crowd. "We're going to load the ring with everyone we've got and I want them to beat the shit out of each other."

"Why aren't you going to let the natural thing happen out there, boss?" Ricky asked

"No. We're going to go out there to finish. It might not be the finish they paid for, but we will give them everything we have," Danno said. He pulled the top off a Sharpie and began to write out different match scenarios on a paper tablecloth. "I need a list of everyone who is ready to work. Ricky? Go and find yourself some gear."

"If they riot then we might at least get paid after all the shit we've been through."

"I fucking know that, Ricky. We can still work our way out of this. Get booted up."

"With all due respect, Danno . . . this whole place paid to see Babu versus Gilbert King, and I don't see either of them here."

"Do you not think I fucking know that?" Danno said.

"You sure you still want to work this angle, boss?" Ricky asked as he approached Danno.

"I don't want to talk about it here, Ricky," Danno replied.

"There's nothing to talk about, Danno," Ricky replied. "We can't give the crowd what they paid for, so now we have no choice but to make sure they riot."

"I have no other choice now, Ricky. We stay and finish the card," Danno said.

Ricky butted his head against Danno's. "You've done nothing but fuck this territory since you got your greedy hands on it."

Danno pushed him away. "Don't ever get in my face again, Ricky."

A few half-dressed wrestlers silently stood between the men.

Ricky paused and looked around the room. "You people realize what's happening here? No payday. After all that's happened. Years of fighting. Some people getting fucked up, never to wrestle again. The biggest pile of money we've ever seen and he's going to give it back."

"I'm not fucking this crowd over." Danno continued to write out his revised card on the tablecloth.

"But you're willing to fuck us over. The truth is, you couldn't draw money with a green fucking crayon. Asshole."

Ricky spun on his heel and sucker punched Danno hard in the side of the head. The old promoter stumbled helplessly into the tables, which collapsed under his considerable weight.

Tiny Thunder grabbed Ricky around the waist as some of the roster hurried to Danno's aid.

"Are you fucking crazy, man?" Tiny shouted. Ricky easily shrugged him off and moved for the exit. His strides exploded into a sprint when he saw some of the other wrestlers running toward him with bad intentions.

"Did everyone forget we're here to make money?" Ricky shouted as he bolted through the exit door.

The room melted into chaos.

Danno immediately rose up and tried to steady himself. There was a nasty gash above his left eye and a lump was already starting to form. He pushed his revised plan into Tiny Thunder's arms. "We go out there and finish the card. We take what's coming our way. Then we are going to rebuild. No matter what happens out there, we can come back from this."

Danno staggered out of the room and used the stadium walls to steady his shuffling movements toward the restroom. He opened the door and hid in one of the dirty, smelly stalls. From outside a panicked voice shouted, "Boss, Proctor King is looking for you."

"You didn't tell him I was here, did you?" Danno shouted back.

"I meant on the phone, sir."

"Well, *say* that, then. There's a big fucking difference."

The messenger paused. "What should I tell him?"

Lenny pleaded and begged to make a call, but the arresting officers never even acknowledged him as they threw him and Babu in the holding cell.

Knocking out a cop for calling you fake was a no-phone-call move.

The only thing keeping Lenny together was knowing that Babu was a veteran at this. Tales of his overnight stints in lockups around the country were legendary among the other wrestlers. Every territory where Babu went, there was another story of a ten-man brawl and a heartbroken woman. Babu, the Savage from South Africa, was a living myth to all the Boys in the back.

Lenny snuck a look from the corner of his eye. Maybe Babu was having an off night, 'cause he didn't look all that comfortable in this cell to Lenny.

"You okay, champ?" A few years in and Lenny was so far outside the loop he didn't even know Babu's second name. Or even if he had one. Driving and being around backstage meant he had one foot in and one foot out, in Babu's eyes. Danno had shown way more faith in Lenny lately, and so had Ricky. Babu barely acknowledged he was alive.

Wrestling was built on paying your dues before you were allowed in. It was one of the most rigid fraternities ever constructed. So

Babu, as champion, customarily ignored Lenny's every breath. It could have something to do with the fact that Lenny had just plowed them into a wall under the bridge on 72nd Street.

"I don't remember what happened, but I'm sorry. I know tonight was huge for the company," Lenny said.

Babu might have been playing mute, but he certainly wasn't deaf. He followed every sound from the front of the police station with focus and intent. He was on edge and it was beginning to become more evident to Lenny.

The cell was not nearly as nice as the ones on *Dragnet*. Lenny did notice that the walls in the hallway were that pea-soup green that was everywhere now. Then he wondered why he even noticed that. A little decor distraction couldn't totally drown out the reality that Danno Garland was surely looking for him. Lenny wanted to go home and sleep in his own bed and eat in his own kitchen.

The silence in the lobby of the building was replaced with energy, which in turn was replaced with noise. Plenty of noise. The aggressive kind.

Babu stood instinctively and cradled his severely injured forearm.

"What?" Lenny asked.

Babu acknowledged Lenny with a look of frustration. "Who do you think that is out there, you dumb fuck?"

The end of the announcement was drowned out by ferocious boos. "And there will be refunds for anyone—" The announcer ran from ringside to avoid the avalanche of missiles that rained down at him from the stands.

"Get the fuck out of here," Tiny Thunder shouted to his fellow wrestlers as he abandoned the ring too. All the wrestlers ran back toward the wrestler entrance.

The whole ringside area pushed forward and dismantled the retaining barriers like a swollen sea swallowing a storm wall. Pockets of fighting had broken out between New York and Florida fans in the huge crowd, each blaming their man for the no-show. There were tunnels of people crushing and jamming themselves into all the available exits as the temperature rose to boiling point. The more scuffles that flared up, the more the peaceful people struggled to maintain their calmness and reason.

Bodies, arms, legs, chairs, bottles, barriers, shirtless people, bleeding people, angry faces, stunned children, sneaky punches, threats, and promises of beatings, all could be seen as Danno watched from a box at the top of the stadium. He nursed his own cut eye, picked up the phone, and delicately laid it to his ear. "Hello," he said.

Proctor's voice on the other end of the line was cold, measured. "You're doing this to fuck me over, aren't you? You were going to make sure that I didn't get that fucking belt no matter what you did. Isn't that what's happening here on my TV? Are you fucking me over, Danno?"

Proctor was standing in his hotel room watching the scene unfold.

Danno didn't even know where to begin. "No, I don't know what—"

Proctor paced his room. "Where is he?"

"Who?"

"What do you mean who? My boy. That's fucking who."

"He's not my responsibility. What are you asking me for?"

Danno had never gotten the message Babu left at the box office. The lady who had taken it just rolled her eyes and moved on with her day. Danno knew that Gilbert was with Lenny, but nothing more than that.

"One of my guys just called and told me that your champion dragged Gilbert out of his room," Proctor said.

"What?"

"Said your giant and your driver took him."

"Took him? What the fuck are you talking about?" Danno asked.

"You better find my boy, Danno, 'cause if I find out that there's anything wrong with him . . ." Proctor paused. "Find him."

The ice was helping. Kind of. The ring was mostly ripped up and pissed on. A few stadium employees swept their way through the considerable amounts of wreckage and rubbish that lined the aisles. The main lights were still on and there was a deep quiet after the explosion of madness.

At the end of row A stood an officious beige figure. Melvin Pritchard knocked the center rail with his car key to get Danno's attention. Danno duly raised his weary head, ready to unload on whoever was trying to further annoy him. He thought better of it when he saw who was standing there waiting for him.

"One week, Mr. Garland. And unfortunately you can't fix the end of this matchup." Melvin put on his hat and walked away.

Babu looked around the cell for something, anything. His arm was in bad shape; the pain was radiating in his elbow, shoulder, and down his rib cage.

"What is it?" Lenny asked anxiously.

Babu grunted at the sheer inconvenience of Lenny being alive. He sized up the bench that they were sitting on and stomped on it with his giant foot.

Lenny rushed to the bars and tried to look down the hallway to see what was agitating Babu so much. The giant stomped on the bench again. Lenny could see shapes and figures form behind the frosted glass in the door to the hallway. It looked like the booking room was filling up fast.

On the third attempt, Babu drove his size eighteen-and-a-half extra-wide foot through the six-inch-thick timber bench. He dropped to his knees and tried to pull a usable sliver of wood from the broken options available.

Lenny noticed the handle begin to turn on the door at the end of the hallway. "Someone's coming," he informed Babu.

Babu worked faster to split the wood with his one working arm. "Help me."

His tenseness made Lenny move faster. Babu shoved a partially split piece of bench into Lenny's hand. "We're going to wishbone this. Hold it as tight as you can."

Lenny's knuckles whitened. Babu abruptly yanked the wood and sent Lenny flying across to the other side of the cell. Lenny could feel a difference in his shoulder. Babu knelt down beside him and lifted him to a sitting position.

"Thanks."

"Move it, asshole. You're sitting on the wood." Babu reached down between Lenny's legs and retrieved it, folding Lenny in half.

The noise and shouting was now mounting and moving toward them. Nine or ten, Babu thought. Lenny sheepishly made his way toward his cellmate. "I think my shoulder is out."

Tyler, the aggressive officer from the crash scene, appeared with a huge spread of yellow bruising on most of his face. Lenny had never seen anything like it before. It was as if he had been hit in the face with a typewriter. He was lucky that Babu hadn't been able to use his right arm.

The cop removed a huge bunch of keys and warily unlocked the cell door. "They let me bring some friends of yours here."

Several other officers dressed in riot gear marched the aggressive mob into the cell. Individuals were getting clubbed and punched, and the door was slammed shut after everyone was beaten into place.

"Enjoy," Tyler shouted to Babu above the rising madness.

Babu sat down and grabbed Lenny by the arm to sit too. Babu made himself as small as he could, pulled off his cap, and turned away.

"Who are these people?" Lenny asked.

All the cops left and the cell was filled with belligerent and drunk people. "This is bullshit, man. Let us out of here."

In the huddle, Babu checked his arm. He could see the bone.

The cell door was rattled by several pairs of drunken hands.

"We got ripped off. Do you hear me? Let us fucking out of here," one of the mob shouted.

The roars of protest gradually stopped as the crowd realized they weren't doing anything. Lenny turned to Babu. His heart was galloping in his chest. He had never felt anything like this before. This was fear. The real kind. The meeting-a-black-bear-in-your-bathroom kind. He could feel a shortness of breath.

"I want to go home," Lenny whispered.

The men's focus shifted from through the bars back into the cage. Lenny's instinct kicked in. Sometimes you don't have to look to know that someone is staring at you.

"What the fuck?" Some of the new visitors stopped their incoherent protest and turned to Babu and Lenny.

"Is that Babu?" one of the people in the group wondered loudly. "That's fucking him."

Babu rose up and stood before the crowd. For years he had been provoking hatred in these very same people. Cowardly attacks. Bloodying their heroes. Burning their local team jersey. Humping the American Flag. Babu was so good at his job that when he went to Boston, they had to erect Plexiglas around the ring. He was the most hated man along the East Coast, who made a lot of money on the premise that no one could beat him.

But tonight was the night he was going to get it. Finally, after years of dominance, Babu, the South African Savage, was going to be whooped in Shea Stadium. The people could feel it. They all paid to witness it. They were promised.

Except he never showed up.

"Man, you're the biggest fucking pussy I've ever laid eyes on," said one of the horde as he stepped forward. "What happened, did you wet your big giant panties on the way to the show?"

The mob roared their approval and the self-assigned leader was clearly enjoying the verbal battle with a mute. "Well, one way or the other, we're going to see you get bloody tonight, Babu. You fucking white nigger."

Everyone agreed with a series of "woohooo"s and "yeah"s. Lenny involuntarily stepped out between the crowd and the champ.

"We were in a crash—"

Babu grabbed Lenny around the face and tossed him back behind him.

The leader continued, "I ain't no Florida kid, but I bet I could break you up."

Babu began a visceral bellow. The self-appointed leader tried to backpedal back into the collective, but he was met by a wall of anxious flesh. They all knew that when the Savage began his "weird shit," the end was near for his opponent. The bellowing continued through the short faux-tribal dance. The bravado was gone and replaced with a vacuum. The South African Savage had arrived. He pounded his chest with his good hand and his noises became louder, his movements more confrontational. And then he abruptly stopped.

This was the part where the bad stuff usually happened. And they all knew it.

The swarm was halfway between spectator and prey. They knew what was going to happen next, but their fandom slowed down their alarm.

Babu snapped forward and dropped two of them instantly with the same huge elbow hook. He produced his split of timber and cracked another over the head with it.

Those remaining upright automatically rushed him to try to stem the momentum of hurt that was plainly coming their way. They threw everything they had: kicks, punches, bites, and nut shots, but it was like throwing snowballs at a tree. Lenny wanted to do something. This was what he was waiting for. It was his opportunity to become one of the Boys once and for all.

He saw the giant trying in vain to protect his seriously injured arm while fending off a mass of out-of-shape attackers. Bodies were flying in all directions. Babu was kicking ass and, more importantly to him, staying in character.

This was Lenny's chance.

When he was young, Lenny had jumped from the dilapidated Villa Rosa mansion into Long Island Sound. He couldn't swim. Until this moment, it was the bravest, stupidest thing he had ever done. He was about to get wet again.

Lenny closed his eyes and jumped in. He was immediately knocked out and trampled.

CHAPTER TWENTY-THREE

October 1, 1972—The Next Day.
New York.

It was that unusually calm time between sunrise and the city waking. The noise wasn't at its peak or the traffic at its busiest yet. It was a nice time—if you weren't Lenny Long.

His head was hinged back as far as his neck could go. Both nostrils were blocked tight with tissue, and he was having a hard time breathing without pain. There was a dried lump of blood at the back of his head, and his stained and tattered clothes were barely staying with him.

The night before, when things had quieted down inside, Babu had pulled Lenny's arm back into place. Lenny thanked him, but Babu ignored him. Worse still was Lenny's lack of contact with his family. He couldn't remember how often they'd spoken in the last two months. Maybe three times. He'd been home even less in the last six months. All the physical pain, the emotional torment, and yet he knew there was a real good chance that something even worse was coming his way.

Both men were on the steps of the police department while Danno's lawyer, Troy Bartlett, haggled inside the station. "You tell me why I had to call around to every fucking jailhouse in the city to find my clients, officer," Troy said across the counter.

"Just tell your friends out there not to run off anywhere now," the police officer replied before taking a call.

Bartlett scraped his briefcase off the counter and headed for the door. It was probably going to cost Danno a pretty penny to make the charge of assaulting an officer go away, but no doubt he'd pay it for his champ.

Troy cracked the doors open and approached the two men sitting on the steps of the police department. Danno had only asked him to deal with one of them. The one who got them into all this. The small one.

Troy handed Lenny a piece of paper. "Danno wants to see you at this address, seven-thirty tomorrow," he said before he walked off.

Babu was beginning to shake with the effects of his injured and possibly infected arm.

"We're going to have to get you to a hospital," Lenny said.

Babu began to walk. "We need to pick up someone on the way."

Lenny followed after him, trying to keep up like a child with a grownup. "Have you got change for a five? I just need to make a call."

Babu ignored Lenny's question. "We need a car," Babu said, turning the corner with purpose.

"You saw what happened to my wheels last night."

Babu stopped. "You get a car."

"Why?"

"'Cause we have to collect Gilbert King," Babu said as he walked on.

Lenny knocked on the peeling white door. He took a look around the yard and noticed the wire fence was gone. He had promised he would get rid of it when he came back off the road. Looked like he was too late.

The only contact he had had with his wife for the last couple of months was their short argument in the car lot. Based on that, Lenny figured that things might get awkward.

Babu waited in the yard while Lenny waited for the door to open.

Bree answered. She was taken aback by Lenny's appearance, but was too angry to ask if he was okay. Lenny missed her immediately. He just couldn't tell her what trouble he was in.

"Hey, honey. I lost my key," he said as he tried to enter the house. Bree stood firmly in her doorway.

"I don't want you to come in," she said.

"Why not?" Lenny asked.

"Because breezing in and out of this place is turning your kids upside down."

Lenny looked back at Babu. He was getting a little embarrassed that he wasn't allowed into his own home. "I'll just be a minute."

"That's the fucking issue, Lenny."

"What?" he asked.

"Tell me Lenny, do you think I'm the kind of wife that's going to sit around here and wait for you to make me happy? Do you think I think that's my job?"

"I—"

"Do you think that I sit in here every night changing the wallpaper in my head or baking cakes just in case you happen to grace me with your presence some night? Is that how you've decided my life is to be?"

Lenny tried desperately to direct Bree's eyes to the waiting giant behind him.

"Him? Fuck him, Lenny." Bree stepped onto her porch and looked over her husband's shoulder to Babu. "Do you understand me, mister? This one likes to stay away from his family. You can keep him."

Bree started to close the door, but decided she wanted to have another go at Babu, who seemed to symbolize the business for her. "I fucking hate what you do and I hate what it does to my family."

"I just need the keys to the car, Peaches."

Bree stopped her struggle. "You want what?"

"The keys."

"You're not even going to argue with me or push me over to see your kids? You just want the car? Where's that van that you just had to have?"

"What van?" Lenny pleaded innocently.

"Are you going to tell me you didn't get the van, Lenny? 'Cause I will scream right here if you're going to come home and lie to me."

"I'm coming back later. We can talk then."

"Yeah, what time? Gimme some time to put on a nice dress and warm up the foot massager for you."

Lenny couldn't answer. Bree took the car keys from a homely little hook plaque.

"Get the fuck out of here," she said.

Lenny took the keys and walked back down the steps. His oldest boy peeked around the door and father and son looked at each other briefly before Bree closed the door.

Lenny quietly passed Babu and opened the car door. Babu stuffed himself into the passenger side.

Babu took the receiver off the dash. "What's this?"

"CB radio."

Lenny turned the key and prayed that one of the blinds in his house would move, even just an inch. That he'd get a sign that someone was watching him leave.

His prayer went unanswered.

"She never asked what happened to me," Lenny said.

"Hardly anyone in this business gets to go home."

Lenny turned the key in the ignition. "Where's Gilbert King? Where am I driving to?"

Babu looked straight ahead. "Back to where we crashed."

The bridge was unmoved. Not a scratch. Lenny tried desperately to squeeze out a memory of what had happened the night before. Did he really ruin the biggest match in professional wrestling history because he was tired?

If he couldn't come up with something else, he was going to get hurt. And probably by several different groups of people.

Babu was sweating profusely in the seat next to him.

"We have to get you to a hospital, man," Lenny said.

"Turn here and pull over by that gate," Babu muttered.

Lenny drove along Roosevelt and stopped at a black gate that hung crookedly between two graffiti-covered buildings. Babu struggled to release himself from the car. Lenny leaned over to help, but Babu warned him off without saying a word. The giant opened his own door and fell out onto the road. He made his way to the gate as people stopped and watched.

"Fuck you, Babu, you pussy," a voice shouted from the other side of the road.

Lenny followed his injured passenger as he opened the gate. They could see a heavily bloodstained dumpster sandwiched by a small and filthy alleyway.

"Where the fuck is he?" Babu muttered to himself as he walked to the soiled dead end.

"Gilbert?" Lenny asked.

Babu struggled to stay standing. Lenny tried to hold his arm in support. Babu suddenly turned and grabbed him by the neck. "This is all your fault. You hear me? You couldn't keep your fucking eyes on the road, where they were supposed to be—and now we're all fucked."

Babu released Lenny just in time. Lenny slid down the wall and fought for breath. Lenny had never felt so helpless against harm in all his life. "I don't know what happened last night," he said.

"You started something that's going to finish us all." Babu kicked open the gate and marched to the driver's side of the car. A small pool of onlookers had gathered across the road.

"Babu, your momma sucks dicks. Fuck you, man."

The giant started the car and took off on his own before Lenny found his feet.

The bouquet of flowers was half hidden by Lenny's side as he walked down the busy hospital hallway. He was ready to present them or drop them. Truth was, he didn't know which he was going to have to do. He just knew he couldn't tell Danno that he lost the giant again. He had already tried a few hospitals closest to the crash site.

"Sorry, miss," he said to the nurse at the front desk. "I'm looking for a friend of mine. He's a really big guy who would have come in with a damaged arm?"

Down the hall in the same hospital, Gilbert was in a bed and sleeping. His face was unrecognizable from the bruising, cuts, and swelling. The tubes ran in a pack from the machines to his nose and hand. His mother reached out a shaky arm to lightly touch his face. "Why would they do this to him?"

Proctor stood at the foot of the bed, seething.

Gilbert moaned as he woke. He looked toward his father. "Sorry."

Proctor wasn't sure if he heard Gilbert correctly. "What?" he said as he moved closer to his son.

Gilbert took a second to take in the room. "I tried to get Lenny to stop driving, but he was drunk," Gilbert said.

Proctor could hardly contain his anger. "It's okay, son."

Gilbert ran his dry tongue across his drier lips. "He tried to get me to drink, Pop. Said it would loosen me up for the match. And the giant held me down when I tried to stop the van to get out."

Proctor's knuckles whitened as he strangled the thin blanket on the bed. "It's going to be okay."

Out in the hallway, the adrenaline running through Proctor's body made it hard for him to pinch the coin from his own hand. "Fucking . . ." He tried again, but suddenly became aware of the patients in the hallway staring at him. "What are you looking at?"

he said, scowling. Lenny, still waiting at the desk, heard the roar of Proctor's familiar voice. He moved stealthily into the crowd.

Proctor finally deposited the money and dialed the number.

"New York Booking Agency—" answered the voice on the other end of the line.

Proctor cut in. "Put me through to Danno," he demanded.

Danno's secretary knew the voice well and connected the call immediately, as Danno had instructed her to do if Proctor called.

"Hello?" Danno answered.

Proctor squeezed the phone like it was Danno's throat. "You fucking cunt. I swear to God I'm going to kill them, Danno. Then you."

Lenny watched Proctor from a safe distance down the hall.

"What are you talking about?" Danno replied.

"This is how you keep your fat, greasy hands on the belt? You take out my boy? Is that where we've gone in all of this?"

"We didn't plan anything . . ."

Proctor removed the phone from his ear and just screamed down the line. "Where's his fucking foot, Danno?"

Proctor slapped the phone off the wall and fired a potted plant through the candy dispenser glass in front of him.

"Move him," Proctor shouted to no one in particular. "I want to bring my boy home to Florida with me."

Lenny quickly left the building.

"Listen, baby. I'm sorry," Lenny said as he tried to jam his foot in his own front door.

"You lost the car, Lenny? You were only gone an hour," Bree said.

Lenny mustered his best "pity me" face. It didn't take much. "Some Mexican guy took it. I was trying to buy a gift for you and when I came out it was gone."

Bree stood outside and gently closed the front door behind her. "What do you want?"

Lenny stopped struggling. "I just want to see my family. Get cleaned up a little and maybe take a nap if I have time."

Husband and wife focused on each other in silence.

"Please," he said. "It's been a bad day."

Lenny sat opposite Bree at the table in their modest kitchen. She was smoking and he was finishing up some eggs.

"Do you think the boys might be back soon?" he asked his wife.

"I don't know. Your mom usually takes them to her house after church."

Lenny scraped his last piece of bread around his plate. "So you're smoking now?"

"So you're an asshole now?"

Lenny wiped his hands on his trousers. "I'm sorry."

Bree stubbed her barely lit cigarette out in the ashtray. "I'm trying to start smoking, but I just can't do it," she said as she wiped her tongue on her sleeve. "Thirty-nine years old and I'm still trying to fit in with all the other kids."

Lenny smiled. "Have you been getting the money okay?"

"I want you to come home," she said. "I don't care about the money."

Lenny rested his sore, tired head in his hands. "Do you think I like being out there weeks at a time? Just look at me. We have a nice TV, and that rug looks like it would be nice to lie on with my boys . . ."

"I know about the knapsack," Bree said.

Lenny slowly pushed himself away from the table. "What knapsack?"

"Thing I hate most about all of this is, you're making me into one of these women that snoops. Do you want to be married to one of these women?"

Lenny shook his head.

Bree walked to Lenny with a damp cloth and kissed him on the forehead. "Well, then you're going to have to start telling me things."

She began to gently wipe away some of the dry blood around her husband's ear. "There's ninety-two thousand dollars in our basement," she said.

Lenny turned to her. "I—"

"Don't say it, just let me finish," she said. "That money is the only reason that I've stayed here, Lenny. Not because I'm greedy. It's because I know you. You're a good man and that knapsack is your way home. And I know you're trying—but we just want you."

Lenny stood up and put his hands on his wife's hips. "How much of it did you spend?"

Bree didn't want to say, but he was going to find out one way or the other. "A couple of grand. Me and the boys have been to Coney Island a couple of times and last week I got them some Space Walker toys."

"That's not a couple of grand."

"It is when you're angry."

Lenny tried to kiss Bree, but she moved her lips just out of reach. "You smell like a hippie."

"Bree?"

"Yeah?"

She could feel a moment between them. A space for truth.

He said, "Why is our whole house orange?"

She broke away from him. "Asshole."

"I liked it better when my furniture didn't give me motion sickness."

Bree couldn't help but smile. Lenny was right. Their house was a little loud. "When are you coming home?"

He knew what she meant, but downplayed it. "I want to make sure we're going to be okay before I come off the road."

Bree rested her arms on Lenny's shoulders. "We're not going to be okay if you don't come off the road. I'm not threatening you, I'm just telling you. Those kids are growing up fast and they're making do without you, all the time."

Lenny knew she was right. Her words broke through. They weren't that different or more impactful than what Lenny had heard from her tons of times before. But these words, on this night, broke his heart. He knew what he needed to do. He needed to get out of the wrestling business. "I've got something that I have to finish—"

Bree turned away. Lenny followed her.

"No, I mean it," he said. "Trust me. I'm going to put this one thing to bed and then I'm done." Lenny gently moved Bree's chin back in his direction before kissing her.

Danno threw his father's picture on the bed. He clicked open the safe and dragged the remaining blocks of cash into a waiting bed-sheet on the floor.

In the kitchen, he pulled out his drawers and dipped his arm into the body of his cupboards and pulled out more bags of cash.

In the barn, he hurriedly pulled out more money that was wrapped in plastic from the bales of hay.

"Annie?" he shouted as he rushed through the barn doors.

"Danno?" said a male voice from behind.

Danno stopped dead and waited for something. Something bad.

"Danno?" the voice repeated.

It sounded familiar. Behind him stood his no-nonsense, gray-faced lawyer, Troy Bartlett. "I've got the papers you asked for. Is everything okay?"

Danno nodded happily.

"Would you like to go inside?" Troy asked.

"I don't have time," Danno answered as he looked around for his wife. "I just need someplace safe to move some of my . . ." Danno lowered his voice. ". . . In case the government tries to fuck me over."

Troy nodded knowingly and held out a prepared file. "I've got the papers for your businesses here like you asked. I've placed Mrs. Garland—"

"No," Danno simply said.

"Excuse me? I thought you were wanting to shift your assets into . . ."

"I am. But not her." Danno felt his words betray his wife. "Not that I don't . . ." Danno's embarrassment caught his lawyer off-guard.

"I'm just here to do as you say, Mr. Garland," Troy said.

"We'll just think of someone else, that's all," Danno said as he hurriedly opened the file.

October 2, 1972 — The Next Day.
Atlanta.

It was a public place, but even that didn't make Wild Ted Berry feel totally safe. It was a neutral place, but that didn't bring him any great comfort either. Being a messenger on behalf of Danno Garland was dangerous work after what had happened around the Shea match. Ted had just a glass of water in the busiest restaurant in town. The menu looked good, but he didn't know how long this was going to take.

Beguiling Barry Banner entered the restaurant and walked toward the big Texan sitting at the table. He seated himself and got straight to it. "Is your fat piece of shit boss too fucking chicken to come out in public now, Ted?"

Ted raised his head from the table. He hadn't seen Barry Banner since Barry broke the ankle of Ted's good friend, the Folsom Nightmare, in the ring.

"Danno said he'll make it up to Proctor, and he wants you to tell Proctor that they can still make money from this," Ted said.

Barry scoffed at Ted. Ted didn't like that one bit.

"Listen to me, you little fuckface. If I had my way, your jaw would be broken by now for what you did to Folsom—but Danno wants to do a deal," Ted said. "And he asked me to come here and give that message."

Barry kept his counsel for a few seconds before replying, "Proctor wants the belt dropped in Florida this Friday. Four days. No bullshit.

That gives us time to put the word out and sell the tickets. Babu comes down and does business in the middle of our ring. Proctor keeps a hundred percent of the gate and you all fuck off back to New York—and thank your gods that's all he's going to do to you."

Ted seemed unfazed. "Danno wants to give him a hundred percent."

Banner was knocked a little sideways, but wasn't going to show it. "Well, that's nice of that fat pig."

"One more quip from your face, boy, and I'm going to open you up right here all over this nice tablecloth," Ted said.

Barry backed down and signaled for a glass of water too. "Proctor wants Danno to know that the NWC is behind us now. They were shocked at the way you guys left a boss's son. They also don't tolerate fake handovers. We all know the belt is coming our way, Ted. Tell Danno to just let it go, and let happen what's going to happen."

Barry's water arrived.

"Would you like to order now, gentlemen?" a long, perfectly-pressed waiter asked.

"Another minute," Ted said.

The waiter walked away.

Ted decided to have a look at the breakfast menu after all. "Aren't you getting worried about Proctor chasing Ricky Plick to be his number two, Barry? Doesn't that leave you without a cock to suck?"

Again, Barry worked hard to hide his anxiety. "You think I trust that all that nonsense is aboveboard, Ted?" Barry stood up. "Proctor wants Lenny Long to ref the match. That's non-negotiable."

"Lenny?" Ted asked.

Barry nodded. "Proctor feels it will sell tickets to have the man responsible for all of this down there in the match."

"Do I look like some green fucking mark to you, Barry?" Ted said.

"Just make sure Lenny is there, and all this bullshit goes away. If he's not there, then this all gets a lot messier for your side."

Barry left the restaurant to find a phone. Ted walked to the back of the restaurant to find a phone too. Speed was key here.

Florida.

Proctor was in the empty TV studio where he taped his weekly wrestling show. He waited there long after everyone else left for the news from Barry's meeting. He watched the phone in silence until it rang. At the sound of it he released a long breath.

"How is he?" Barry asked.

"We just moved him down here and he's going to be okay," Proctor answered.

Barry got straight to it. "Well, they agreed."

"A hundred percent? Danno agreed to that?" Proctor asked.

Barry replied, "He's scared stiff of you, boss. No one even knows where he is. In four days, you get the belt and one hundred percent of the gate, too."

Proctor watched as Ricky Plick entered Studio Two for the first time. "And Lenny Long?" Proctor asked.

"There's no way Danno can justify protecting him. That won't be a problem."

Ricky nodded to Proctor and began to walk toward him. "Okay. I have to go and sell this on TV now. I mean, the least we can do now is make some money, huh?"

"Some money, boss? You're going to have the biggest first night as champion in all of wrestling."

It was different kind of taping than usual. There were more people huddled in behind the camera. Less noise. More concentration. An air of uncertainty around the studio.

Heels and babyfaces put their weekly differences aside and stood in unison in the ring. Rule after ironclad rule was broken. No production, no storylines, no costumes this week. This wasn't the usual

TV night for wrestling in Florida. But then again, this wasn't going to be the usual wrestling TV show.

Sean Peak, the local TV boss, was more nervous than he normally would be. He normally wouldn't attend anything to do with professional wrestling, but in recent days pro wrestling had been pulled into the local news for all the wrong reasons. Sean left the two-hundred-seat studio and walked down the hallway as he counted down to show time. He had relied heavily on God to get him this far in life. One more request for clear passage couldn't hurt. Even though he made his request to on high, something didn't feel right. Live TV was never a good place to air something that didn't feel right.

Another prayer couldn't hurt.

Maybe he shouldn't have taken the money. Maybe he should have told Proctor to stick to his ordinary slot. The bottom line was, if Sean had that much of a problem taking money from these guys, he might as well sell up, or shut the station down. Whether the station owner liked it or not, pro wrestling was by far the biggest earner for his channel. And his annual national conference told him that it wasn't just his area, either. Wrestling and horse racing were proving to be two sure-fire hits across all regions of the US.

Outside the studio, Ricky questioned himself and his ability to get the job done. He straightened his head and braced himself before he entered the arena. What a first day. What a way to break into a new territory.

From behind him, Flawless Franco whistled for Ricky's attention at the door. "Hey, I was looking for you out here."

Ricky put out his hand and Franco coldly shook it.

"I hear you punched the old man Danno in the face. Good job," Franco said as he opened the studio door.

Ricky nodded.

"How did it feel?" Franco asked with a perverted smile on his face.

"Great," Ricky replied.

"Well, Proctor appreciated it." Franco held the door open for Ricky to enter. "Welcome to your new home."

Ricky entered the hallway and noticed a deathly quiet around the building. Sensing Ricky's question, Franco quietly said, "Proctor hasn't spoken to no one since he got his boy back to the hospital here. Your Boys did quite a job on Gilbert, so these guys might not be your best friends in the world right now."

Ricky looked down the hallway at the pissed tough guys scowling back. "Do I have to watch myself in here?"

"Yeah," Franco said plainly as he overtook Ricky to lead the charge. "We all know what's going on."

Ricky grabbed Franco by the arm and stopped him before he could open the door. "What do you mean?"

"I'm not a fucking mark. What do they call this in politics? Damage control. That's why you're here."

"I don't want to be on TV. You tell Proctor that I'm all about the work here; that's no problem. But I don't want to kick Danno when he's already on his way down."

"No kicks. Just sucker punches." Franco discreetly opened the doors of Studio Two.

The lights dimmed in the studio and the cameras were counted in.

Ned Theodore, Florida's wrestling announcer, stood with his comb-over in front of camera one. "Ladies and gentlemen, I would, at this time, like to inform our viewers that an event occurred two nights ago that shocked us all. It is to that end that we join you tonight and try to fill you in on what is happening in the world of professional wrestling. What was to be a heavyweight championship match turned into a dangerous and ugly affair in the back alleys of New York City. The images that you see here tonight should only be viewed with caution and by a mature audience. These images are graphic, to say the least."

Proctor could be seen trooping to the ring over Ned's shoulder. He rolled under the bottom rope and snatched the microphone.

Ned chimed back in with a confused tone. "It seems we have something going on in . . . we'll get to those images . . ."

"New York, New York," Proctor shouted while signaling the camera to get closer to his face. "You took something of mine and you abused it. You took something of mine and you broke it. You took something of mine and you tried to kill it. Why? 'Cause you're animals."

The troop of wrestlers huddled closer together behind their leader.

"Yesterday, I had to take my wife to your stinkin' city. I had to take her to see her son, lying smashed and broken on a cheap hospital bed. Why was he there?"

Proctor wiped the spit from his lips and pressed his fingers closer together.

"That close you left him from God. That close. And not 'cause you showed mercy. You didn't spare him 'cause you grew a heart. My son made it back from New York because you're incompetent. You couldn't do it. In a dark alleyway with your best men. You couldn't get the job done on my boy. You want to know why?"

Proctor ripped off his jacket and started to punch himself in the face.

"Because he's *my* boy. He's *my* boy, New York. Made of the stuff I'm made of. And we are the opposite of you. You're cowards. Yellow, all of you from your fat Mick boss all the way down. Do you think he'll see me? Do you think he'd take my calls? No. I tried to talk to your boss. Danno Garland, you Mick piece of shit."

Sean looked around in shock. No one used bad language on WDBO. Certainly not at six o'clock. Proctor knew his language would cause concern.

"Sue me, mister TV, if you want," Proctor shouted as he took off his watch and threw it to the station boss.

"If you think that I'm going to be censored . . ." He took his wallet from his pocket and threw that, too. "You can take my TV slot.

You can take my company. But I'm going to get revenge. You hear me? You're a coward, Danno. Piece of shit. You wanted to break our deal. You snake bastard."

Sean Peak jumped from his seat to cut the shoot. He was immediately derailed by Ricky Plick, who grabbed the station owner's hand before he could stop anything.

"We need to talk, Sean," Ricky said as he walked the station manager out of sight.

"Ricky? What are you doing down here?" Sean asked as he walked.

Ricky whispered, "My boss wanted me to thank you again for the advice you gave us down in Texas."

"Tell him he was more than kind. I enjoyed the whole trip." Sean was still unsure as to what was going on.

"That same man is now willing to pay you three and a half times what those guys out there pay you for this same slot."

"He wants TV in Florida?" Sean asked.

"He wants Proctor's TV in Florida. He's willing to pay you three and a half thousand a week for five years—half up front. What do you say?"

Ricky looked over his shoulder to make sure their departure wasn't raising any eyebrows. His nervousness made Sean even more nervous.

"I . . . I . . ." Sean struggled to string a sentence together. It didn't feel right. Who did business like this? "Can't we talk about it? Meet up—"

"No," Ricky cut him off. "This offer expires in five seconds, Sean." Ricky lifted up his shirt and showed Sean several flat packs of money taped around his waist.

In the ring, Proctor continued to punch himself in the face. Drops of blood stained his white shirt from a slit in his eyebrow. "You knew that your time was up with the title, and this was how you wanted to handle it. We shook on it like men, Danno. Well, you were right. Your time is up. You have nowhere else to hide.

Nowhere. Jacksonville Coliseum, one week from tonight. And I'm going to fill the seats with eleven thousand rabid fans. I'm going to fill the locker room with every single wrestler who wants to see you get yours. And I'm going to fill the ring with . . ." Proctor grabbed the camera lens and brought it right to his face. "Me."

The wrestlers could hold back no longer and exploded into cheers.

"That's right. Me. Crazy King. I'm going to be in the ring to take the title off your champion myself."

The wrestlers roared for their leader. Proctor jumped from the ring and walked right past the lens of camera two.

Ricky slipped back onto the studio floor. Proctor finished by slapping the camera around to reveal Ricky Plick waiting to embrace the exiting Proctor. "Even your own have jumped ship, Danno. We're coming to get you, and that's a shoot."

Proctor dropped the mic to the floor. Pictures of Gilbert King, severely bloodied and battered, silently looped to end the program.

That Evening.
New Jersey.

Lenny chugged to a stop in his mom's Datsun. He nervously stepped outside and checked the rooftop of the motel for a shooter, like he had seen in the movies. The parking lot was quiet. Lenny took out the piece of paper with the address Troy had given him outside the jailhouse. Lenny looked for a face or sign in one of the many windows to let him know he was in the right place.

This grubby little place didn't look like somewhere Danno Garland would end up.

Lenny had washed his wounds and his scrapes were treated and patched. His polyester suit was replaced by bell-bottom jeans and a loudly printed shirt. He wasn't at all sure what to expect. Some part of him wondered if he would make it out of this situation at all. If it went bad, at least he'd gotten to spend a morning with Bree.

Danno whistled to Lenny from a balcony on the second floor and slipped back inside his room.

Lenny walked to the door and tapped lightly.

"Come in," Danno shouted from inside.

Lenny pushed the open door and entered the small room. Danno sat facing the dressing table with his back to Lenny.

"I'm sorry for everything that happened. I have no excuse," Lenny said. "I know you put your trust in me, boss. I've never been as sorry about anything in my whole life."

Danno pushed a seat out beside him. "I'm in real trouble, Lenny." He lit a cigarette. "There's nothing I can do."

"What is it, boss?" Lenny asked as he slowly approached.

Danno stood suddenly and drove his closed fist down on the dressing table. "Did you fall asleep? Is that what all this is over?"

Danno turned to reveal his severely swollen and bruised eye.

"Jesus, boss. What the fuck happened?"

Danno approached and grabbed Lenny by the face. "What the fuck happened is right, Lenny!"

Danno wanted to break Lenny's fucking neck, run him through the door, and throw him down to the lot below.

But he couldn't. Not to Lenny.

"It's time you were smartened up." Danno slammed the door closed. "I have nothing I can barter with here. You've left me with nothing. Proctor thinks I tried to kill his son *and* fucked him out of his split and the belt all in one night."

Lenny wiped the smoky sting from his eyes. "Let me talk to him."

"You're going to. I have no other choice." Danno paused and Lenny could see that he was having a quiet argument with himself. Danno's nod punctuated an internal decision. "There's nothing I can do, Lenny. He's on his TV this evening calling us out and telling the world that we jumped his son and tried to kill him on purpose."

"But that's bullshit," Lenny said.

"Well, tell me what happened, then."

Lenny couldn't answer that question. He wished more than anything that he could, but all he remembered was driving one second and picking himself up from the ground the next.

"I can't even hold Proctor off. The other bosses would make sure I wasn't around if I went into business for myself. You understand?" Danno said.

Lenny wasn't sure he did, but he nodded.

Danno tried to think again. Maybe there was some last-second thing that could turn this all around. Something he was missing, something he could barter with. But nothing came. The crash had taken all Danno's power away. Whatever happened now, happened.

Danno looked at Lenny and struggled to hold in the tears. He hated that Lenny was making him do this. Hated that it was Lenny that Proctor wanted.

And Danno had to deliver him. Even if Lenny didn't know it.

"I want you to bring Babu to Florida so he can drop the belt to Proctor," Danno said, his voice almost choking. He turned back into the room. His eyes were full and a single drop fell out and slid along his face. Danno quickly wiped it away.

"There's nothing I can do," Danno said.

Lenny pulled the motel door closed behind him and Annie came out of the bathroom where she had been listening. Danno didn't want her out of his sight while he met with Lenny.

She tried to comfort her devastated husband.

Lenny walked somberly to his mom's car. He thought that Danno might be watching him out of his window and Lenny wanted his walk to say *sorry*. Inside, he was fucking partying.

That's it? Drive the giant to Florida and have him drop the belt? I thought they were going to file my dick and burn my eyeballs. Drive Babu to the sun? Is that all?

That wasn't all.

CHAPTER TWENTY-FOUR

Danno stared into the open pizza box that was on the motel dressing table. He could see it and smell it, but he couldn't bring himself to eat it. Annie sat on the tired bed behind him, looking out the window at the traffic rushing past.

Danno ran through clips in his mind of all the times in his life when he'd been pinned down. All the people who'd mocked him. All the situations where he'd felt like a worthless piece of shit. The way the world beat on him sometimes. The way he was told how his life was going to play out. Crying didn't come easily to a man like Danno Garland. He just wasn't allowed to act like that, like a fucking pussy. He had to be hard and silent. No emotion, no whining, no sobbing. But in this situation, he would have simply broken down—had he been on his own.

Every time he breathed, he could feel the ball of painful anger in his chest. How could he go back to being a nobody? Lose everything. All because Lenny fell asleep.

"Dan?" Annie's voice pulled him slightly out of his head. But only slightly.

"Yeah?" Danno answered. He forced a slice into his mouth to avoid raising questions.

"You want to tell me what he said?" she asked.

He didn't really, but how long could he keep her away from all this stuff?

"Proctor just went on TV in Florida and told the people that we tried to kill his son."

"Can't you put him right?"

"He doesn't care if that's the way it was or not. The story sounds better if we tried to kill him. There are more tickets in that story. Maybe that is what he fucking thinks. I don't know."

"Dan?"

"Yeah?"

"Can't we get a better room if we're going to be on the run?"

Danno turned around angrily. Annie's attempt to lighten the mood a little had landed on a raw nerve. "Who said we're on the run?"

Annie was taken aback by her husband's sharpness. "Well, we're not at home and not telling anyone where we are. What else do you call it?"

Danno fired his pizza at the trashcan and missed. "Do you think I'm afraid of him or something? I came out here to protect *you*, Annie. I don't know what this fucking nut is going to do."

Annie slid closer to her husband. "Is that right? You came out here to save me?"

Danno was getting more offended at Annie doubting his motives. "Yeah, that's right."

Annie picked up a magazine and put her feet on the bed. Danno stared at her just long enough to prove that he won that particular exchange.

"Everyone's dropping like fucking flies. I can't risk it with you," he mumbled as he turned back to his pizza box.

Annie began to loudly and sharply turn the pages of her magazine.

"What?" Danno asked.

She threw down the glossy pages and stood up. "When are you going to realize that you're the boss? What's got you so . . . paralyzed?

You have all the cards. Start fucking playing them, Dan," she said before walking into the bathroom and slamming the door.

"Fuck," he shouted in silence. It was the perfect word for a quick and meaningful release of tension. He quickly settled himself and walked to the bathroom door. "You decent in there?" he asked.

"Well, I'm mostly just standing here looking at the wall because I have nowhere to storm off to, Dan."

"Okay, can I come in?"

Annie opened the door and Danno entered like a shy guest. "I . . . don't know where to start with all this stuff. It's bearing down on me, is all. People are getting hurt and I don't know what that senator has on me. And then Proctor and all the madness that's going on there."

"You will figure this out," she said as she hugged him. "We will figure this out."

"I fucking ambled into this wrestling thing and I was doing an unremarkable job at it, until I found this giant. Luck . . ."

Annie could tell her husband was about to talk himself down again. "Dan—"

Danno broke away from his wife. "No, hear me out. I have to say this to someone or I'm going to fucking lose my mind. I had no business coming into this world. My father was good at the wrestling business. He was a tough guy. And it got to him in the end. When I got the belt, I thought I was good at this business too. All the other bosses did what I told them, business was great . . . I even began to think that I was a tough guy."

Danno caught a look at himself in the bathroom mirror and tried to suck his belly in a little. "I ain't no tough guy, Annie. People walked on me my whole life."

Annie wondered if that last sentence was made for her. If it was, she knew she deserved it.

"They walked on me and I let them, because without that belt I have nothing that separates me out from the jackals. I lose this title and I immediately slip back down into the hole where all the other bosses are waiting to settle old scores. It's that belt that keeps me safe. Or safer than I will be if I don't have it."

In the middle of the bathroom of an old motel room on the outskirts of New Jersey, Annie Garland hugged her husband again. She knew she was one of the ones who had done him wrong, and it was tearing her up.

"You're better than tough, Dan," she whispered. "You're smart. None of these guys have nothing on you in that department. You just need time to figure this out."

Annie spoke with such conviction and honesty that Danno began to believe it. And it was in that belief that a germ of an idea began to scratch away at his thoughts. An idea that just might work.

"I need to give up," he said.

CHAPTER TWENTY-FIVE

October 3, 1972 — The Next Day.
Atlanta.

Barry Banner came marching back into the same restaurant where he had met Ted Berry the day before. He surveyed the busy tables, but couldn't see Ted's big frame.

"Barry," Ted called from a small booth in the corner. Barry approached. "What the fuck is it now?" he asked abruptly. "You dragging me all the way up here every time you want to talk. You never heard of the fucking phone?"

"Sit down," Ted said.

Barry remained standing. He could see that Ted was a lot more downbeat—maybe a little more deflated—than he was the previous day.

"What is it?" Barry asked. "I'm planning a fucking title match, in case you hadn't heard."

"Danno is going to rat," Ted said.

Before Barry could speak, Ted leaned back to let the busy waiter freshen his cup of coffee. Ted flipped over a spare cup for Barry, opposite him, and had that filled also.

Barry sat down. He waited for the waiter to leave.

"What are you talking about, Danno is going to rat?" Barry asked.

"He's going to meet with the Senate guy in private and smarten him up on the business."

Barry wasn't buying it for a second. "Bullshit."

"Believe what you like. But the Senate hearings are this Thursday. That's a fact. Danno isn't going to be pulled apart in public. Not on his way out—"

"His way out, huh?"

"You think he's going to hang around this business after you guys piss all over him this weekend? He's done. And he's going to fuck you over on the way out. That's what's happening here."

Barry sat in silence while he tried to figure out what the play was. He wanted desperately to be Proctor's second in command, and bringing back a win this big could seal it. "What are you saying?" Barry asked. "Are you saying there's going to be no title match again?"

Ted shook his head in frustration. "No. I'm saying that if Danno opens his fucking mouth to this senator and wrestling gets banned in New York—where does that leave you?"

Barry's head dipped as he thought and muttered to himself. How the fuck was he going to tell Proctor this one? "Doesn't matter, the title match is happening in Florida."

"But the belt, the current champion, is booked out of the New York Booking Agency. You hear what I'm saying? Danno is old. He's made his money. You really think he wouldn't use this to fuck Proctor on his way out the door?"

Barry looked close for a sign—a tell. "Why are you telling me this?"

"You know how this game works, Barry. I need to know I can still earn a living after Saturday. You know what I mean?"

Barry still wasn't sure, but he couldn't afford not to take it seriously. He knew Danno was capable of anything.

"He's going to rat, huh?" Barry said.

Ted nodded.

New Jersey.

Annie knocked on the bathroom door. Danno was taking a shower. "Proctor knows," she shouted through the door.

Danno shook the water from his ears. "What?"

"Proctor knows about your meeting . . ."

Danno hurriedly stumbled for his towel. "Okay, make the call."

Annie sat at the small table at the head of their tiny room. She opened Danno's address book and dialed.

A lady answered. "Hello, New York State Athletic Commission."

"Hello, may I speak to Melvin Pritchard, please?" Annie said.

Within the hour, Danno was starting to feel like his old self. He pulled down on his tie and slicked back the remaining hairs on his head. Annie brushed the dandruff from his shoulders. Tiny Thunder came out of their bathroom.

"I'm not fucking wearing this," Tiny said, holding up a schoolboy outfit.

Danno was confused, "It's a disguise, Tiny."

"Well, you wear it, then," he replied. "If I go into Manhattan dressed like a schoolboy, someone is going to try and fuck me. Sorry, Mrs. Garland."

"You have to be able to blend in," Danno stressed.

"And you think a thirty-nine-year-old midget in a schoolboy out-fit won't draw attention?"

Danno gave Annie a devious little smile. Seemed like he liked fucking around with midgets in his spare time.

New York.

Danno wanted his money back. He specifically mentioned the sum of ninety-two thousand. That was why Lenny found himself trying to break into his own garage at ten at night.

It was lashing rain; the wind drove through the fence and across the front garden. Lenny thought that explaining a robbery to Bree was easier than explaining that the money wasn't theirs. He pulled his black hood over his head and made his way to the side of their house. All the lights were off inside except for the one on the landing. That was for Luke, because he thought the bathroom sink next to his room was trying to kill him.

Lenny did all that he could to stop himself from simply putting his key in the door and slipping into his own bed for the night. He wondered if ninety-two thousand dollars was that big a deal in the grand scheme of things.

It was.

He cracked open his side gate and the unkempt dog of the alcoholic next door barked like a coked-up lunatic.

"Shut up, you fucking dog," Lenny hoarsely shouted.

The dog ignored him and kept up the alarm. Lenny decided to just run to the garage. He wiped the rain off his face and ducked under the workbench, where he pulled aside the never-opened toolbox. He stuck his hand back behind the workbench. He groped around, but his hand couldn't find anything that felt like the knapsack.

He panicked, quickly forgot the stealth part of his mission, and pulled the bench out from the wall, causing old broken appliances to crash to the ground. He slid his head painfully into the small gap behind the workbench and eyeballed the dark empty space.

He immediately felt sick. The knapsack was gone. Lenny sprang up and tried to think if he had moved it to a better place one day or maybe he . . . something.

He looked through the cobwebbed garage window toward his house and knew that Bree had taken the money inside to a safer hiding place. He switched off the light and closed the garage door. Before he could turn away from the door, a gardening shovel took a brutal swipe to the back of his neck. Lenny dropped to his knees and tried to cover up.

"Wait," he shouted. "Wait."

He could make out the shovel being raised again in the light of the moon. "I live here."

The shovel stopped.

"Lenny?" Bree asked. She was shaking with fright.

Lenny couldn't move to get up but he rolled over onto his side and saw his wife, as white as a ghost, standing over him, crying.

"What are you doing, Lenny?" she shouted.

"I'm sorry."

"I thought you were going to come inside and go after the kids next." Bree's voice was trembling.

Lenny struggled to his knees. He wanted to hug his wife and make her feel safe. He thought he might cry himself, seeing her so upset.

"I heard the dog barking and I didn't know what to do," Bree said.

Lenny made his way up to his unstable feet and tried to move her head onto his shoulder, but Bree was standing rigid. "What are you doing to me?" She pushed him away. "What are you doing?"

"I need the money."

Bree shivered. "What money? The bag?"

Lenny nodded. "Where did you put it?"

"Inside."

Lenny tried to walk past Bree into the house, but she stood in his way. "What's wrong? What are you doing?" she asked.

"I just need it."

"Why, Lenny?"

Lenny paused and tried to think of a good enough lie. "I can't tell you."

"Lenny?"

"I just fucking need it. How much of it is gone? I need something to make up the difference, Bree."

Danno sat silently opposite Melvin Pritchard in the cafeteria of JFK International. He had a plane ticket in his hand and the knapsack, which Lenny had delivered, by his feet. Over Melvin's shoulder, and across the room, Annie sat incognito beside the pay phone.

"Mr. Garland, not that I don't like your company, but . . . it's past two in the morning and you did say you were going to talk to me. 'Tell me everything' was, I believe, what your secretary said on the phone."

Danno covertly looked to Annie for a signal, but she shook her head.

"Mr. Garland? We've been here for nearly two hours."

Melvin might have been there for two hours, but Danno and Annie had been there a lot longer.

"You have to know how hard this is for me, Mr. Pritchard. The workings of wrestling have been kept guarded for . . ." Danno said.

Annie checked her watch and quietly left for the exit.

"I've changed my mind," Danno quickly said as he stood up and threw the bag over his shoulder.

"Excuse me?" Melvin said.

"If I'm going to say anything about how our business works, I want Senator Tenenbaum here too. I want to do this once, and I want to do it right. No press, no public. Just me, you, and the senator."

Danno, too, walked for the exit, leaving Melvin wondering about what had just happened.

Florida.

Proctor watched as the sides of the cage were fitted around the ring. He had wanted to make himself relevant again for many years, but could never justify placing himself at the center of the territory. Now the paying public was demanding it, and he was ecstatic.

Revenge money traveled quicker to the box office than any other kind. People would pay double the price to see a father defend his son against the New York City cowards. There would be a packed house for his crowning as the new champion, and the nearby towns on the touring loop were all sold out too.

"Ricky?" Proctor shouted across ringside. He enjoyed making Danno's former right-hand man dance in front of his own Boys. "Read me that schedule again."

Ricky took out his hardcover book and began to read. "Mondays, West Palm Beach. Tuesdays is the Fort Homer Hesterly Armory in Tampa. Wednesdays, TV in the day and Miami that night. Thursdays in Jacksonville and Friday is Fort Lauderdale, or maybe Arcadia? Saturday in Lakeland or St. Petersburg, and Sundays are Orlando or Ocala."

Proctor quickly began to realize how Danno got rich so quickly. It was almost a pity the big fat pig wouldn't be there to see him hold the belt over his head.

"Everyone hear that?" Proctor shouted to all the various people milling around. "We're going to make this place the hottest territory in the US." Proctor proudly sat down, only to quickly spring back up and offer a half-hearted salute, "For Gilbert."

There was a dribbling of respectful applause. Proctor sat back down and bathed in his own excitement.

Barry Banner slid into the seat behind Proctor. "He had a meeting with Melvin Pritchard today. Looks like he's serious," Barry whispered.

"But we don't know that," Proctor replied.

"Can we afford to find out one way or the other?" Barry asked.

"I can't have five fucking peaceful minutes to enjoy this without Danno fucking Garland creeping into my thoughts and ruining my moments." Proctor turned in his seat toward Barry. "You think he's serious about this? You think that fat fuck is going to rat out our business?"

Barry leaned in, covered his mouth, and whispered even softer, "We can't let the meeting take place. You'd be ruined for good if you didn't deliver the giant and the belt down here."

Proctor could see himself in the middle of the ring in his packed arena with no giant to wrestle and no belt to take.

"He waited until I announced the match to the world," Proctor said with a begrudging smile. "He knows I can't let him talk to the senator."

Proctor was going to have to take a risk, and he knew it.

"Want me to arrange some of our guys to go visit Danno and make him see sense?" Barry asked.

Proctor shook his head. "Not Danno."

CHAPTER TWENTY-SIX

October 4, 1972—The Next Day.
New York.

Mickey Jack Crisp didn't know the city that well. The cab had taken him to right outside Fraunces Tavern in lower Manhattan. He'd been standing outside in the freezing cold for a couple of hours, waiting for his man to appear. He walked up and down the street to find a suitable alley or dark corner to deliver his message. There was no place quiet, no place really fitting—a doorway might have to do. Mickey didn't want to let his target get to the openness of Broad Street. He knew there was no time for anything elaborate, just a straightforward delivery in a short amount of time: Mickey's specialty.

When Ricky heard what the plan out of Florida was, he had made the careful tipoff call to Danno, who in turn immediately instructed Tiny Thunder to follow the action. Danno wanted to know the second Proctor moved on the senator. Nothing was going to happen when the senator was at his office. It was too busy and too well protected. If Proctor were to order anything, it could only be in the time it took the senator to get from work to home. Tiny had followed the senator home the night before, but nothing happened. He had even slept in his car outside the senator's house just in case Proctor sent a late-night caller.

But this night was the last chance. This night was the last before the hearings. If anything was to happen, it had to be now. Watching Mickey Jack pace the street outside, it looked like Tiny might get the pleasure of phoning the boss with good news after all.

Danno sat at the mouth of the departures lounge eating a cup of yogurt. He again had the knapsack that Lenny had been hiding for him by his side. Melvin stared at him as he demolished the treat in his hand.

"It helps settle my stomach," Danno said.

"Listen, Danno. I don't know what's going on here, but if you don't begin to talk, we're going to have to leave our discussions for the hearings tomorrow. Is that what you want?"

"I want to meet the senator," Danno said.

"Not going to happen," Melvin replied.

Danno licked his spoon and dumped it in the bin beside his seat. "You don't like me, do you Melvin?"

"I don't know you enough to have any thoughts on you, personally."

Danno watched Annie by the phone. "You know, I didn't get into this business until fifteen years ago. In wrestling terms, I'm still a blow-in."

Melvin began to write in his waiting yellow pad. "But your father was one of the top guys, according to my office."

"I won't speak to his name, but one thing I can tell you is that he did everything he could to keep me out of it. When he . . ." Danno found it hard to even finish that sentence. "Anyway, he left the business to my mother," Danno said with a laugh. "Who in turn kept it away from me until *she* died."

Melvin was furiously taking notes.

"Then the lawyer kind of just gave it to me. Like a booby prize. There was no one else left to give it to, so I got it."

Melvin's eyes were alive. "Now, what year did you seize control?"

Danno lit a cigarette and leaned into Melvin. "You're getting off on this, aren't you, Melvin?"

"Excuse me?"

"Don't you Athletic Commission people usually just sign stuff and go to meetings about stuff? What are you doing out here with me?"

Melvin stopped writing. "I think what you do is a con and a black eye to real sports, Mr. Garland."

Danno smiled. "Oh, we're back to Mr. Garland now, are we?"

"Furthermore, I think that children can't tell the difference and try your choreographed moves as real, with dire consequences."

"In your opinion."

"Well, we hope to prove that as fact tomorrow. But until then, yes, my opinion."

Danno sneaked a glance over at Annie. She again shook her head. No news. No update to what was happening on the street.

"Don't you have to minute and date those notes you're taking there?" Danno asked Melvin.

Senator Tenenbaum left the Fraunces Tavern and walked a little woozily toward Broad Street. Mickey briskly moved between two parked cars and pushed the senator down the steps of a basement apartment. The senator rolled down to the bottom and before he could react with any noise, Mickey was on top of him with his gloved hand over his face.

"Listen to me very carefully. What's on your schedule for tomorrow?" Mickey asked.

The terrified senator tried to answer, but Mickey wouldn't remove his hand. "Exactly. Nothing. Do you hear me? You have no business tomorrow. Isn't that right?"

The senator nodded in agreement. Mickey reached into his pocket and tried to open a hunting knife with his teeth. The senator tried to struggle free and scream for help, but Mickey was too strong. He sat atop the squirming and horrified man and kept trying to pick open the folded blade with his teeth. "Fucking thing."

Senator Tenenbaum continued to make muffled screeches into Mickey's hand.

"Wait,"Mickey said with a terrifying calmness. The struggle continued. Mickey jabbed his gloved thumb in the senator's eye to get his attention. "Shut the fuck up," Mickey said. "I'm going to remove my hand for a second. If you scream, you won't be leaving here alive. Do you hear me?"

The petrified senator nodded and began to cry with terror. "Please," he whispered. "I can do . . . pay you ten times—"

Mickey punched him hard in the face, breaking the senator's nose.

"What did I fucking tell you?" Mickey warned. "No talking."

The senator grabbed his face and the blood from his nose ran through his kneaded-together hands. Mickey opened the knife and put his hand back over the senator's mouth. He looked right in the senator's eye before stabbing him deeply, twice in each thigh. The senator howled in agony.

Mickey said, "You stay away from business that's not yours. If I hear you saying anything other than you were mugged by some niggers tonight, then I'm going to come back and cut you in half."

Mickey finished his job by knocking the senator out cold with an elbow smash to the chin.

Still no talking. Melvin was starting to lose his composure. "You haven't really said much about anything at all."

At the other side of the airport, the pay phone rang and Annie quickly answered. Danno's eye was caught by sight of her standing up and getting ready to move.

"When did you become aware that the business you're now in was fake, Mr. Garland?" Melvin asked, unaware of Annie conducting business behind him.

Danno waited for Annie's signal.

Melvin tried to catch Danno's attention. "Mr. Garland? When did you know that professional wrestling outcomes were prearranged?"

Annie gave Danno the thumbs up. He released a huge sigh of relief. "Mr. Garland?"

Danno focused back on Melvin. "How many clocks do you suppose are in this place?"

Melvin was getting tired of the games. "I have no idea."

"Enough to know it's the fourth of October at roughly half past eight and we've been in each other's company for two hours."

Danno stood and lifted the knapsack full of money before he calmly walked off. Melvin was left baffled at Danno's behavior.

Danno and Annie didn't know just how brutal the elimination of Senator Hilary J. Tenenbaum was. Tiny could only see Mickey take the senator out of sight and then reappear in a hurry, only to disappear. The senator was one roadblock out of Danno's way, for now.

It was time to deal with the other one.

CHAPTER TWENTY-SEVEN

October 5, 1972—The Next Day.
Texas.

Annie tried to read the in-flight magazine, but she couldn't get her husband out of her head. She had asked Danno to catch her up and, for the first time in their marriage, he did so without any side-talk or lies. She was genuinely taken aback by all the maneuvering that went into keeping afloat in his business.

She could see the temptation to make it simpler. To have fewer voices at the table. She just wasn't sure how long Danno could keep it that way. He told her about the deals he had been cutting behind the scenes. She wanted to be filled in before she had to represent him. Annie Garland was studious and logical. She couldn't figure out what her husband's play was in Texas. She knew it was all going to be different after the title match the next night in Florida. And she was learning that it was almost impossible to get from one end of the wrestling business to the other without getting your hands dirty.

Maybe Danno's father, Terry Garland, had known better than anyone what it took to stay on top of the business. Maybe that was why he hadn't wanted Danno involved. Maybe he knew his son just wasn't that kind of person. But that's not to say that Annie Garland wasn't.

Annie was a master of keeping secrets.

New York.

Danno locked the door on the way out of his house after a good night's sleep in his own bed. His bag was packed for the long trip to Florida. He still hadn't been able to check in with his wife, Ricky, Babu, or Lenny, and probably wouldn't until the chain of events began to flow. He wondered anxiously if they had all been successful in their parts.

"Danno," Melvin called from his car, which was parked in Danno's driveway.

"Just on my way to the hearings now, Melvin. Where is the meeting taking place again?" Danno asked, checking his watch.

Melvin got out of his car. "Don't fucking talk to me like that."

Danno was surprised by the usually placid man walking toward him.

"What?" Danno asked innocently.

Melvin couldn't contain himself. "Senator Tenenbaum has just been released from the hospital, you lying bastard."

Danno passed Melvin at the bottom of his front steps. "That's terrible. Give him my best."

"Danno?" Melvin shouted. "I'm going to do everything in my power to get this done. Do you hear me?"

Danno stopped walking and turned back suddenly. Melvin wasn't as brave when Danno was facing him. "What did you say?" Danno asked as he dropped his bag. "What did you say?"

Danno took a few steps forward like a man half his age and weight. Melvin backpedaled in fear until he nearly tripped on Danno's steps.

"Listen to me, you asshole, go back to your meetings or whatever it is you do before I figure that you're a real problem to me. 'Cause if I do figure that out, it won't end up good for you. Do you hear me?"

Melvin nodded quickly.

Danno paused. "And I don't like your suggestive tone here today, either. I don't know what happened to the good senator, but I'm very sorry to hear about it from you this morning."

Melvin struggled to regulate his breathing in the face of such aggression.

"Now, let's clear up your innuendo toward me and my part in this unfortunate event, shall we?" Danno said. "What happened—or, more importantly, *when* did this happen?"

Melvin struggled to answer the question, so Danno upped his volume. "Fucking *when*, I said."

"Last night. It was last night."

Danno pushed forward even further. "And where was I last night?"

Melvin stared hard at Danno. "With me."

"At what time?"

Melvin didn't want to answer.

"At what fucking time?"

"The time it happened."

"So I was with you, looking for a meeting with the senator so that I might fully comply with his questions—and you come here this morning implying that I had something to do with this? Shame on you, Melvin. Shame on you."

Melvin paused. Danno balled his fist and held it to Melvin's face. "Does that logic, alibi, or timing stand up to you, Mr. Pritchard?"

Melvin couldn't answer.

"Exactly. Now get the fuck off my property," Danno said.

Danno stepped aside and let Melvin scurry to his car.

"I would suggest that you use every means necessary to find out exactly who was behind it, though," Danno shouted as Melvin sped down the driveway.

Florida.

Luke answered the phone. If it weren't for that, Bree would have let it keep ringing. Hearing her little boy talk with his father over the phone broke Bree's heart. Luke couldn't understand why he never got to see his pop anymore. Bree couldn't, either.

She took the phone when their son said good-bye and let Lenny sit quietly on the other end for minute. Just a minute to catch his thoughts, to think about what he was going to say.

"Lenny?" she eventually said.

"Yeah?"

"I'm leaving tonight with the kids. I don't want to fight. I just want you to know what's happening," Bree said.

"You're not taking my kids, Bree."

Bree calmly replied, "Don't do that, Lenny."

"What?"

"Don't start to act interested in them now."

Lenny slid down the wall in another hotel lobby in another part of the country. "Where are you going?" he asked her.

"I don't know. Back home to California." Bree was reluctant to speak and Lenny could sense it. "Are you meeting someone else out there?" he asked.

"No, you asshole."

"Sorry."

"I'm . . . going to set up something for me and the kids."

"A business?"

"Yeah."

"How are you going to do that?"

"My dad said he would help me out. Like an investment. We'll be fine."

"I want to go with you," Lenny said.

"Lenny . . ."

He could feel the likelihood of an argument—and Bree hanging up—edging closer, so he tried to settle the conversation back down. "What is it? The business?"

Bree paused. She wasn't sure about telling him.

Lenny was just trying to keep her on the line. To hear her talk some more. "What is it? What did you decide on?"

He listened keenly to the sounds of his children playing in the background.

"Bicycles," Bree answered simply.

"Bicycles?" Lenny asked, hoping she misunderstood the question.

"Yeah."

Lenny was puzzled. "Is that a business?"

"Yeah. The numbers are impressive. There are more bikes being made in the US than cars right now. The sales of bikes have risen over fifty percent in the last year alone. The manufacturing—"

"I'm sorry I took your rings, Bree," he said. "I'm sorry I did that."

Bree went so quiet that Lenny wondered if the call had been dropped. "Hello?"

"Yeah, Lenny. I don't know what you've got yourself into, but it's making you a different person and it's broken your family too. So I hope it's worth it for you."

Lenny shimmied back up the lobby wall. "Gimme one more chance. I love you. I swear I'm done here. I'll sell bikes with you, or make them, or whatever your plan is. I will. You can come down here to Florida and we can go to Disney World and then wherever you want. I promise, Bree. I think I'm going to lose you. I really do, and it's terrible. I think I'm going to . . . I don't know, Bree. I'll take the kids around the park, and then we can stay, or go, or do whatever you want to do . . ."

"Lenny?"

"No, please. I'm just . . . it's just hit me. I swear. I'm done here. Just tomorrow night and then that's all. Come down here and meet me."

"I've got to put the kids to bed."

Lenny paused. He knew that there was no point in continuing. "Okay."

"Okay, Lenny." Bree hung up.

CHAPTER TWENTY-EIGHT

Babu sat at the sleepy bar and downed another drink. He was quite enjoying being away from New York. Not because he didn't like the city, but at least down here he could find a little out-of-the-way bar and have a quiet drink.

Or at least, that's what he thought.

Proctor's promo and the subsequent pictures had traveled far and wide in the state of Florida. Wrestlers who usually wouldn't be known from the New York scene were all over the TV, Babu being the biggest.

Proctor, like an old pro, played brilliantly to his people. He was a simple man, a father, looking for revenge for what was done to him by the big-city folk. A gang attack that was "real." Everyone could understand that story. This wasn't some wrestling bullshit. The people of Florida thought that someone could actually die in the Jacksonville Coliseum.

And they would gladly pay to watch.

Flawless Franco had Proctor in a loose headlock in the middle of the ring in the otherwise-empty Florida arena. "Drop down, leapfrog, dropkick," Franco said.

Proctor pushed Franco, who duly ran to and sprang back from the ropes. Proctor dropped onto his belly in the middle of the ring; Franco jumped over him and continued running into the ropes at the other side of the ring. Proctor followed behind Franco and kissed the side of Franco's head with a drop kick. Franco bumped to the mat like a sniper had just shot him.

"Perfect," Franco said from his position. "Nice and snug."

"My timing is off," Proctor said with frustration.

"You're not going to have to worry about too much of that with the giant anyway, Proctor," Ricky offered from ringside.

"Is that big asshole going to call the whole match in the ring?" Proctor asked.

Ricky was happy to chime in further. "Yeah, he usually does. Babu doesn't like to prepare anything beforehand. He just wants to know the finish."

Proctor didn't like that style. He liked the match to be worked out in detail before he got in the ring. What were the big moves going to be? How long would the match go on for? Proctor wasn't so sure that Babu was going to stick to the script.

"What can I do if this big fucking lug starts shooting on me for real in here?"

Not much, Ricky thought. If Babu wanted to hurt Proctor for real in there, there wasn't much anyone could do about it.

"He won't do that, boss," Franco said. "He knows the consequences of something stupid like that happening. I'd kill him and all his fucking family if he embarrassed you like that in here on the biggest night of your life."

The loyalty of Proctor's Boys was at its peak. It wasn't anything to do with Proctor, really—it was that they knew the belt was coming to their territory. They were all about to make a lot of money.

Proctor laid his head on the top rope and thought. He wanted to trust Ricky in a situation like this, but he didn't believe for a second that he could. Certainly not yet.

"And what about Lenny Long? What's the plan for him, Ricky?" Proctor asked.

If Ricky was still sending love letters to Danno, then this was a good way of Proctor knowing for sure.

"What do you want to do?" Ricky asked.

Proctor fell onto his ass and rolled under the bottom rope. "What would you do to someone who messed up your family that badly?"

Ricky wanted to answer Proctor with a bat across the face. He was responsible for injuring the person Ricky loved.

Proctor continued, "Someone who hurt the one you love that badly that they're probably never going to be the same again?"

Ricky wasn't sure if Proctor was saying those exact words in that exact way just to antagonize Ricky. "An eye for an eye," Ricky replied.

"Exactly," Proctor said with a little slap to Ricky's cheek. "You make sure Lenny's here and I'll get me that eye in the ring."

Lenny snuck in through the door and quickly walked up to the bar. He was wearing a hat and sunglasses and acting very twitchy.

"Where were you, man?" Lenny asked Babu.

Babu looked at Lenny and didn't bother answering him.

"Did you hear me? I was supposed to bring you down here. If Danno finds out that I didn't get you down here . . . do you know how much shit I'm in already?"

Babu just kept drinking. Lenny pulled up a stool and took up residence beside the giant. He seemed way more jumpy at being out in the open than Babu did. "Lucky you're not too hard to find in a town like this."

Lenny waited for a response. Something. But there was nothing. Babu had a way of making him feel like the shit on his shoe.

"Listen, I know that if you hit me, I would probably disintegrate, but I'm telling you now, as God is my witness, if you don't stop ignoring me, I'm going to punch you in the fucking face," Lenny said.

The phone call he just had, the week that went by, the pressure, the loneliness. Lenny was on the edge of not giving a fuck.

Babu turned and looked at Lenny with a bottle to his lips. "Go home," he whispered before taking a swig.

"And what do you think will happen to me if I do that?"

Babu knew what would happen to him if he stayed. "I don't much give a fuck what happens to you, Lenny. You're the reason we're all in this situation. Whatever your outcome is, it's all the same to me."

Lenny was immediately silenced with a wave of guilt. "I'm sorry about that."

"Yeah, well, now all the grown-ups have to deal with it. So you go home to that wife of yours so she can whip you some more."

Lenny instinctively punched Babu in the shoulder. His action surprised even himself. "I'm sorry."

Babu never moved from his hunched-over position at the bar. Lenny slid off the stool and noticed the small patronage of the bar looking in his direction. A small old man in the corner encouraged Lenny, through mime, to wallop Babu in the back of the head.

"You'd be better off leaving," Babu said. "They can get themselves another referee for this match."

"What?" Lenny asked, not quite sure if he heard the giant correctly.

Babu spun around on his stool. "You've got five seconds to get in your car and go back to New York. One . . ."

Lenny stood firm. "Did you say I'm going to be the ref?"

"Two . . ."

"Did you?" Lenny asked.

"Three . . ."

"Stop counting. Is that what you—"

"Four . . ." Babu took one last drink.

Lenny turned to the onlooking locals. "Is that what he said?"

"Fi—"

Lenny bolted for the exit and ran into the small, sticky parking lot. The perfect black sky was dotted with stars and the crickets chirped in the background. It was kind of a perfect night. Too hot. But perfect.

Fuck it. Why not?

If Danno, Ricky, or Babu were going to start respecting him, he'd have to earn it. Why not earn it now when his standing in the company was lower than it had ever been?

Lenny opened the door of the bar and didn't even bother to look in. He simply stood in the open doorway and said, "You want to come out here like a man, champ?"

Lenny let go of the door as he exited again. He could hardly hold in his pee as he walked to the center of the parking lot and waited.

Nothing.

What's going on in there?

Lenny shouted. "Did you hear me in there? Or do I have to say it in African?"

Lenny walked to the windows and started to slap them all as he went the length of the bar outside. "Hello?"

The bar door swung open and Babu filled the doorframe. "I'm serious, Lenny. You better fuck off home."

Lenny nearly keeled over with panic. "Fuck you," he said, his voice shaking with adrenaline.

Babu walked toward him and every muscle in Lenny's skinny body screamed at him to run. "I'm sorry for what happened in the van, but I know I didn't fall asleep and I deserve to be treated with some respect from you."

"You don't know shit about how this whole thing works," Babu said.

"Well, teach me. Everyone is mad at me 'cause I don't know anything, but no one is offering to teach me."

"You want to know what it's like in this business?" Babu lifted Lenny off his feet with an open-hand slap to the jaw. "You want to be part of this business? Do you?"

Lenny struggled back up and stood on severely shaky legs. "Yes."

Babu slapped him with his other hand on the other side of his face. Lenny was driven the other way to the dirt. That slap hurt Babu's damaged arm. He turned toward the doorway of the bar. "Get back in," he shouted at the overly nosy patrons who looked on. The small crowd trampled on each other trying to re-enter the bar before the giant caught up to them.

"You still want in?" Babu asked Lenny.

Lenny stumbled to his feet, but fell headfirst into the wheel of an old broken-down truck in the parking lot. "Yes," he said from the ground.

Babu grabbed him by the collar and lifted him over his head. "You think they want you to ref 'cause they like you, Lenny? Is that why they suddenly needed you down here?"

"I don't care why," Lenny struggled to say. "It's an opportunity."

Babu launched Lenny into the windshield of the old truck.

"Hey," shouted the small old man from the open window of the bar. "That's mine, asshole."

Lenny took a fifty from his pocket and stuck it under the broken windshield wiper. "I can take a bump."

Babu was starting to get legitimately angry with Lenny. Taking bumps was what you got trained for. It was the bread and butter of the wrestling business. Taking good bumps would make the crowd believe. Taking a shitty bump got you booed and lost ticket sales.

"You can take a bump?"

Lenny rolled off the hood and fell to his knees. "Yeah. I practice all the time."

Babu wondered if someone had broken Lenny into the business already and not told him. "With who?"

"On my own at home. When no one is looking, I just fall down." Lenny fell straight back and spread his weight perfectly across his body.

Lenny forced out a breathless "See?" before curling up into a winded ball.

Babu stared at Lenny uncertainly for a few seconds.

"Do what you like, Lenny," Babu said as he walked away, leaving Lenny winded and disoriented.

Lenny held the phone to his ear and tried to adjust the air conditioning. His ribs were sore, his face was numb, and his lower back was in agony—but he felt kind of good for having taken the beating.

He was a little apprehensive about calling home at nearly two in the morning, but he didn't have that much time left.

"Hello?" Bree answered.

"Hello, missus. It's me again. Now, I know it's late, but . . ."

"I can't talk now, Lenny."

"What? Why not?"

"'Cause we're all about to get in the car."

Lenny was afraid to ask. "For what?"

Bree paused, not all that sure that she was making the right decision. "We thought we'd take you up on your offer."

Lenny thought he was going to erupt into tears.

"You there?" Bree asked.

"Yeah," Lenny said, trying not to bawl.

"Where are we going to meet you? The kids are desperate to see you."

"I don't know this place well. How about you find the arena here, Jacksonville Coliseum, and I'll meet you by the entrance at ten tomorrow night?"

Bree was still wary. "Do you promise you won't let these kids down again, Lenny? They miss you. I miss you."

"I promise you I'll be there." Lenny started to get emotional. "I'm sorry about everything, Bree. I really am. I'm a good guy, really."

"I know you are, Lenny. That's why I married you."

"Okay," Lenny said, winding up the conversation. "I love you."

"Lenny?"

"Yeah?"

"If you're not there, I will have to go."

"I know. I'll be there."

"Okay. Love you."

"Me too. Drive carefully."

Lenny put the phone down and jumped all over his room in celebration. Then there was a knock on his door.

"Lenny?"

Lenny stopped jumping around and looked through the peephole. "Yeah?"

"You want to know how to work?" Babu asked.

CHAPTER TWENTY-NINE

October 6, 1972 — Match Day.
Atlanta.

Barry Banner was angry. He was so angry he was sure that when he saw Ted Berry's smiling face in that fucking restaurant that he was going to smack him there and then.

Another meeting. And Ted wouldn't shift the meeting to Florida or talk over the phone. Something big needed to be discussed and there was no way New York would do it any other way than in person.

And that person was Barry Banner.

Three of these meetings in four days. All of them in Atlanta. All of them a huge trek. Barry wanted Proctor to call the shots and set up the meetings. He thought that Danno was still trying something on.

If it was all up to Barry, he would have cut the head off the snake and dealt with Danno a long time ago.

He pulled his car to the curb outside the restaurant and didn't even bother rolling his windows up. This was going to be short and sweet. He'd make sure of it. Barry wanted to be back in Jacksonville to see Proctor finally take the belt later that night. He also wanted to be there in case Proctor named him as his number two.

Barry slammed his door shut and checked his watch. He was fourteen minutes late, but just let Ted try to say something to him about it. Standing in the street, he pocketed his keys when a battered limegreen 1960 Rambler hit him straight on. Barry bounced face-first off the windshield and got caught under the front of the car, where his pelvic bone and sternum were shattered. The Rambler continued until it clipped another parked car. Its back wheel lifted as it drove over Barry's already crushed torso.

The Rambler continued down the road calmly as the Folsom Nightmare looked out through the back window.

Revenge had started. More was coming.

Texas.

Annie made her way down to the hotel bar carrying the knapsack from Lenny's house. This was what she wanted: a piece of business to handle, to help her husband get through this.

The bar was quiet and mostly empty. She looked for the man her husband had described as "a really brown fuck with a white mustache and shaky hands."

Annie scanned the room and ordered a drink. She noticed a man looking out the window by the door who fit the description. At least the first two parts of it.

"Curt?" she asked.

"Yes?" Curt answered, a little confused. He seemed nervous and edgy.

Annie offered a handshake and he obliged as he stood up. "Hello. I'm Annie Garland," she said. "I think we met briefly in New York at a party."

"Oh, yes. Mrs. Garland. Your anniversary party. I'm sorry, I wasn't expecting to see you down here. I was in a world of my own."

Annie and Curt sat down. Curt seemed more confused as to why Annie would be joining him and Danno for a business meeting. "Has your husband been delayed?" he asked.

"He's not coming," she replied.

"Excuse me?"

Annie pulled herself up to the table. "As you may know, my husband is otherwise engaged tonight. Although he is anxious to complete the deal here in Texas before the main event begins later in Florida."

Curt stood up. "I'm sorry, darlin', but him sending you is a slap in the face to me and a waste of my fucking time."

Annie didn't flinch. "Sit down, Mr. Magee, or your deal with my husband will be pulled immediately," she said while opening the knapsack. On top of the stacks of cash, she noticed an envelope with "Sorry" written on it.

The handwriting wasn't Danno's.

"Excuse me?" Curt said.

Annie was a little thrown by who could have written on the envelope and what could be in it. Had Danno asked someone to send her a message?

She steadied herself and pulled her thoughts back to the table. "I said there will be no second go-around, here today or any other day, Mr. Magee. My husband's offer expires the second you leave this bar."

Curt struggled to contain his contempt for the power this woman seemed to have over him. "What's going on here? I thought we had a deal? I have a line of people who are looking for payments off me, Mrs. Garland. Going out of business is not a cheap pursuit."

"We want to do a deal," Annie said.

Curt slowly pulled his seat back out and lowered himself into it like a lobster being eased into a pot. "And he gave you full permission to make the decisions to get this deal done?" Curt asked.

Annie couldn't contain her curiosity any longer. She opened the envelope under the table. Inside there were two ladies' rings. One looked to be an engagement ring and the other a wedding ring.

Now she was totally perplexed.

"I don't want to prolong this humiliation any further, Mrs. Garland. Your husband promised me a cash deal here today." Curt's nerves were beginning to show on his face. It looked to Annie like both of his hands were shaking now.

Annie quickly pocketed the rings and read the note that accompanied them: "I'm sorry, boss. I couldn't get all of the money. I will pay you back what's not here. The rings are my promise to you. I'm sorry. Lenny."

"Is there a problem?" Curt asked, starting to get nervous and a little paranoid as to what Annie was silently reading under the table.

Annie knew now she didn't have the money to close the contract. Not in the amount her husband had promised Curt. At a bar in Texas, Annie and Curt were both starting to feel the pressure of this deal.

Florida.

Danno leaned over the hospital bed, keeping a keen eye on the door. Gilbert was asleep in the bed. Danno knew that being there was a stupid move to say the least, but he had to know.

"Hey?" Danno whispered into Gilbert's remaining half-ear. Gilbert's eyes opened and immediately revealed fear.

"Lenny didn't do what you said he did. Did he?" Danno whispered.

Gilbert opened his lips to speak, but Danno hushed him up. "Just nod. Do you hear me?"

Gilbert nodded.

"He didn't fall asleep, did he?"

Gilbert nodded that he had. Danno leaned in closer. "I'm going to ask you once more, Gilbert, and then I'm going to take the results of your answer out on your old man. Do you understand?"

Gilbert nodded again. The monitor beside his bed began to beep faster.

"Was all this started by Lenny Long?"

This time Gilbert slowly shook his head. Danno felt a weight rise from his chest.

"Was the van crashing Lenny's fault?" Danno asked.

Gilbert again shook his head. The beeping was twice as fast as it had been before Gilbert woke up.

"It wasn't?" Danno said.

Gilbert shook his head.

"Now, you see . . . now I'm pissed. You know why?" Danno didn't wait for Gilbert's nod. "Because I like Lenny. He's a good guy, and you made me want to fucking kill him. He didn't deserve that. Lenny Long didn't deserve what you put on him. You understand?"

Gilbert nodded.

Danno took a long, mind-clearing breath. "I feel better now, Gilbert. Do you?"

A scared tear rolled down the side of Gilbert's face. "I didn't mean to . . ."

Danno grabbed Gilbert by the throat. "You shut your fucking mouth or I will choke you to death right here."

Gilbert stopped trying to struggle or speak.

Danno continued. "When I've done my business here in Florida tonight, I'm going to call my secretary and tell her to clear a day next month so I can concentrate on tracking you down. Until then . . ."

Danno turned and strolled out of the hospital room. Gilbert's eyes widened when he saw what was coming next.

CHAPTER THIRTY

Babu and Lenny sat in a van outside the Coliseum. The parking lot was packed with cars, but there were no people around. Everyone who was coming was already in their seats watching the opening matches.

Lenny was quiet and thinking about his way home. He knew it didn't have to be back in New York. He was absolutely happy to go wherever his family wanted to go. He just needed to exorcise the wrestling demon first. He needed one time in front of the crowd, to make them believe that what they were seeing was real. Lenny was a short time away from living his dream and he had never been so scared.

"You know what happens to you if you go in there?" Babu asked.

Lenny was resigned to the possibility that he wasn't going to walk out of there unaided.

Babu said, "Danno sent word that he doesn't want you involved no more."

"What about Proctor having him by the balls?" Lenny said.

Babu smiled. "I got word before I left the hotel. You don't have to do nothing you don't want to do."

Lenny looked at the giant defiantly. "I want to work him."

What could Babu do? If Lenny entered that ring, Proctor was going to hurt him for real. It wouldn't be the first time that the "trapeze" situation was used to protect wrestling malice from the law. If a wrestler with an agenda dropped another wrestler on his neck and retired him, all the offending wrestler had to say was that he slipped. What could the law do? Could a trapeze artist get arrested for dropping a colleague?

Proctor had had Lenny marked for the trapeze angle since Danno's anniversary party. He was almost glad when Gilbert fingered him for this whole situation. Proctor knew that Danno couldn't protect the man who nearly killed his son. That was why Lenny was in trouble.

Babu took no pleasure in saying to Lenny, "When I'm out there, I have to be professional. I have to work a match with this old fuck. I can't break character and protect the referee."

"I know."

"He's going to try and work a little something between you and him into the match. Then he's going to hurt you as bad as he can."

"I know that too."

"So, I'm not your mother. Danno asked me to pull you from the match, but you're old enough to take your medicine if that's what you want to do in there."

"I want to work Proctor. I want to know I can do it."

Babu thought Lenny was insane. He also thought it was none of his business what another man chose to do with his body.

Texas.

Annie counted the remaining blocks of cash in a stall in the ladies' room. Eighty-four thousand. Saying she had eighty-four thousand made her look like an amateur. A round, concise number conveyed confidence. She composed herself and packed seventy back into the knapsack. That would be the new offer. The rest she crammed into her purse.

Out in the bar, Curt was waiting anxiously at the table. The fact he was still there led Annie to believe that this deal wasn't dead. He looked sweaty and twitchy and constantly scanned the room.

"My apologizes, Curt. Had to—"

Curt was far past Annie's faux charm. "I want a hundred and twenty thousand now, Mrs. Garland. Your husband's disrespect toward me has been shocking and upsetting, quite frankly. He and I have served together on the National Wrestling Council for—"

"I'm going to give you seventy thousand now, Curt. You get less for being an asshole."

Annie sat down.

Curt laughed. "This is why I don't deal with the wives, Mrs. Garland. They are crazy one hundred percent of the time."

She'd had enough. "If you disrespect me one more time, I will pull the money from this deal altogether."

"What are you talking about?"

"You've been without TV down here since December two years ago. If you want to know my feelings on this matter, I think my husband is being overly generous to you. You have nothing to sell in my view. No TV equals no company in the wrestling business."

"Bullshit."

"Really? How was your attendance six months after the TV dispute began?"

Curt tried to think of a way of answering without having to tell the truth.

"You didn't have any, Mr. Magee. It only took one month without TV before your gates halved. Then three months in, you were back to running high school gyms, and six months in, there was nothing. Your wrestlers all moved elsewhere."

Curt was getting angry. "Do you think I don't know how much of a hand Danno's played in my TV being pulled off the air down here? Do you think I don't know he was the one who made this dispute with the TV company and paid them well to make sure it continued?"

Annie wanted to defend her husband, "Yes, we have bought your old TV slot, Curt. We've also bought the TV in Florida and Ade

Schiller sold us her company in San Francisco, so we've got her TV slot, too. Danno would now like to pay you for your company, but we both know he doesn't have to. Quite frankly, he can simply come down here and take this territory if he wanted to. Now, do we have a deal at seventy thousand?"

Curt shoved the table angrily back toward Annie, which knocked both their glasses onto the floor with a smash. "Who are you to be sitting in judgment of me? You fucking don't think I know what you've been doing behind his back? Do you think that somehow this fucking cesspool of a business is too good to talk about you, Mrs. Garland?"

Curt left the hotel bar. Annie waited for him to walk past the window before she exhaled. "Fuck," she whispered to herself. She didn't expect him to be that intense or jittery. She couldn't get it done. She didn't have the money to play it straight, but even if she had, she wasn't sure if he was all that keen on dealing with Danno's wife. And now she wondered if he was going straight back to Danno to let the cat out of the bag.

Florida.

Ted Berry swung the van as close to the Studio Two doors as he possibly could. Danno got out and quickly entered the building. The anxious TV owner, Sean Peak, stood waiting for him in the hallway.

"Are you sure this is going to be okay, Danno?" Sean asked.

"Sean, nice to see you again. I look forward to working with you." Danno peeled off his coat. Underneath, he was dressed like a man who was about to make his Florida TV debut.

"What's going to happen?" Sean asked.

"We're all going to make a lot more money than we do now, that's what's going to happen," Danno replied.

Outside, Ted Berry unloaded Gilbert King, still dressed in his hospital gear, from the back of the van. He carelessly dropped him into a wheelchair and slammed him against every door and wall he could find on the way into the building.

"I want to tape this, Sean, and then you run it at ten o'clock like we agreed," Danno said as Ted wheeled Gilbert into the studio.

"What the fuck?" Sean said to himself as he saw the scene unfolding in front of him.

"Cameraman ready?" Danno asked.

CHAPTER THIRTY-ONE

Bree pulled up outside the Jacksonville Coliseum. She watched the parking lot for signs of Lenny. She felt inadequate, in a way—like she had made her husband choose between the business and her, and she honestly didn't know if she was worth it.

"Is Daddy coming?" Luke asked from the back.

"Yeah, we're early, little man. Is your brother okay?"

"He's chewing his toy. Do you want me to slap him?" Luke asked. "No."

"Is Daddy in there?" Luke asked, craning his neck toward the arena.

"Yeah. Daddy works in there." Bree turned off the engine and checked her watch: four minutes past nine.

She prayed that Lenny wouldn't let them all down again.

It was heavy, but beautiful to look at. Babu had heard that it cost thirty thousand to make, but he knew not to believe anything anyone told him in the wrestling business. He knew for sure that he was going to miss that championship belt though, no matter how much it cost.

"The boss taped the piece and he's on his way down," Ricky whispered to Babu and then walked on. Babu smiled broadly to himself.

Game on.

"What time is it?" Lenny asked the waiting crowd at the curtain. He knew his family was outside and he was cutting it fine.

Nobody bothered to check or answer him.

A member of the ring crew walked past. "Okay, guys, we're having trouble getting the cage in place. There's something wrong with one of the pins on the side. We're going to be a little while."

Lenny pushed forward through the waiting crowd and grabbed the crew member. "There's a cage?"

"Yeah," he said as he pulled his arm back.

"How long is it going to take to get it in place? I have to be somewhere," Lenny asked.

The worker just walked through the curtain and disappeared into the chaos that was growing from either side of the aisle. Lenny stood and watched as the men busily erected and interlinked a steel cage around the ring. Once inside, Lenny, Proctor, and Babu would be locked in with no way out.

Oh, fuck.

"What time is it?" Lenny shouted with more urgency. "Anyone?"

The camera was in place in front of Gilbert King's face. He was more scratched than stitched. His eye was beginning to yellow and his huge lips were starting to deflate a little. He was knee deep into a groveling admission as Danno and Sean looked on.

Danno checked his watch. It was 9:37. "Any word from my wife, Sean?"

He looked around to find Sean in a panicked state. "No. I haven't heard anything."

Danno walked Sean away from the recording behind them and whispered, "We're going to be done in a couple of minutes. When that happens, I'm going to leave Ted here with you to make sure this is played across your fine state in our new ten o'clock slot. We will also be sending this tape to our existing TV in New York, our new TV in San Francisco, and to your station manager friend you helped us with in Texas." Danno checked his watch again. "Who we're now in business with, also."

Danno turned Sean around. Gilbert was crying and Ted Berry was standing off camera with an axe in his hand to make sure they got the full story.

"We're going to be the first wrestling company that's going to reach more than one territory at a time, Sean. That's going to make us very rich indeed."

Lenny pushed through the flimsy curtains and the audience immediately booed him. He was blinded by the lights, but could hear glass bottles smashing close to him. He hurried closer to the ring as his heart kicked against the inside of his chest. This huge crowd hated him for real. He walked up the blue steel steps and entered the open door of the fifteen-foot-high steel cage that surrounded the ring.

Lenny checked the wristwatch that he had stolen from a bag in the locker room. Eleven minutes to ten. Proctor said he wanted the match to last twenty minutes, but Lenny knew he needed to be out of the ring long before then.

This was the one night of his life he couldn't be late or not show up. Bree was just about done with him and he knew she was right. Ten o'clock and she was gone.

"And weighing in at nearly six hundred pounds, from South Africa . . . BAAAAAAAABuuuuuuuuuuu," the exaggerating ring announcer screamed.

Babu ripped through the curtains and immediately started rearing up on the crowd. He dared them to come from the stands and get in his face. Tonight was a new night for Babu. The realness of the situation meant he could leave his mute African gimmick backstage and just be himself out there.

He was splashed with liquid from a cup and someone leaned in from the aisle and grabbed his hair as he passed. In retaliation, Babu just knocked out the first man he saw at ringside. The cops jumped the barrier and circled the giant. They didn't seem sure if it was for Babu's protection or the audience's.

Babu grabbed the microphone from the ring announcer at ringside and threw him over the guard railing into the crowd. "It's part of the show," he shouted at the cops.

It wasn't.

"You people suck," Babu enthusiastically shouted into the mic. "Your town is a dive and your wrestlers down here are all jabronis."

A shower of ringside seats began to crash all around him. Babu entered the safety of the encaged ring and he and Lenny looked at each other. Lenny had clearly made his decision.

Proctor ran through the entrance and down the aisle to a big roar. He looked older in his wrestling gear, but was still visibly tough as nails. He marched up the steps and mugged for the adoring crowd before stepping through the open cage door and into the ring.

Proctor almost licked his lips in anticipation of getting to Lenny and then to the belt.

"Close the fucking door," Proctor shouted at Lenny.

Nine minutes to ten.

Lenny rushed over and grabbed the cage door. Proctor stalked up behind him—and Babu followed.

Proctor zoned in on Lenny's exposed heel and cocked his knee, ready to drop it, but Babu got there first and dropped Lenny like a brick with a punch of his own. One clean shot from the giant to Lenny's jaw and that was curtains for the referee.

The crowd was stunned into silence.

Lenny dribbled down along the ropes and bounced his head off the canvas.

"What the fuck are you doing?" Proctor shouted at Babu.

Somewhere in Babu's head, him getting to Lenny was much better than Proctor getting there first.

"Get him out of here," Babu shouted to the cops at ringside. The cage door was opened and Lenny's limp body was dragged out of the cage.

"No, no, leave him here," Proctor said as he grabbed Lenny by the ankle. Babu caught Proctor and slammed him off the cage before he could do anything.

"Get an ambulance," one cop shouted over his shoulder to no one specific. As they dragged Lenny from the ring, a fellow officer called it in.

Ricky jumped the railing and slid in through the open cage door wearing a ref's jersey. He locked himself, Babu, and Proctor in the cage. Proctor suddenly began to realize that he was being played.

"Ready to go to work, men?" Ricky asked.

Babu smiled and nodded. Proctor wasn't as confident.

CHAPTER THIRTY-TWO

Bree walked a few steps away from her parked car. She was on tip-toes and willing Lenny's silhouette to run toward her from the arena doors. She could hear the roar of the crowd and the rhythmic chants inside. She looked back at the car stuffed with bits and pieces. That was it, that was all she had of home, and she couldn't wait to unpack them in their homeplace.

Maybe things wouldn't be so hard for her in California. Maybe Lenny would settle down a little bit more.

Bree checked her watch and it was ten past ten. Luke's expectant face popped out of the side window. Bree could see an ambulance pull out from the building and drive off into the night. She wondered for a second. *Could that have been him? Maybe that's why he was late. Maybe he was looking for us? Maybe we're just second best again. He knew what time to meet them. He knew where. This was his fucking idea.* But still, no Lenny.

Bree got into the car and turned the key.

"Where's Daddy?" Luke asked.

"Just strap yourself in, little man. We're going to go see Nanna and Granddad," she said as she threw her purse on the floor by his feet.

"Is Daddy coming, too?" Luke asked.

Bree began reversing. "Not this time." She shifted into drive and headed toward the exit opposite the one the ambulance had taken.

Luke was getting upset. "Where is he? Where's Daddy?"

Bree couldn't answer. She didn't know how to. She turned onto the road and tried not to cry herself.

"Daddy!" Luke shouted from the back.

Bree didn't know what to say. "He's not . . . Luke . . ."

Luke began to slap the side window. "No, Daddy. He's back there."

Bree couldn't see in the dark, but she slammed on the brakes. "What?"

Luke jumped up and down in the back seat. Even little James Henry woke up. Bree reversed the car and she could see her husband running as fast as he could down the street to meet them.

Bree was still mad at him for not showing up, but was overcome with happiness that he was running down the road toward them. She stopped and rolled down the window. She was going to play it cool when he caught up. *Ah, fuck being cool.* She got out of the car and began running to him too.

"Daddy!" Luke shouted, startling his baby brother and making him bawl.

Bree and Lenny met a few steps from the car and hugged and kissed. They could hear a roar from the crowd in the arena behind them.

"I love you," Bree said in his ear.

"I love you too," Lenny replied.

She knew by his face that he meant it. That she wasn't second best and that he could be happy with his family.

Lenny opened the back door and kissed his kids over and over. "Where are we going?" he asked.

"Are you coming, Daddy?" Luke shouted.

Lenny jumped in the front and kissed his wife. "You better believe it."

The baby bawled louder, until Bree played a tape that had some lullabies on it. The reaction was instant. Baby was quiet.

"Is that you singing those?" Lenny asked.

"It's like magic," Bree replied.

"Works overtime," Luke said.

Lenny could see his family had a bond, and a way of being with each other, that didn't now include him. He wanted to get where they were. He wanted to feel part of his family again, but he knew it would take time. Time that he was now going to have.

Bree smiled at him and pulled off with her few possessions, her family, and about eight thousand dollars she had managed to take from the knapsack in her garage and hide from her husband.

Lenny and Danno passed each other on the road and didn't even know it. One was driving away from the business, the other to claim it. Danno was pushing down hard on the pedal to get to the arena before Proctor could sneak out the back door. Had Danno seen the condition Babu left him in, he would have known there was no rush.

Proctor wasn't going anywhere quickly.

Gilbert's tape had been aired across Florida and his confessions gave Danno a huge platform to make money. It would be replayed in spots across New York, Texas, and California.

Out of all this came one hell of a money angle for Danno. And that was where he knew his strengths in the wrestling business lay. Outthink them, don't outfight them. However, sometimes he knew he'd have to do both.

In the dressing room, Proctor let the globs of blood tangled with saliva run from his mouth to the floor. He had a hard time closing his jaw without pain shooting through his ear. His head was also bleeding, and his eyes were swollen. He was sure that his right thumb was broken and his shoulder was probably dislocated.

Wrestling wasn't fake all the time. Not when you'd done all that Proctor had done. In the end, the giant did business and gave him the belt. But he sure kicked his ass before he lay down.

Danno came in. Both men remained silent for a while. Proctor couldn't bring himself to look up.

"I want you to stay on board," Danno said to Proctor.

Proctor laughed until his raw chest turned his amusement into a fit of coughing. "You want me to work for you?" he asked with another spit.

"Do you have any other choice?" Danno replied.

Danno knew that Proctor would have been told by now.

Proctor dropped the heavyweight belt to the floor. "Fuck you."

Danno walked closer. "The only thing that's keeping you alive is that belt. The second I take it back, all the people who you've hurt come looking for you."

Proctor slowly rose to his feet. "We were just supposed to make money, Danno. That was the plan."

Somewhere in his head, Danno wanted to scrub it all out. Start again. He knew that Proctor's simplistic look back was, in some way, correct. It had been all about the money. It still was.

"You can go across the territories and defend that title with the giant chasing you, or you can drop the belt tomorrow and take your chances out there. It's up to you," Danno said.

The weight of his beating pushed Proctor back down into his seat. "You know I'm not just going to take this, don't you, Danno?" Proctor said.

Danno opened the door to leave. "You don't have any fucking say in the matter, Proctor."

Danno stepped into the hallway outside the dressing room and closed the door behind him. He said to Ted Berry, who was waiting outside, "Don't let him out of your sight from now on."

Ted nodded and entered the dressing room. Proctor was going to have a hard time doing anything without Danno knowing it.

Danno whistled down the hallway. The Florida wrestlers had already begun to ask about being used for the new TV show in Studio Two. They all knew Proctor was finished as an owner. No

TV meant no crowds, which meant no wrestlers, which meant no company to own.

Danno stopped his victory lap, backed up a little, and sank a quarter into the pay phone on the wall. He took out his little address book and tried his wife's hotel room number himself.

The phone rang, unanswered, on the bedside table in Annie's Texas hotel room.

Annie lay on the floor next to the table, strangled and beaten. Lenny's envelope with his wife's rings had fallen from her pocket and lay by her body.

All the money from the knapsack was gone—and the room had been turned over.

Danno checked his watch and thought it possible that she was on the flight back or something. He shouted down to the crowd at the end of the hallway, "Get Lenny down to the airport to wait until my wife gets in."

"Yes, boss," came the response.

Danno hung up and triumphantly lit a cigar.

"What's the plan now?" Ricky asked as he lay against the wall by his boss.

Danno passed Ricky a cigar. "We just opened up the whole country tonight. It's time we made some real money."